"Miss Fitzmou... repeated sudden... struck a familiar chord.

As Valeria made a stammered acknowledgment, she saw his earlier amusement give way to icy disdain. Though his eyes were blue, there was nothing warm about them. Rather they held the color and density of sapphires, coolly stripping away her defenses, until she felt that his probing, dissecting glance had laid bare her every thought. Bravely, she tried to meet his gaze. Why was he looking at her like this? What on earth had she done to be the recipient of so much animosity?

"I am not a man to mince matters, Miss Fitzmount," he said softly. "Indeed, as a soldier I have grown accustomed to plain speaking, and I have no recourse but to protest your presence in Vienna. Please do not deny or seek to deny your shameless pursuit of one of my young officers—Perry Adaire. When a woman pursues a man as blatantly as you do, Miss Fitzmount, I consider there is every excuse for that man's friends to save him from what would undoubtedly be a lifetime of misery."

Valeria was stunned at the accusation. The village gossip from England had evidently reached Vienna. And she stood condemned without even a chance to defend herself.

Novels By Caroline Courtney

Duchess in Disguise
A Wager For Love
Love Unmasked
Guardian of the Heart
Dangerous Engagement
Love's Masquerade
Love Triumphant
Heart of Honor
Libertine in Love
The Romantic Rivals
Forbidden Love
Abandoned For Love
The Tempestuous Affair
Love of My Life
Destiny's Duchess
A Lover's Victory

Published By
WARNER BOOKS

CAROLINE COURTNEY

A Lover's Victory

WARNER BOOKS

A Warner Communications Company

WARNER BOOKS EDITION

Copyright © 1981 by Arlington Books (Publishers), Ltd.
All rights reserved.

Cover design by Gene Light

Cover art by Walter Popp

Warner Books, Inc., 75 Rockefeller Plaza, New York, N.Y. 10019

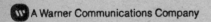 A Warner Communications Company

Printed in the United States of America

First Printing: October, 1981

10 9 8 7 6 5 4 3 2 1

Chapter One

"No, Papa! I am not going with you!"

The speaker's fragile countenance belied her firm tones, but as Sir Edward Fitzmount knew to his cost, his daughter Valeria could be exceedingly strong-minded when the occasion demanded it; a trait she had inherited from his own late, unlamented grandmother as he was wont to declare whenever he felt particularly out of charity with his sole offspring.

Valeria, used to her father's sudden starts, watched him frown heavily, linking his hands behind his back under his coattails. It was a stance he had a habit of adopting whenever he wanted to assume an air of authority. But it was wasted on Valeria, who had transferred her gaze to the rolling parkland of Fitzmount Place.

From the library window she had an uninterrupted view of the lake and the winding ride beyond it, leading upward through the carefully planted woodlands. Fitzmount Place was considered something of a showpiece locally, having been copied from drawings of Italian palaces brought back by Sir Edward's grandfather from his Grand Tour. However, for once the view from the library window failed to hold Valeria's attention.

"Now, you listen to me, Valeria," Sir Edward continued to his recalcitrant daughter. "I have not gone to the trouble of arranging this trip to Vienna just for you to cry off at the last moment. I had the devil of a job securing lodgings for us. With the congress in full swing, all the world is flocking to the city."

"All the more reason for us not to join them, then," Valeria rejoined calmly.

"Not join them! You know full well—"

"I know full well that the only reason you are so set on dragging me there, Papa, is because you hope to constrain Perry to offer for me," Valeria interrupted frankly. "Well, it won't work! Perry has as little wish to marry *me* as I have to marry *him.*"

"Nonsense!" Sir Edward roared. "You've always seemed fond enough of the boy, to me. I mind well the number of times I've seen the pair of you romping about the park together."

"I don't deny that we are good friends, Papa," Valeria agreed patiently. "But we are talking of marriage, and I have no wish to marry Perry."

"Wish! Wish! Who is talking of 'wishes,' miss?" Sir Edward fumed. "How can a chit of twenty-two summers presume to know her own mind, in any case? I suppose the next thing you'll be telling me is that you fancy yourself in love with some parson's son! You know quite well that it has long been my desire that you and young Adaire make a match of it."

Ignoring her father's earlier comments, Valeria left her post by the window and crossed the Turkey carpet to face him. The furnishings in the library were, in the main, old and shabby. It was the only room Sir Edward had not allowed his bride to touch when he first brought her to Fitzmount Place. Certainly it was a lack of funds that prevented Sir Edward from refurbishing the room, for he was well known to be a very generous man. Rather, it was due to a sentimental streak, hidden behind a gruff exterior. Valeria knew nothing on earth could induce him to change a single item of furniture in the room that had originally been furnished by his grandfather; and she also knew that it was this same streak of sentimentality which inclined him toward a match between herself and Perry Adaire.

Valeria had nothing against Perry. Indeed, she was exceedingly fond of him—in a sisterly fashion. Twelve months her junior, Perry had been the constant companion of her childhood until he went to Eton. The bond between them was, perhaps, stronger than it might otherwise have been, because they had both suffered the loss of their mothers. Valeria's mama had died in childbirth when Valeria was scarcely eighteen months old, and Perry had lost both parents in a carriage accident six weeks before his first birthday.

From long experience of her papa's choleric temper, Valeria knew quite well what manner of tirade would follow her avowal that she had no wish to marry Perry. Normally an indulgent father, Sir Edward was immovable in his desire to see his daughter betrothed to Perry Adaire. Valeria knew why, of course, and even sympathized with him. Marriage to Perry would unite for all time the neighboring estates of Fitzmount and Adaire. Her father's hopes in this direction were shared by Perry's grandfather, Lord Adaire, but—whilst appreciating the wishes of their elders—neither Valeria nor Perry could submit to a loveless marriage for the sake of several thousand acres of land.

Valeria had hoped, when Perry joined a particularly illustrious cavalry regiment, that her father and Lord Adaire would abandon any notions of their eventual marriage. However, no sooner had her papa heard that Perry's regiment had been posted to Vienna as an escort for Lord Castlereagh, Britain's foreign minister, than he had announced that he was taking his daughter there to participate in the peace celebrations.

After the fall of Paris, and Napoleon Bonaparte's subsequent surrender, Britain and her allies had elected to hold a congress in Vienna. The original purpose of the congress was to decide upon the fairest method of restoring Europe to what it had been before Bonaparte annexed so much of that continent to his empire. However, such serious and high-minded intentions soon became secondary to society's desire to turn the congress into a hectic whirl of frivolous gaiety.

When the venue of the peace congress had first been announced, there had been a general exodus amongst the ton; gentlemen in search of entertainment which the congress promised, and ladies with marriageable daughters to provide for, hurried across the Channel.

Reports from Vienna tantalized those who stayed behind. There was no gayer city on earth: balls, routs, promenades, all on a scale of such magnificent lavishness that they were impossible to describe without employing trite superlatives.

It was Sir Edward's announcement that he intended to remove himself and Valeria to Vienna that had provoked their present quarrel. Although a very good-natured girl, with a fondness for her papa and the sense of humor necessary to cope with his fits and starts, Valeria had been dismayed by his plans.

It was an open secret in the neighborhood that Sir Edward and Lord Adaire would like to see their offspring united. Valeria was not so blind as to be unaware of the acid comments and assessing looks exchanged behind her back. At two-and-twenty she was the older by a handful of years than the other girls in the immediate locale, and she knew that she was talked of as being "at her last prayers," or even "on the shelf." Hurtful as these remarks were, she had learned to shrug them off, concealing her feelings behind a smiling facade.

It was less easy to accept calmly the unthinking comments about her height. She had always been self-conscious about it, even though her father had assured her that *all* the Fitzmounts were tall. But the discomfort she had experienced in the country was nothing to that which she suffered when she went to London for her coming out.

As she had complained to her papa at the time, at Almacks and all the ton parties, she had felt like a giantess in the presence of dozens of dainty little fairies. With the added wisdom of the intervening years, she was now able to look back upon her agonizings with affectionate amusement.

But some things could not be forgotten. Her height had made her feel awkward, thus causing her to be brusque with those gentlemen who did approach her at balls, fearing that they did so merely out of pity. Self-consciousness had been hidden behind a wall of freezing politeness, frightening off the young men who would have liked to approach her and confirming her own opinion that gentlemen had no partiality for long, tall women.

Only with Perry, and gentlemen of her father's generation, did she feel able to be her natural self; and she had to admit that since Perry had joined up, life had been sadly flat. A fault of her own nature, she fully admitted, for she had long ago given up accepting invitations, fearing to look foolish and out of place amongst a crowd of simpering pocket Venuses.

It was true that both Perry and Papa topped her by a good four inches, but since they were each over six feet tall in their stocking feet, she felt this was little consolation; and she had long ago abandoned earnest treaties to her fairy godmother that she might somehow shrink overnight. There was little use in denying that dainty, fragile females had a far better time of it than tall, capable ones.

Sir Edward interrupted her reverie.

"I cannot think why you do not wish to marry Perry," he exclaimed pettishly. "You have known each other for ever and. . . ."

Valeria smiled humorously.

"I do not wish to marry him, Papa, because I do not love him as I should want to love my husband. Nor does Perry love me, except as a sister, which is hardly surprising. Look at me. I am a positive bean pole!"

As she spoke, she directed a look into the gilt mirror hanging on the opposite wall. A reflection she considered too familiar to be worthy of any comment stared back at her— a neat oval face, well-spaced green eyes, tidy russet braids. She had adopted the braids after her first season, much to her father's disgust. He said her hair was the color of beech trees in the autumn sunlight and that it was a crime to bundle it up in plaits, but Valeria refused to be swayed. Her height had given her a craving to make herself as inconspicuous as possible; and so obsessed had she become with her inches, that she failed to realize her body had a grace not given to her smaller sisters.

"Nonsense!" Sir Edward replied gruffly. "There's nothing wrong with being tall, my girl. Told you so before. Makes for elegance."

Elegant or not, Valeria was determined that she would not accompany her father to Vienna. However, as she soon discovered when she voiced this intention, she had been neatly outmaneuvered.

"Stay here?" Sir Edward exclaimed. "You cannot. I have let the place."

"Let it? To whom?" Valeria asked suspiciously, suspecting that her father's claim was just a ruse. His next words demolished this hope.

"Arthur Gervaise," he told her, with a great deal of satisfaction. "His father died recently and a nephew inherits the title. Arthur was the youngest son. He and his family lived with the old boy, and now he needs to find a place for them. Met him in London when I went up there the other week. Told him he couldn't do better than to look round these parts. Outcome was—offered him this place. Told him we were off to Vienna."

9

Valeria's sensitive spirit writhed at this blithe disclosure. She well knew her father's predilection for exchanging confidences with all and sundry over a bottle of port. By now, no doubt, the entire Gervaise family would know of his aspirations concerning her marriage to Perry. Well, it would serve no purpose, she decided crossly. She would go to Vienna—but she would *not* marry Perry.

Later in the afternoon, whilst her papa was engaged in appraising the household of his intentions, Valeria went up to her room. Chin on hands, she stared heedlessly through the window. *Vienna!* She had been following the progress of the congress via the pages of the *Morning Post,* and couldn't quite repress a small surge of excitement at the thought of traveling to the city which was reputedly the most exciting and dashing in all Europe.

If only her papa did not have this bee in his bonnet about herself and Perry. She knew him too well to suppose he would keep his intentions to himself. Within a sennight of their arrival it would be all over the city that he was trying to throw them together. Somehow she and Perry would have to find some means of persuading him that they would not suit, but although Valeria wracked her brains she could think of no way to convince her father to accept that she and Perry did not want to marry. Perhaps Perry might be able to provide a solution.

Despite all her doubts, Valeria could not help looking forward to their journey—and their destination! *Vienna!*

Naturally, Sir Edward's plans could not be kept a secret. Nor indeed did he desire that they should be, and before the week was out he and Valeria were subjected to a series of morning calls from their neighbors, all intent on discovering the truth of the rumor that Sir Edward was bent on sallying forth to Vienna.

There was also correspondence between Fitzmount Place and the Viennese agent Sir Edward had hired to secure lodgings and make arrangements for their arrival. Within a month of Sir Edward's first informing Valeria of his plans, they were almost ready to depart.

Four days before they left for Dover, Arthur Gervaise and his family arrived to take up occupation of Fitzmount Place.

Valeria found it impossible to like the small, fussy

gentleman or his strident, overbearing wife. As for their four children! Several hours after their arrival she caught the eldest boy in the stable yard, tormenting one of the many cats that made their home there. With his ears still ringing from the sharp boxing Valeria had given him, he took himself off to his mother, loud in his complaints about the treatment he had received.

It was over the dinner table that Euphemia Gervaise chose to launch her first salvo in retaliation for this usurpation of her maternal role.

"Such a very tall girl," she remarked with an acid smile to Sir Edward, before turning pityingly to Valeria. "You must find it very awkward, my dear. What height are you? Five feet eight at least, I dare say."

"Five feet nine, actually," Valeria returned calmly, "and on the contrary, I find it gives one great advantages. For instance, one may never fear becoming lost in a crowd, or . . ."

Fortunately for her powers of invention, Sir Edward came to her rescue by suggesting that he and Arthur Gervaise retire to the library with the port, leaving the ladies to enjoy a comfortable coze.

"Comfortable" was the last adjective in the world to apply to Euphemia Gervaise's conversation, Valeria thought ruefully an hour later after she had been subjected to a rigorous cross-examination! Just when she thought the arrival of the tea tray would save her, her companion fired her final shot.

"Is it true that we may be seeing an interesting item in the *Post* following your arrival in Vienna?" she asked archly, with a smile which in no way deceived Valeria.

In that instant she was glad of the control she had taught herself, for it enabled her to continue pouring the tea as though Euphemia had commented on nothing more noteworthy than the weather. Her best form of defense, she decided, lay in feigning ignorance, and this she did. However, it was obvious that Euphemia was not deceived. Her eyes narrowed unpleasantly, and Valeria suspected that she would have been subjected to another barrage of questions if the butler had not interrupted to inform them that Master James Gervaise had made himself thoroughly sick on some plums he had stolen from the kitchen whilst cook was not looking, and was calling for his mama.

• • •

Sir Edward had one final duty to perform before they left, and this was to pay a visit to his old friend, Perry's grandfather, Lord Adaïre.

They found him in the library, and whilst the two gentlemen discoursed, Valeria went to look out onto the gardens. The house had been designed by Inigo Jones, during the time of the Stuarts, and the gardens abounded with exquisite topiary work, shady walks and rose arbors enough to delight the heart of any poet.

Whilst the two gentlemen discussed the implications of the peace congress, Valeria listened in silence.

"Lord only knows what they want with the regiment in Vienna," Lord Adaire commented testily. "War's over, now."

Valeria smiled sympathetically. Despite his brusque manner, she knew he thought the world of Perry and longed to have him home. He had not wanted him to join up, and pride had warred with fear when Perry announced firmly that Adaires had always been to the forefront when English history was being made, and he was not going to be the first to break that tradition.

"A diplomatic move, I expect," Valeria heard her papa say. "The czar is surrounded by his personal guard, and Castlereagh will not want—"

"Castlereagh, that old fox. They should have sent Wellington." Lord Adaire snorted.

Valeria hid a small smile. When politics came into the conversation the two men could talk for hours, as she well knew.

"I'm afraid I cannot give you Perry's direction." Lord Adaire apologized, reverting to the reason for their visit, "for when he last wrote he did not know where they would be billeted. I should inquire of the British Ambassador, if I were you." He turned to Valeria: "And what about you, my dear? Looking forward to all the festivities? The country's all right for dull old dogs like me, but a pretty girl needs balls and parties to keep her amused. If I were twenty years younger, young Perry would need to look to his laurels. Bought yourself plenty of geegaws, I suppose," he added genially.

Sir Edward answered before Valeria reply.

"Like as not Val will need to replenish her wardrobe once we get to Vienna. With the peace celebrations, my agent tells me that the cream of the nobility is flocking to the city. He's never seen anything to rival the entertainments. I don't want my daughter to feel her clothes can't match those of the other females."

Honey to sweeten the pill, Valeria thought wryly. To tell the truth she was not particularly addicted to fashion. For her coming out she had had several new gowns, all in white or palest pink—as befitted a very young lady—and she had hated herself in them.

"I've already collected the family jewels from the bank," her father surprised her by adding. "Took 'em round to Rundell & Bridges the last time I was in London to get 'em cleaned. Came up very well, too. Especially the emeralds."

"Oh! Not the emeralds, Papa," Valeria protested despairingly. She had worn them at a supper party at Almacks one night during the season, all too uncomfortably aware that the size and quality of the jewels drew all eyes. She considered them far too opulent. They were a legacy from an Elizabethan Fitzmount, who had given them to the bride he had snatched from the fires of the Inquisition. It was that bride whom the Fitzmount women blamed for their height, for she was Andalusian with a dash of Berber blood.

"Ahem! Seem to recollect there's a very fine emerald ring amongst the Adaire finery," Lord Adaire harrumped, avoiding Valeria's eyes. "Dare say I could dig it out of the safe, if you'd like to look at it?"

"Thank you, but no," Valeria answered firmly.

Really, the pair of them were quite impossible! Papa was all set to hound down the bridegroom, and Lord Adaire was ready with the ring. If it weren't so embarrassing the situation would be positively amusing!

Lord Adaire escorted them to their carriage, leaning heavily on his stick.

"You can tell that rascally grandson of mine, when you see him, that it's high time he gave up his soldiering and settled down to rear a family," he told Valeria gruffly. "If he leaves it much longer, I'll have received 'notice to quit' before I've dandled any great-grandchildren on my knee. A house without children is a cold, empty thing," he added somberly, "and to tell the truth, I miss the young jackanapes."

Valeria shook her head chidingly at the reference to his eventual demise, reminding him that Dr. Chadburn had pronounced that he had many years left to him if he took things quietly and did not excite himself.

"Aye, and that means no port, no hunting, no rich food. Might as well *be* dead," he grumbled. "Wish I could go with you, Edward," he added to Valeria's father, "but my old bones aren't up to the journey."

At last, the morning appointed for their departure arrived.

Sir Edward surveyed the well-burdened chaise waiting for them outside the porticoed main entrance.

" 'Tis just as well we're traveling post, Valeria. What do we need with so much luggage? I thought you were to purchase new clothes in Vienna?"

"I think that you will find the majority of the luggage is *yours*, Papa," Valeria informed him. "I believe Timkins has packed enough cravats to last you for the next ten years, and then there was that special port you did not wish to leave behind. . . ."

"Certainly not! Unless I miss my guess, it is exactly right for drinking. I have no intention of leaving it for our tenant, having cherished it so carefully these last fifteen years!"

The household lined up to wish them a safe journey: Hardwicke, the butler, stern and seemingly imperturable—everything that a good butler should be; Mrs. Bramford, the housekeeper, wiping her eyes on the corner of her apron; the two footmen and the maids; Sir Edward's groom and the stableboys; the three gardeners who, between them, cared for the park and the succession house; plus a host of general estate workers.

Only Sir Edward's valet, Valeria's personal maid, and the coachman were to accompany them, Sir Edward's agent having procured Viennese household staff for them.

Hester, Valeria's maid, was another subject of speculation amongst the local gentry. With her Cockney accent, thin body and fierce frown, she was not fashioned in the accepted mode of ladies' maid. However, she suited Valeria, who privately disliked the condescending manner some of her acquaintances' dressers adopted toward their mistresses.

Hester had been Valeria's devoted servant ever since the older girl had discovered her in a shivering heap by the railings of Sir Edward's elegant London house one cold November morning, when she had risen early intending to take a walk before breakfast.

The groom who had been with Valeria had been all set to drive the girl off, but Valeria had prevented him, moved to pity by the skeletal body and huge, terrified eyes. Gently, she had spoken to the girl, instructing the groom to hurry round to the kitchen and procure some food from the cook.

A back stiff with resentment had informed Valeria of his feelings about her instruction, but he had complied nevertheless; and by the time he had returned, Valeria's sympathetic manner had dragged the whole sorry story from the girl crouching at her feet. The daughter of a washerwoman who lived in the slums of St. Giles, Hester had been orphaned when her mother was killed by a runaway carriage. Destitute, she had been thrown out of her lodgings by the landlord, and had been desperately looking for work. It was four days since she had eaten, she confided to Valeria's horrified concern, and a full sennight since she had known the luxury of sleeping with a roof over her head.

Valeria had gone at once to Sir Edward, begging him to take the girl into their household. At first he had demurred, commenting that he would not bring his daughter to London again if she was going to fill his house with the riff-raff of the gutters, but Valeria had persisted and Sir Edward gave way to her pleas.

After Hester had been bathed and given a new gown by the disapproving housekeeper, the "waif" turned into a very presentable girl, quick to learn, and nimble-fingered. Valeria decided that she should become her personal maid, replacing the rather frosty creature who had originally been engaged for that position. It was a decision she had never regretted.

The last persons to wish them *bon voyage* were their new tenants—Arthur Gervaise stiffly self-conscious, his wife coldly unsmiling as she acknowledged Valeria's farewell.

"I'm sure you will be comfortable here," Valeria said impulsively, unwilling to part from their guest on a sour note. "I have always thought it a particularly happy house."

Euphemia Gervaise sniffed disparagingly.

"Happy? I dare say it might very well be, but it cannot compare with Searle."

"Searle?" Valeria queried, thinking it an odd name for a house.

"The house takes its name from the title," she was told. "The Dukedom of Searle was created by William the Con-

15

queror, and my husband's late father would have it that there was no finer nor more honorable name ever written in the history of England."

It certainly did have a rather arrogant ring to it, Valeria decided as the steps were folded away and the carriage door closed. And then she put aside all thoughts of Euphemia Gervaise and her pretensions. Their journey had begun. For better or for worse they were on their way to Vienna, that city of ancient and modern; and music and laughter, flanked by beautiful woodlands.

They had a long road ahead of them, with the Channel crossing and its attendant discomforts only a small part of it. They were traveling post which would ensure that they had every luxury; fresh horses at every stage, and only the best rooms in the inns at which they broke their journey. But Valeria had heard that continental posting inns could not be relied upon to offer the same standards of cleanliness and order one might expect from an English inn. She had received numerous warnings from their neighbors, several of them urging her to ensure that *only their own sheets* were placed upon the beds, and the water never drunk unless it had been cleansed with wine beforehand.

If she were to believe every unpleasant tale she had been told, Valeria reflected humorously, she should be anticipating their journey with the liveliest dread. Instead, she was forced to confess to a small frisson of excitement, despite her doubts concerning the wisdom of allowing her papa to overrule her original protests.

Chapter Two

Sir Edward had been lucky in his choice of agent. For despite the fact that Vienna was crammed to capacity, with many of the reputed seven hundred foreign diplomats—complete with secretaries, households and everything that goes with them—squashed into tiny boxes of houses within the old city walls, the agent had managed to secure for Sir Edward a very fine suite of rooms, in one of the elegant palaces lining the Josephsplatz. Once the home of the nobility and minor princelings, many of these buildings had been abandoned by their owners, who, ruined by their contributions to the war against Napoleon, had been forced to retire to more modest dwellings.

As they crossed the Danube, Valeria stared interestedly about her. The waters of the canals lay still in the clear, afternoon sunlight.

The variety and splendor of the buildings they passed drew more than one gasp of admiration from her. After London's cool Regency facades, the unashamed magnificence of the baroque and rococo architecture was almost too lavish. Scarcely a single palace was without its winged cherubs and gilding; satyrs and nymphs peered down from every building.

And it was not merely the lavishness of the architecture that drew Valeria's attention; she lost count of the number of parks they passed, all of them thronged with people. She had enlivened the long drive across Europe by familiarizing herself with a guidebook of the city, and now she amused herself trying to recognize her surroundings from the descriptions she had read. They drove past the Prater Park, past the Schonbrunn Palace, which she knew was the Empress Maria Theresa's favorite summer home.

Valeria already knew that Vienna was divided into two cities, the old and the new. Old Vienna lay within the ancient walls of the city, called the "Linie." These walls had been partially destroyed by the Turks when they besieged the town in the seventeenth century, but now they were being repaired so that visitors might pass a pleasant hour walking along the ramparts and enjoying a fine view of the city.

New Vienna lay outside these ancient ramparts, and was comprised of fine, new palaces, set in beautifully designed gardens. The wall that lay between these dwellings and the open countryside was called the "Glacis," and consisted of a ring of defensive bastions built during the previous century.

The guide book provided a wealth of detail about the city. In the back was a list of churches, telling when services were held. Following it was a description of the orangery in Augarten Park where musical concerts were given every morning.

There was also a recommendation that no visitor should quit the city without having first enjoyed the pleasure of sailing along the Danube in one of the gaily painted barges kept specifically for that purpose, perhaps completing the outing with a meal at the Gólden Rose at Nussdorf, where exquisitely dressed shellfish were a delicacy of the house.

Never had Valeria seen such a merry throng of people. Even where the streets were narrow and crowded, they made way for the carriage with good-natured smiles.

The guide book was forgotten as Valeria espied the Burgtheatre, and the outline of the Hofburg Palace.

Gentlemen and ladies strolled by in groups and pairs, and always Valeria was struck by the elegance of their apparel. The fashions were quite unlike those she had seen in the *Ladies' Journal;* the ladies' gowns were far prettier and richer, and even the gentlemen's more sober-hued garments were of a cut and style that could not help but draw attention to their wearers' undoubted elegance.

Sir Edward had told Valeria that there were reputed to be one hundred thousand foreigners in Vienna, all told, and as she watched the crowds from the carriage window, Valeria could well believe it.

Before she left the city Valeria was determined to explore it to the full, visiting the parks and gardens, strolling in the woods, or perhaps, just, sitting in a coffeehouse watching the world and listening to the musicians for which Vienna was justly famous.

At last, the carriage rumbled to a halt.

Stiff and sore, Valeria allowed her maid to assist her to the flagway.

A very correct butler welcomed them to their apartment and informed Sir Edward that his agent had been called out of town, but would pay his respects upon his return.

"Place seems all right to me," Sir Edward commented. "What do you think, Val?"

"If Vienna is as crowded as they say, I think we have done very well indeed."

The apartment was arranged on two floors of the building. An elegant oblong hallway with a rich marble floor gave access to a curving flight of stairs, a balconied landing, and the bedrooms.

Off the hall was a well-proportioned salon, furnished in the French Empire style, with chairs upholstered in pale blue watered silk to match the wall panels. Several Chinese rugs were scattered on the floor on which stood a quantity of sofa tables, which Valeria privately thought a trifle inferior to Mr. Chippendale's work.

There were also a small dining room and a small library, the latter of which Sir Edward elected to use as his study.

Although the apartment was really quite compact, by the time they had finished inspecting their new abode, Valeria felt quite fatigued and was grateful for her father's suggestion that they both retire early and leave the unpacking until the following day.

Having partaken of a late breakfast, Sir Edward enquired if Valeria would care to explore the city with him.

"I had best go and make our presence known to Sir Charles Stuart, our ambassador. We have several mutual acquaintances, and I have been charged with many messages for him. I must discover Perry's direction, and Stuart is bound to know where the regiment is billeted."

Refusing her father's invitation, Valeria explained that she wished to oversee the unpacking of their trunks herself.

It was well into the afternoon before the last box was emptied. Valeria had just dispatched the maid with a final

19

pile of cravats, when she heard the unmistakable sounds of someone's arrival in the hall below her.

From her light tones, the visitor was plainly female, and, cursing her lack of forethought in not warning the butler to deny visitors, Valeria paused uncertainly on the stairs—who on earth could be calling upon her?

Her gown was creased, her hair faintly mussed, and she was totally unprepared for visitors. Just as she was debating whether or not she could take refuge in her room, a light, feminine voice called her name. An enchanting vision in rose pink and blond lace was revealed to her through the wrought-iron tracery of the balustrade.

"Val!" the vision shrieked in a hoydenish manner, abandoning the pink parasol she had been carrying and rushing up the stairs to envelop Valeria in a perfumed embrace.

"Camilla!" Valeria exclaimed in a dazed fashion, when she had finally managed to disentangle herself. "What on earth are you doing in Vienna?"

She and Camilla Verne, as she had then been, both had attended the Bath Seminary for Young Ladies and had come out together. But whereas Valeria had been a gauche, uncertain debutante, Camilla had taken to the social scene like a duck to water, teasing, flirting, gathering about her a positive covey of admirers, and delighting her mama by marrying the Marquis of Normanton before her first season was out.

No two girls could have been more dissimilar. Tiny, sprightly, with soulful blue eyes and a mop of golden curls, Camilla was fashion's darling personified. Even so, despite the vast gulf between them, the two girls had remained fast friends, although Valeria had steadfastly resisted all Camilla's attempts to lure her to London to participate in the giddy, hectic round of pleasure that she herself so enjoyed. Now, as Valeria led her companion into the salon, she waited for an explanation of her friend's presence in Vienna.

It was delayed for several minutes, whilst Camilla examined her surroundings, exclaiming over the richness of the carpets and furnishings.

"How fortunate you are, Val. Hart could only get us a tiny little house inside the old walls. Wait until you see it! I swear it looks just like the dollhouse I had when I was young. But then, everything was such a rush. Hart was given only *days* to prepare himself to come to Vienna, and just because one of Lord Castlereagh's aides had to drop out at the last minute because his mama died . . . ."

Valeria knew that Hart, Camilla's husband, was attached to the Foreign Office in a diplomatic capacity, and that because of this, Camilla had traveled widely since her marriage, often being absent from England for months at a time.

"This time I have brought little James with me, and baby Lucy, as well—but I haven't spent as much time with them as I had hoped." She wrinkled her dainty little nose. "Nanny Hoskins, who was Hart's nanny when he was a baby, will not let me near the nursery. I do believe she thinks me too feather-headed to have a proper care for the children. Hart says I must not mind her, and it *is* wonderfully reassuring to know that when we are away they are being properly taken care of. One hears such dreadful tales about some nurses, and I well remember one I once had. She used to take away our food and lock us in the nursery cupboard, if we were naughty!" She sighed and frowned, as though suddenly remembering the reason for her visit.

"My dear, I could hardly believe my eyes when I saw your papa. He was just about to call on the ambassador, and so I begged him to give me your direction. We have it all planned. You will need a chaperone whilst you are in Vienna, and who better to fulfill that role than I? I promise you, you will have the gayest time. I swear I am quite exhausted with balls and routs—" She broke off and eyed Valeria's doubtful expression with mischievous eyes. "Your papa has brought you to Vienna because he hopes its romantic air will cause you and Perry Adaire to fall in love, but I have a much better idea! Perry is a nice boy, but he is not for you, Val. No, I intend that you will be the toast of the season, and shall secure yourself a husband of the foremost rank. I have long wanted to try my hand at matchmaking, and you have been very naughty, hiding yourself away in the country, but you cannot escape me *now!*"

Valeria started to protest, but it was no use. As she knew from past experience, trying to stop Camilla once she had set her mind on something was like trying to stop a river in full spate. On and on she chattered, full of plans for launching Valeria onto the social scene, stopping now and again merely to catch her breath, before hurrying on.

At last she paused, head to one side, like a small, exotic bird, as she considered her friend.

"If you wish to make me into a 'toast,' I fear you will have an impossible task on your hands!" Valeria commented humorously.

"Certainly not," Camilla objected stoutly. "You are far too modest and self-effacing, Val. I have always thought so, and so too does Hart. He told me once you reminded him of a tiny sea anemone, curling up and retreating inside yourself every time someone approaches. You have the loveliest eyes, Val, and such a very elegant carriage. Oh, I know you have grown into the habit of hiding yourself away because you consider you are too tall," she continued, when Valeria would have protested, "but that is all the greatest piece of nonsense. It is true that when we made our come-outs, you were a little awkward and unsure of yourself, but that was four years ago. When you are not concerning yourself with what others think of you, you have a grace that makes me positively green with envy."

Valeria could not believe this, even allowing for her friend's well-known propensity for exaggeration, but before she could say so, Camilla was rattling on, barely pausing for breath.

"You could take the town by storm, if you wished it, Val. I have often remarked that it is girls who are not quite in the common run who capture the gentlemen's hearts."

"And I am certainly not *that!*" Valeria agreed with a gurgle of laughter.

For a moment Camilla looked rather crestfallen at her companion's perversity in treating her words as a joke, but she soon rallied.

"I am quite serious, Val," she said firmly. "I have discussed it with your papa, and he is fully in agreement with me."

"Because he hopes it will make Perry fall in love with me," Valeria commented wryly.

Camilla shrugged dainty shoulders. As Valeria's oldest friend she was well aware of Sir Edward's hopes in that direction.

"As to that, I cannot say, but before this congress is over I intend that several gentlemen will fall in love with you, and I hope that you will fall in love with one of them. You cannot imagine how delightful it is to be married, my dear. Hart is the most adorable husband. Mama does not approve.

22

She says he spoils me too much. But there, I must not go running on about Hart."

Adopting a businesslike manner, she surveyed Valeria's shabby gown with an air of affectionate resignation.

"If that isn't just like you, Val. To come to the most fashionable city in the world, dressed in a gown that is at least two seasons behind the times. And such a drab color! From now on you shall wear gowns that make you stand out in a crowd, not fade into it. All is arranged. Your papa has given me carte blanche with his purse. By the way, do you waltz?"

Valeria shook her head. The matrons of Surrey did not permit that wild, fast dance, which allowed a young lady actually to be held in the arms of her partner, to be performed in their salons.

"Then you shall learn," Camilla declared firmly. "I shall ask my own teacher to call upon you. You will love it, I promise you."

Still trying to catch her breath, Valeria shook her head. Events seemed to be moving at a pace far different from that to which she was used. Fond as she was of Camilla, she felt it incumbent upon her to point out the flaws in the rosy picture her friend was painting. Not for one moment could she visualize herself as the 'toast of Vienna,' or even creating the mildest stir, except as an object of pity. But when she tried to voice these opinions, Camilla swept them aside.

"Nonsense!" that young lady declared, when Valeria announced that she had no desire to waltz. "You will love it, and if it is a shortage of partners you fear, pray allow me to tell you, dearest Val, that the Czar of Russia has brought with him his own personal guard. Each and every gentleman in that regiment is reputed to top six foot, by order of the czar himself." She darted Valeria a wickedly teasing smile. "What do you say now!"

Valeria was weakening, and she knew it. A vision of herself, dressed in a pretty gown, waltzing round the dance floor clasped in the arms of a handsome gentleman in an impressive uniform, crept traitorously into the mind she had hitherto considered to be properly sensible. Was she succumbing to Vienna's spell already? It seemed so!

Camilla, reading her friend's expression correctly, pounced.

"So it is all decided. We shall have such fun. Balls, routs, parades: you will attend them *all*."

Useless to go on protesting in the face of Camilla's enthusiasm, and, truth to tell, Valeria was becoming infected with her friend's excitement.

There were still many plans to be made and matters to discuuss before Camilla was ready to leave.

"Tomorrow, we shall visit my modiste," she announced as she stood up and drew on her gloves. "It is just as well that your papa is a wealthy man, my love, for I promise you, you are going to be vastly expensive. I am holding a small musical evening, tomorrow. Provided Madame Bertine can have a gown ready for you in time, you will attend. It will do very nicely to give you your first taste of society. The Princess Orsini will be there. She is Russian, you must know, and one of the foremost hostesses. Her ball was the first to open the congress festivities, but it was nothing compared to the one the empress plans to give. We must procure you an invitation, for it will be the most glittering social event of the congress. Simply *everyone* will be there.

"Tonight Hart and I are engaged to dine with the Castle-reaghs." She pulled a face. "So stuffy! Lady C. cares nothing for fashion, and as for his Lordship! He thinks of nought but the Congress. I swear I am quite fatigued with listening to who is to have Poland, and where it will be safest to send Bonaparte. Hart maintains that Elba is too close to France, but the other countries are all jealous of England's victories, and argue against everything that Lord Castlereagh suggests. I do not like Prince Metternich, the Viennese first minister. All the ladies are swooning over him, but I find him too suave, too knowledgeable of our sex. You will see that I am correct, when you meet him."

She chattered on for some time, bombarding Valeria with gossip concerning all the major personalities attending the Congress, until, ears ringing with names and titles, Valeria learned that the Czar of Russia, a boyishly handsome gentleman, was to be avoided at all costs, if she wished to preserve her good reputation.

She learned also that the Emperor of Austria, Francis I, was a very insignificant, tired little man, who looked more like a bourgeois shopkeeper than a ruler, and that the King of Wuttenburg was so grossly fat and ugly that everyone who could, avoided him.

24

"And Hart says," Camilla finished with a patriotic flourish, "that it is no wonder that Talleyrand managed to survive the Terror and Bonaparte's rule, for he is the most wily politician he has ever met."

Valeria, who had read a great deal about the astute Frenchman, agreed that this must be so. For a member of the ancient regime to become a trusted aide of Bonaparte, and then to survive that gentleman's downfall and become prominent in the very congress that had been set up to dispose of his ill-gotten gains, spoke of a skill at intrigue far beyond the scope of most mortals.

"They say Talleyrand claims that, during his service with Bonaparte, he was secretly supporting the Bourbons," Valeria commented. "But there is grave doubt at home that the French will accept Louis."

A startled frown wrinkled Camilla's alabaster brow. She paused in the act of buttoning her gloves, to exclaim worriedly, "My dear, never say you are becoming bookish! I promise you it will not do. There is nothing the gentlemen hate more than a lady who concerns herself in matters of politics!"

Recalling all she had read of the great Whig hostesses of London, whose salons drew the foremost gentlemen of the day, Valeria could only repress a small smile. Throughout their shared adolescence, she and Perry had always debated freely and fiercely upon current affairs, and whilst in no way considering herself a 'bluestocking,' Valeria could not close her eyes against what was going on in the world around her, nor considered it right that other members of her sex did. However, she conceded that nothing was to be gained by pointing this out to Camilla, whose thoughts, she knew, centered on gowns, beaux and balls. And yet those who judged her friend to be nothing more than an empty-headed flirt did her a grave injustice, for no mother could have been fonder of her children, or more concerned for their welfare. And no young wife was more serenely in love with her husband.

For more than an hour after her friend had departed, Valeria was too bemused to do much more than stare foolishly at the now empty trunks, littering her bedroom floor. What on earth had possessed her to agree to Camilla's impossible suggestion? She made a small moue. Could it be that the romantic air infecting Vienna was contagious? A smile

25

curved her lips. If so, then it was a very heady disease, indeed. It would do no harm to buy a few new gowns and attend several balls, she allowed, gathering her thoughts. But as for being a 'toast'—that notion was completely ridiculous!

By the time she had restored herself to a more ordered frame of mind, Sir Edward had returned, calling loudly for his daughter as he stepped into the hall.

"Has Camilla called?" he inquired jovially, handing his hat and cane to the waiting servant.

"She has, indeed," Valeria agreed severely. "Papa, what could you have been about, saying she could be my chaperone? I am quite exhausted already, just listening to the entertainments she has in store."

"Time you had some fun," Sir Edward replied, gruffly. "Damn it all, Val—"

"Don't think I don't know what you are about, for I do; and I promise you it will serve no purpose," Valeria interrupted before her father could finish. "If only you and Lord Adaire would just accept that Perry and I are not suited, Papa."

Sir Edward gave his daughter an irate glance.

"Fifty years ago, young lady, you'd have been banished to your room on a diet of bread and water, until you did marry him. Same thing goes for young Perry. This modern generation . . . Which reminds me. I have discovered the direction of the regiment's headquarters from the ambassador. He does not know where the individual officers are billeted, so I shall have to call at the headquarters to make further inquiries. Apparently, they're situated in the Minoritzenplatz, where Lord and Lady Castlereagh have been given a suite of rooms.

Valeria, whose dismay had been growing since she realized that her father intended to call at the regiment's headquarters, tried to think of some way of delaying her papa's visit until she herself had had an opportunity to seek out Perry and warn him of what was afoot. It would undoubtedly come as a great shock to him to learn that they were in Vienna; and whilst the relationship between them was more that of brother and sister than mere friends, Valeria wanted to suggest that it might be as well, if, during her stay in Vienna, they treated each other a little more distantly than was their wont.

However, before she could call to mind any way of

dissuading her father from hurrying round to the Minoritzen-platz, he coughed in a rather hesitant manner and inquired if she would object to dining alone.

"Fact is," he explained, "the ambassador asked if I wanted to take potluck with them. Seems he's entertaining several cronies of mine from the Foreign Office—an all male affair, I'm afraid, Val. But if you don't wish to be alone . . . ?"

Valeria's brain worked at top speed. Fortune was certainly disposed to favor her. With her father out of the house she hoped she would be able to hurry round to the Regimental headquarters and warn Perry of their arrival. Quickly reassuring her father that she had not the least objection to dining alone, that in fact she was not particularly hungry, she went up to her room to scrutinize the pages of her guide-book and decide upon the best way of reaching the Minoritzenplatz. By the time her father was ready to leave for his evening engagement, Valeria had laid her plans. No sooner had the door closed behind him than she summoned Hester and bade her put on her bonnet and clock.

"Surely, we aren't going out, Miss Valeria?" she asked dubiously.

Inured to the girl's deep mistrust of anything unfamiliar, Valeria replied briskly, but not unkindly, "If you do not wish to accompany me, Hester, I can always take one of the other maids," knowing quite well that she would never allow another to take her place. Her small deception worked, as she had known it would, and ten minutes later Valeria, with Hester dutifully, if reluctantly, at her heels, was walking down the street in the direction of the Minoritzenplatz.

It was a good deal farther than she had thought, but there was so much to see, so many fine palaces and beautiful gardens, that the long walk was more of a pleasure than a hardship. Eventually she reached the crowded Minoritzen-platz. The square was busy with carriages, and Valeria re-called Camilla's telling her that the emperor had ordered three hundred new ones especially for the Congress, all exactly the same in every detail. No one paid much attention to her as she crossed the square. Indeed, why should they when handsome hussars strode arrogantly through the throng, in the white and gold dress uniforms of the Imperial Guard; and ladies, in the filmsiest of pastel muslins, leaned graciously from their carriages to address the gentlemen riding at their sides. For once, even Hester had fallen silent.

At last the impressive bulk of the Hofburg Palace loomed up in front of them, and beyond it Valeria could see her destination.

Pray Heaven that Perry was on duty, she thought feverishly, as she entered a vast hallway, bustling with important-looking gentlemen, all seemingly bent on hurrying past her in varying directions.

Just when she felt she must have been rendered invisible, a liveried servant espied her and came solemnly forward.

To Valeria's relief he spoke English, and in a very short space of time she was being escorted down a long, polished corridor to a room which overlooked a small, enclosed courtyard.

A burly sergeant rose to his feet as she entered the room. Rather breathlessly, she explained her mission.

"Captain Adaire. Of course, miss. I'll go and see if I can find him. There's a small antechamber through here. Why don't you and your maid wait in there?" he suggested kindly.

Grateful for his tactful understanding, Valeria allowed him to usher her through what was obviously his office, into a small room off it.

Little more than fifteen feet square, it too looked out onto the courtyard, and was furnished with a table and several hard wooden chairs.

A regimental flag leaned drunkenly against one wall, a pack of well used playing cards on the table.

"Very rough and ready, I'm afraid, miss," the sergeant apologized, "but we don't get very many ladies here. I'll just go and see if I can find Captain Adaire for you."

Left alone with her maid, Valeria stared out into the courtyard. It faced south and caught the sun, tumbling geraniums cascading from terra-cotta pots, a brilliant splash of color against the golden stone. In the center of the cobbled enclosure was a pool, and from her vantage point, Valeria could see the goldfish swimming lazily from lily pad to lily pad.

"Begging your pardon, Miss Valeria, but please don't sit down," Hester exclaimed respectfully as Valeria turned toward one of the chairs. "Just look at the dust," she added, in scandalized accents.

Valeria laughed. "I don't think gentlemen care very much about dust, Hester," she said gently, her attention caught by the deep sound of male voices, and the clinking of spurs.

The sound came from the courtyard, and she glanced hopefully at the four men crossing it, hoping one of them might be Perry. None of the faces was familiar. The uniforms she recognized as belonging to Perry's regiment, but the gentlemen were complete strangers. They sat down on the edge of the pool, disturbing the fish, who darted quickly away. One of the small group remained standing, his back to Valeria as he placed one Hessian-booted foot on the rim of the pool, leaning his weight upon it as he bent down to catch one of his companions' comments.

His head was bare, his thick, black hair ruffled by the breeze. His very evident air of command caught Valeria's attention. In profile his features were severely classical, sculptured almost, and her heart missed a tiny beat. Whoever the gentleman was, he was quite undoubtedly extraordinarily handsome, in a way that was totally masculine. His uniform fitted him like a glove, white breeches tucked into Hessian boots that a London dandy would have envied. His scarlet jacket was unfastened, displaying the strong column of his throat, and the simple white muslin shirt he wore.

One of his companions addressed him, and he turned his head sharply so that for a suffocating moment, Valeria had the impression that he was looking directly at her.

Seen full face, his features had a hardness she would not have expected, harsh lines drawn from nose to mouth.

"Do not stand so close to the window, Hester," Valeria cautioned her maid. "We do not wish to be thought prying!"

The room was high-ceilinged, and Valeria suspected that it had once been part of a larger unit that had been partitioned off. The upper windows were open, and through them she caught fragments of the quartet's conversation.

"I wish I could find that batman of mine," one of the men seated by the pool complained lazily. "My dress uniform is in a shocking state. Indeed, I believe it has suffered more wear and tear than my battle dress did during our campaigning."

All but the gentleman standing laughed.

"That is because you are a far more enthusiastic dancer than fighter, my friend," one of the others replied teasingly.

"Tell us, who is to be your unfortunate victim, tonight?

I heard that the Princess de Lieven complained that you were not to request a dance with her ever again, you trod on her toes so many times during your last waltz."

"Lies, all lies. I believe there is not another man in the regiment as skilled in the waltz as I."

Whilst his companions jeered, the tall, handsome gentleman moved away to examine a horse that a trooper was walking round the courtyard.

"What the devil's the matter with Leo?" Valeria heard the gentleman who had been boasting about his waltzing prowess ask the others. "I've never seen him so blue deviled. Always was a serious cove, I'll admit, but I don't think I've seen him smile once since we got to Vienna."

"That's probably because he prefers fighting to dancing," one of the others replied dryly. "You know how he feels about the men being turned loose in a city like Vienna. You know the C.O. has issued an edict that any men caught gaming or fighting will be court-martialed?"

"A bit stiff, isn't it? God knows, we deserve some relaxation after what we've been through, and Vienna's certainly the place for that. I don't believe I've ever seen such beautiful women, and there's certainly no lack of festivities, even for the ordinary privates."

"Stiff or not, that's the way it is," the object of their conversation said dryly, catching both his companions and Valeria off guard. She had been so intent on listening to them that she had neglected to observe that he had rejoined them—and obviously they were guilty of the same omission.

"It's all very well for you, Leo," one of the others complained. "But we don't all have your iron control," came the unsympathetic response.

"Are you dining with the ambassador tonight? We've all been invited," one of the others asked.

"I don't think so. You know what Stuart's dinners are like." His voice was cool and crisp, well modulated and yet plainly used to issuing orders. "Besides," he continued, "I'm getting a little tired of being besieged by anxious mamas newly arrived from England, intent on marrying their gawky daughters off to some hapless man. You wouldn't believe the number of women who think that an officer is easy game. I soon disabuse them of that notion. I haven't brought my men safely through the Peninsular Wars, to be snatched up by some sharp-eyed harpy desperate to get herself a husband."

"You're too hard on the fair sex, Leo," someone objected. "Marriage is what they're bred up to expect, and why not?"

"It is all very well for you to say that, Bennington, but spare a thought for those a little less sophisticated than yourself. How must they feel after months of campaigning, when they are confronted by a prinked-up young miss, carefully lessoned in feminine wiles?"

"Come on, Leo. It's only natural, after all."

"Natural or not," the other retorted crisply, "if I had my way I'd put a stop to it. Now, if you'll excuse me, I have an appointment with Lord Castlereagh."

"What's wrong with him?" one of the remaining trio asked irreverently as he strode away. "I know he's not precisely what you would call a ladies' man, but I've never known him to blow his top like that before."

"I did hear that he didn't want to come to Vienna," one of his companions replied. "Went to see the C.O. about it, apparently, but to no avail. He's a damned fine soldier, you know. I believe his men would follow him to hell and back."

As the officers started to disperse, Valeria saw the sergeant hurrying back across the courtyard.

When he entered the small office his expression was apologetic, and he was frowning unhappily.

"I'm afraid I can't find Captain Adaire," he explained. "Perhaps if you could give me your name and direction I could pass a message on to him."

Disappointed, Valeria did as he suggested, hoping that Perry would have the good sense to call upon her the moment he received the message.

The conversation she had overheard lingered on, disturbing her as she recalled the tall, dark officer's acid denigration of her sex. His disparaging comments still rankled, even though she tried to banish them, telling herself it was no concern of hers that he chose to regard women in so jaundiced a light. Plainly, he had a bias against her sex, although for the life of her Valeria could not understand why. She considered his remarks to be both ill-founded and prejudiced.

There were mothers, of course, who thought of nothing from the moment of their daughter's birth other than how to contrive a wealthy, titled marriage for them. But Valeria was convinced that they were in the minority. And whilst she was forced to admit that she could not number any young lady

31

amongst her circle of acquaintances who would voluntarily remain unwed, she knew of several who had refused more than one proposal, thus disproving the officer's contention that females lived for nothing save entrapping some unfortunate male.

They returned to the apartment at a leisurely pace. There was so much to see that Valeria was constantly having to stop. A party of masked revelers rode past her on their way to a ball, and from the open windows of several houses Valeria caught the strains of music heralding some form of entertainment. The gardens of the nobility were festooned with colored lanterns, illuminating the night with rainbow colors as dusk fell.

In the distance she could hear fireworks exploding and the excited shrieks of children, as the multicolored stars burst into the sky. Her earlier trepidation was forgotten as the atmosphere of the city engulfed her.

Indeed, so infected was she with the gaiety of Vienna, that Valeria found it impossible to contemplate going to bed when she eventually regained the apartment. Dismissing Hester, she repaired to the salon, picking up a book she had purchased in London. However, the story failed to hold her attention. Time and time again, her eyes were drawn to the windows as carriage wheels rattled merrily through the street, snatches of laughter and conversation wafting up to her from passersby.

She was still up when Sir Edward returned. He greeted her jovially, exclaiming over the lavishness of the dinner he had enjoyed.

"Stuart's a capital fellow," he enthused. "Knew him from London, of course, and his being half brother to Castlereagh means that he is well informed of all that goes on. He's given me the name of Perry's commanding officer. A Major Carrington. A good officer by all accounts, although inclined to be somewhat stiffish. You know how it is with these army men." He paused. "I mean to seek him out, tomorrow. Want to appraise him of the situation. He could be of help to us and—"

"I wish you would not, Papa," Valeria exclaimed faintly. "It is not at all the thing. It smacks too much of constraining Perry into a match."

Sir Edward frowned, eyeing her downbent head consideringly. "I cannot see that it would do any harm merely to speak with him."

"I would prefer it if you do not," Valeria reiterated calmly. Oh! Why couldn't her father see the construction that would be placed upon such an action?

"You would not want it bruited all over Vienna that I was on the catch for a husband, would you?" she asked him.

Sir Edward's frown deepened, a choleric tinge coloring his cheeks. "Who has dared suggest such a thing?" he demanded angrily. "This marriage is desired by both Lord Adaire and myself; you know that, Valeria."

She sighed patiently.

"But, Papa, it is not desired by Perry. You must see that if you were to let it be known that you had brought me to Vienna purely for the purpose of seeing me betrothed to him, it would be bound to give rise to a good deal of unpleasant speculation."

She watched whilst he digested her words. While the acerbic assertions she had so recently heard had certainly not weakened her determination to prevent her father from declaring his hopes to the world, they were by no means the sole reason for her actions. They should never have come to Vienna, she thought unhappily. She could not endure to have people gossiping about her behind her back, as they had at home.

She endeavored to explain a little of her feelings to Sir Edward, but he was so patently astonished that she should have so low an opinion of their neighbors that she was forced to abandon her attempt.

"Promise me you will say nothing about Perry to a soul, Papa," she urged her father.

"Very well, then," he agreed reluctantly. "But do not think I have abandoned the notion, for I have not!"

At least she had his promise to maintain silence about his wishes, which was better than nothing. Valeria reflected tiredly. Somehow she and Perry would have to find a way to convince him that there could be no marriage between them.

And yet, it was not of Perry that she thought as Hester helped her to prepare for bed, but of the disdainful "Leo," who so disliked her sex.

Indeed, from the first moment she had seen him, she had been beset by an emotion she was at a loss to comprehend.

Had she not known herself better, she might almost have considered herself to be in danger of conceiving a *tendre* for the handsome officer. Which was, of course, quite ridiculous, for she did not know the first thing about him, and what she had overheard of his conversation, despite his undeniable good looks, was not designed to recommend him to any female!

The last sound she heard before her eyes closed was the faint strains of a waltz. She fell asleep dreaming that she was performing that dangerously permissive dance with none other than the gentleman she had first caught sight of in the courtyard of the Minoritzenplatz.

Chapter
Three

"Valeria, do look at that bonnet. Isn't it the most ravishing thing you have ever seen?"

Dutifully Valeria examined the hat adorning the window of a very superior establishment that she and Camilla were just passing.

True to her word, Camilla had called for her friend punctually after breakfast and, having directed her coachman to set them down in the thoroughfare lined with the shops which the fashionable beau monde patronized, was busily engaged in steering Valeria toward her favorite modiste. Or had been until the very fetching concoction, consisting of a few scraps of lace and a multitude of pretty green ribbons, had caught her eye.

"It *is* very pretty," Valeria agreed at last, having submitted the bonnet to a close inspection. "But only reflect, my love. Green ribbons, with your blue eyes?"

Regretfully, Camilla allowed that this would present a problem of too great a magnitude to be overcome.

"No. It would not suit," she agreed dolefully, brightening a little when a sudden thought struck her.

"But your eyes are green, Val, and if it weren't for those perfectly horrid braids you persist in wearing, you would look quite ravishing in it. Do let's go in and try it on."

"Certainly not," Valeria refused firmly. "We are shopping for gowns, remember?"

In point of fact, she did not want to absent herself from their apartment for too long, lest Perry chance to call when she was gone, but she could scarcely tell Camilla as much. A pretty chatterbox, without meaning to, her friend would soon have confided Valeria's problem to half of Vienna, and *that* was the last thing Valeria wanted.

To Valeria's surprise, the modiste's was situated off the main street, and down a narrow culvert, lined with buildings whose upper storys leaned over until they were almost touching one another.

The woman who emerged from the nether regions of the building was as unlike Valeria's imaginings of an expensive modiste as it was possible to be. Small, with a face as seamed and wrinkled as a walnut, she had, nevertheless, the carriage of a woman of great pride, and her dark, flashing eyes put Valeria in mind of a painting of a gypsy girl she had once seen.

The woman greeted Camilla, listening carefully whilst she explained the purpose of their visit. Without speaking, she studied Valeria, the black eyes flashing as they took in every detail of her appearance.

"Your bones, your skin, your eyes, these are all excellent," she pronounced at last. "But as for the rest! That dress. The way you wear your hair . . ." She shook her head.

"Let me see you walk!" she commanded at last.

Bemused, Valeria did as she was bid, something in the old woman's eyes making her straighten her back and tilt her chin proudly.

"Excellent. Excellent. At least you know how to carry yourself. So many women do not. But you were not walking thus when you entered my salon. Why not? You have the carriage of a queen. *Use it.* Show the world that you are proud . . . and beautiful. How can they know it, if you do not tell them? I shall tell you a secret. Before anyone else can think her beautiful, *a woman must think it herself.* When you came in here you were ashamed of your height, is this not so?"

Numbly, Valeria nodded her head. This small, fiery woman was like no modiste she had ever known before.

"So! You will never walk like that again. You will remember always that God has given you lovely, long limbs so that you might show them to the world. They give you dignity, poise. When you wear my gowns I shall wish you to do them justice." She clapped her hands and a girl emerged from another room.

"Mitzi will take your measurements. I understand from Madame la Marquise that you need an entire wardrobe?"

Feeling as though she had somehow stumbled into a dream, Valeria agreed that this was so.

"Excellent. I do not shrink from telling you that I am the most expensive modiste in all Vienna, Miss Fitzmount. I am also the best. I will not have my gowns worn by ladies who seek to ruin their effect by wearing them with ensembles purchased elsewhere. The line, this season, is one of extreme simplicity, admirably suited to you. You will wear greens, blues, softest peach and lemon, all shades which will enhance your lovely coloring. You will need at least one grand toilette. Tell me, do you have any particular jewels?"

"There are the Fitzmount emeralds," Valeria began doubtfully.

"Excellent," the modiste approved. "Nothing could be better with your eyes and hair. You will bring them to me before I decide upon your gown. Jewels and gown must complement one another. My gowns are works of art, but subtle works of art. They enhance rather than swamp the wearer. Now, your hair." She shook her head as Valeria's hands went to her coronet of braids.

"It is the style of a spinster aunt, no?" She clapped her hands again and another girl appeared. "Go round to Monsieur Jacques's house and request him to spare me a moment, if he will, Leone."

When the girl had gone she turned again to Valeria.

"Monsieur Jacques is an artist with hair, Miss Fitzmount. He will know what can best be done with yours."

Valeria wanted to protest that she was quite happy with her hair the way it was. But was she? Since coming to Vienna she had been made painfully aware of how far her appearance fell behind those of the ladies she saw.

Camilla had had her blond curls cropped into an artless confusion of tousled curls, giving her the appearance of a cherubic angel. Valeria stared rather wistfully, into the pier glass. She felt sure such a style would not suit her. Her face lacked the gentle contours of Camilla's.

Whilst they waited for the girl to return, the modiste drew a few quick sketches.

"No frills or bows for you," she told Valeria firmly. "Severe, elegant lines to emphasize your excellent figure. Yes. It is excellent," she insisted, when Valeria would have demurred. "Remember what I told you. You are beautiful, you will be beautiful. Always you must tell yourself this, like a magic charm, no?"

She handed Valeria the sketches she had done.

"For the afternoon, palest peach, trimmed with écru lace —the discreetest hint, no more. You must have a riding habit, of course. Olive green, I think, with hussar frogging. The military style is very dashing when worn by a female, but unfortunately few women have the figure to carry it off. On you, it will be très chic. Ah, here is Monsieur Jacques!" she exclaimed, as the door opened to admit a small, dapper Frenchman.

He bowed briskly to Camilla and Valeria, before turning to listen to the modiste. When she had finished, he smiled at Valeria and, with a polite 'Permit me?' began unwinding her braids.

There was silence for a moment as the cloud of dark red hair cascaded down over her shoulders.

"It is like living fire," the Frenchman exclaimed reverently. "The fashion is for short-cropped curls, but I cannot commit the sacrilege of denying some fortunate gentleman the sight of so much beauty on your wedding night, m'selle. However, those braids are too repressive. One must give the gentlemen a hint of what they may expect should they ever be fortunate enough to win m'selle's hand, is that not so? A moment, whilst I consider." He lapsed into a deep silence for a second, and then exclaimed triumphantly, "I have it!"

With a few deft twists of his hands he gathered up the shining mass of Valeria's hair, securing it here and there, before turning her round to face the mirror.

So swiftly had he worked that she was barely able to comprehend the transformation. Her expression of delight gave her away, as she waited for Camilla's delighted nod of approval.

Gone were the severe plaits, and in their place were soft, flattering loops of hair that was surely a darker, richer red, than she remembered, coiled artfully round a face that suddenly seemed to have developed an elusive elegance. Valeria turned her head and caught a glimpse of the pure line of her throat and jaw, revealed by the new hairstyle.

Camilla clapped her hands.

"Oh, how clever you are, Monsieur Jacques," she complimented. "Valeria, it is so flattering."

"Not flattering, Madame," Jacques corrected. "I have

merely revealed the true beauty of that which nature had already bestowed."

"It is . . . it is very becoming," Valeria allowed uncertainly, staring a little nervously at the soignée, elegant creature facing her in the mirror. She barely recognized herself. This tall, sophisticated redhead was patently not a woman who needed to pursue a husband. The thought lent her the courage to inquire, rather tentatively, how she was supposed to imitate the deftness of Monsieur Jacques's clever fingers.

"The style is quite simple," he assured her. "If you will allow me to call upon you, it will be the work of a few moments only, to instruct your maid in its arrangement."

"Of course you will allow him to, won't you, Valeria?" Camilla urged. "You could not think of returning to those stuffy old braids, now!"

Rather weakly Valeria found herself giving the Frenchman her direction, whilst Camilla begged the modiste to do what she could to produce a gown for Valeria by that evening.

"I am to give a small, musical party," she added by way of explanation, "and Miss Fitzmount has nothing fit to be seen in!"

"The gowns we have just discussed could not possibly be ready before the week is out, at the earliest," the modiste protested. "However . . ." She eyed Valeria thoughtfully. "There is a dress I had promised to the czar's sister, the Archduchess Catherine. She too is tall." She murmured an instruction to the girl waiting behind her, and then explained to Valeria that the archduchess had given orders for the gown to be made up, although the modiste had not considered the material suitable for her dark beauty.

"She was to collect the gown last week," she informed them. "And since she had not done so, I can only assume that she has thought better of her choice."

She turned aside to speak to Monsieur Jacques, who was on the point of leaving, and Camilla hissed urgently to Valeria, "Do not let her persuade you into the gown if you do not want it, Val. You may depend upon it that if Catherine has refused to accept it, she fears to have it left on her hands."

Valeria had harbored exactly the same doubts as her friend, but the moment she saw the gown, she knew them to be groundless. It was made of the very palest peach ninon, over an underdress of peach satin; the tiny puff sleeves were slashed and trimmed with rows of tiny seed pearls, the same motif being repeated around the scalloped hem.

"It may be a little bit short," the modiste warned her as she helped Valeria into the gown, "but we could overcome that problem by lengthening the satin underdress so that it protrudes several inches below the ninon."

As she had predicted, it was a little on the short side, but otherwise the fit was excellent.

"For a musical evening, it will serve," the modiste agreed disparagingly, when Valeria had removed it. "I shall have it sent round to your apartment this afternoon. As for your other gowns, some I shall have ready within the week. The others, including the ball gown we spoke of, must wait upon my other orders."

As the two girls prepared to leave, she handed Valeria a tiny piece of the peach satin.

"You will need slippers and a reticule. Madame de Fontaine in the Lindestrasse will have exactly what you need. She is expensive, but if you tell her that *I* sent you, she will treat you fairly. The next time you come, you must bring your emeralds. You will, of course, be attending the court ball on the fifth of October?"

Valeria looked questioningly at Camilla.

"My friend has only just arrived in Vienna," she explained to the modiste. "But I myself have received an invitation from the empress and hope to procure one for Miss Fitzmount."

As they left the shop, Valeria whispered anxiously to her companion. "Will the empress permit me to attend the ball, or—"

"I'm sure she will," Camilla assured her. "She is altogether delightful, and very fond of the English. Besides," she added teasingly, "I have a feeling that from now on, no ball can hope to be a success if Miss Fitzmount is not to be present! If you could have seen your face when Monsieur Jacques was talking about your hair! He is right, though," she added as Valeria threw her an indignant, quelling look. "It is very lovely. You see, Val, I am not the only one to consider that you hide your light behind a bushel. You just wait and see," she promised. "All Vienna will be at your feet!"

Valeria had hoped, on her return, to find a message waiting for her from Perry, but instead there was one from Sir Edward, informing her that he had gone out to visit the

English ambassador. Sighing a little, Valeria hoped that he would remember the promise he had given her. She could place no reliance on Lord Stuart's discretion, for it was well known that he had a free tongue.

The dancing teacher promised by Camilla arrived shortly after three o'clock and was shown into the salon. Valeria had been engaged with some embroidery, which she put aside as the footman ushered him in. He spoke English with a very marked accent, and at first she found it difficult to understand him.

A pianoforte had been brought into the room in readiness for the lesson, and Valeria waited expectantly for him to strike up the music.

"We cannot make ze music because no partner you have, m'selle," he explained painstakingly to her when several minutes had elapsed.

"For ze valtz one must have ze partner, no?"

Valeria stared at him, of course. How could she have been so stupid? But what was she to do? She could scarcely summon one of the footmen into the salon to partner her. Dear, scatterbrained Camilla had completely overlooked her lack of a partner.

Whilst she debated on her best course of action, she heard the sound of someone tapping discreetly on the salon door. At her command, the butler entered, followed by a tall, fair-haired young man with tousled curls and a lazy grin.

"Perry!"

Valeria completely forgot about her dancing master as she sped across the room.

"Steady on, old girl," Perry admonished her, as he returned her warm hug. "What's going on then? What brings you to Vienna—or can I guess?"

Valeria glanced warningly at him, reminding him that they were not alone. "You got my message, then?" she asked, lightly.

Now that her initial delight had faded, she could see that Perry's face was showing signs of strain she had never seen there before, although he had lost nothing of his boyish exuberance.

"Oh, aye. What happened to you?"

Valeria had no desire to explain why she had left the palace so precipitately, and so she shrugged vaguely. "I thought the sergeant mustn't be able to find you." She bit her lip at the dancing teacher. How vexatiously awkward it was that Perry should arrive just when *he* was here. Raising her voice a little, she said hesitantly, "Would you excuse us a moment, monsieur?"

He shrugged his shoulders, gathering his music. "It is as you wish it, m'selle, but I have another lesson at five, and after that I cannot return for another week."

"Lesson?" Perry inquired, glancing at Valeria. "What are you learning, Val?"

"Learning? Oh, how to waltz," she explained absently. "You remember Camilla Verne? We came out together. Well, she is in Vienna and nothing will serve but I learn to waltz. Unfortunately, she neglected to provide me with a partner, and now I am wasting monsieur's time."

"No partner! Won't I do?"

"Oh, but—" She had been on the point of saying that there were many things she wanted to discuss with Perry and that therefore she could not waste precious seconds dancing, but just in time she remembered that they were not alone.

"Well, if you are sure you don't mind?"

"Not at all," Perry agreed cheerfully. "You may strike up the music, Monsieur, and observe how well I teach Miss Fitzmount!"

It was easier than Valeria had supposed, and far more delightful. Perry had obviously had a good deal of practice, for he was a most adept partner, whirling her about the floor until she felt quite light-headed.

"Perry, I must talk to you—alone," she whispered urgently when they had a moment's respite. "Have you seen Papa yet?"

Perry shook his head.

"Don't worry, though, we can talk when monsieur has gone."

It seemed to Valeria that the hour would never end. Her mind was not on the steps she was supposed to be mastering, and it was with an overwhelming sense of relief that she heard the salon door close behind her teacher.

"Now," Perry exclaimed, when they were both seated before the fire. "What brings you to Vienna?"

"You—and our proposed betrothal," Valeria said meaningfully.

Perry frowned, for once seeming to lose some of his

normal insouciance. It occurred to Valeria that he was looking a trifle haggard, his eyes faintly shadowed, his air,
preoccupied.

"Is anything wrong, Perry?" she asked him worriedly.

"Wrong? Lord, no. Whatever could be wrong? After the
peninsula, Vienna is like Heaven. To tell the truth, Val, I am
probably suffering from a surfeit of entertainment and un-
employment. Not a day goes by but I am showered with
invitations to attend this review, that breakfast; and every
night we can choose from at least a dozen balls. I have never
known anything like it. Congress fever seems to have swept
the city and no one is immune! You cannot conceive the
welcome we received when we first arrived. I have never
known people with such a capacity for enjoying themselves.
I confess to finding myself quite done up!"

Valeria laughed. "For shame," she teased. "Do you
honestly expect me to believe that a gentleman who has
survived the rigors of the Peninsular Campaign has not the
strength to dance from dusk until dawn?"

Perry gave her a rather preoccupied smile, and again it
struck Valeria that all was not as it should be. However, before she could voice this suspicion, Perry was asking her for
news of his grandfather.

"Lord Adaire is much recovered," Valeria assured him.
"He is still weak, of course, but much stronger than he was.
He is so proud of you, Perry. He has read all your letters to
us at least a dozen times, and when you were mentioned in
dispatches—"

"A mere nothing," Perry disclaimed uncomfortably.
"Lord, there wasn't a fellow in our regiment who wasn't
mentioned for one triviality or another."

"I only trust you can show as much bravery in facing
Papa," Valeria declared mischievously. "He was all for seeking out your commanding officer, and making himself known
to him. I believe Papa hoped to enlist his aid, and I did not
think either of us would want your commanding officer acting
as a matchmaker!"

"Good God, no!" Perry agreed feelingly. "But I'm afraid
I'm at a complete standstill to know what's to be done."

"It is a problem," Valeria acknowledged. "Camilla has
promised to aid me in persuading Papa that we should not
suit, but if he continues in his present vein, I have little hope
of succeeding. We cannot allow him to put it all about Vienna

that we are on the point of becoming betrothed. It was embarrassing enough at home, but here—"

"Yes. You've had the worst of it, I know, Val. The trouble is that he and Gramps have planned our future for so long that they can't accept that we might have plans of our own. I am thinking of selling out of the regiment," he announced abruptly, startling her. "Much as I have enjoyed my time in the army, I cannot continue to allow Gramps to shoulder my responsibilities."

"Oh, Perry. He will be *so* pleased," Valería told him. "Have you let him know yet?"

He shook his head, hesitating, as though choosing his words carefully. "I intend to write to him. But first, there are . . . certain matters I have to attend to. It is a thousand pities that I have not quitted Vienna before you arrived."

"I doubt it would have made much difference," Valeria said practically. "Papa would then merely have mounted his campaign from home. What are we to do, Perry? I have begged him to say nothing of his intentions, but I go in daily fear that he will confide them in some chance-met crony—you know how he is. He has no notions of the construction less charitable-minded persons than himself would put upon his declarations."

"We shall have to think up *something*," Perry admitted. "It is just as well that Gramps did not elect to come with you!"

Valeria could only agree. She had no desire to hurt either her father or Perry's grandfather, but at some point they would have to take a stand. She said as much to Perry, who gloomily agreed.

"Now that Gramps is a little recovered, I think it is time I told him that we are convinced we shall not suit. When I was in the peninsula the question of our marriage was relatively unimportant, but if I am to return home . . . You may rely upon me to do all that is necessary as far as Gramps is concerned, Val, and should you wish it, I shall speak with your father."

Valeria shook her head. "You will not be able to convince him that we are not suited. I have already tried. I think the best thing will be for us to be as casual with one another as we can. Camilla is determined to turn me into a 'toast,' and whilst I cannot place the slightest reliance on such being the case, I intend to make as many gentlemen friends as possible, without showing any partiality for any one of them. I hope that will convince Papa that I have no desire to be married!"

"Good idea, Val," Perry approved, and yet despite his words, Valeria had the distinct impression that his mind was on other things. However, he took his leave of her, with his usual, cheery bonhomie, just as Sir Edward stepped into the hallway.

The two gentlemen conversed for a few minutes, Sir Edward obviously highly delighted to see the younger man.

"Never have I known a city like Vienna," Sir Edward commented when Perry had gone.

Valeria could only agree. Her experience of the town had only been brief, but it had been sufficient for her to sense the mood which seemed to have swept the city. It was as though the new craze for the fashionable waltz set the pace for every facet of life; where once rigidity and conformity had prevailed—as though life must be conducted to the measured pace of a stately cotillion—now all was whirling, breathless excitement. Vienna was showing the rest of the world how to live at the new quick time, and Valeria could not help but feel her own spirits lift, intoxicated by the special magic of the peace celebrations. Suddenly all things seemed possible. Vienna, she concluded, infected one with a dangerous enchantment.

"You haven't forgotten that we are to attend Camilla's musical evening tonight, have you, Papa?" she asked, reminding her father of this engagement.

Sir Edward groaned. "Not that Beethoven fellow, is it?"

"I don't know who Camilla has engaged to entertain us," Valeria answered, hiding a small smile. An evening devoted to the appreciation of music was not her father's idea of good entertainment. She knew he would far rather be with some of his cronies, talking over a bottle of port whilst they played a hand of whist.

As she went upstairs to prepare for the evening ahead, Valeria could hear her father grumbling under his breath, but she hardened her heart. It had not been her idea to come to Vienna!

The peach dress had been delivered, as the modiste had promised, and Hester was hanging it carefully in the wardrobe as Valeria walked in. However, upon seeing her mistress, she laid it on the bed for Valeria's approval.

"You need not hang it up," Valeria told her. "I shall be wearing it tonight and must make haste to dress if I am not to be late. You know how that would displease Sir Edward."

It didn't take long for Hester's nimble fingers to refashion the rich coils of Valeria's hair and button her into the new gown, whilst Valeria examined her reflection anxiously in the mirror. Seeing herself properly for the first time, she exclaimed a little uneasily over the elegance of the gown, doubtful about the expanse of creamy shoulders it revealed.

"Nonsense, Miss Valeria," Hester chided her, when she voiced her doubts. "It ain't nothing to some of them gowns you see ladies wearing. It's just right," she added approvingly. "There won't be another lady to hold a candle to you!"

Valeria laughed, but could not help being pleased by Hester's outspoken praise, for she knew the girl was not given to fulsome flattery.

Whilst she waited for Hester to hand her her shawl and reticule, Valeria checked her reflection, again. "I think I shall wear my pearls, Hester," she decided. "I believe they will make me feel less exposed, and they will match the gown perfectly."

"Go with it a treat, they do, miss," Hester agreed when the single strand of pearls was in place. "Ever so lovely you look. Sir Edward will be that proud of you!"

Camilla and Hart were lodged in a small house, tucked down behind the city walls, with an excellent view of the Karliskirche, Vienna's finest church.

Despite the smallness of the rooms, Camilla seemed to have packed a good many people into them—far more than Valeria had expected for a mere musical evening, and Sir Edward's face brightened perceptibly, as he noted several gentlemen acquaintances amongst the throng.

In such a crush of persons, it was several minutes before Camilla became aware of their arrival. However, at last she saw them and came hurrying across, exclaiming breathlessly, "Hart and his cronies have shut themselves away in the study to discuss politics, and I am having to be both hostess and host. Poor Mr. Haydn will think all Englishmen vastly unappreciative of his music!"

She paused for a second to admire Valeria's gown, and was complimented on her own by Sir Edward. Camilla smiled roguishly. "Pooh, Sir Edward, who is going to pay any attention to a well-married matron like me? Valeria, my love, I have never seen you looking so well. Am I not right, Sir Edward? Is she not destined to be the season's toast?"

Valeria listened absently whilst her father replied. He had always been fond of Camilla, who could no more resist flattering every man who crossed her path, than she could stop breathing. If anyone could persuade her papa to accept that Valeria and Perry did not wish to marry, it would be Camilla, Valeria reflected.

The fashions in Vienna were richer than anything she had seen before, Valeria decided. It was as though the excitement of the congress had swept away all restraints, including those which had latterly decreed that gowns must be sober and plain. Ladies and gentlemen alike were dressed with unsurpassable elegance.

"Hart has been able to procure you an invitation to the empress's ball," Camilla confided in a whisper, before making Valeria known to a purple-turbaned dowager. The lady acknowledged the introduction in faintly accented English, complimenting Camilla on the beauty of her friend.

Blushing a little at the older woman's praise, Valeria answered her eager questions about England as best she could, before Camilla swept her on again.

"She is lady-in-waiting to the empress," Camilla announced when they were out of earshot. "You made a good impression on her, I could tell. I promise you, your description will be circulating every salon in Vienna before the week is out."

"Everyone is so fluent in English," Valeria commented, taking Camilla's words with a pinch of salt. "Even the dancing master—"

"Good heavens! Your waltzing! I had quite forgot. How did you get on?"

Valeria told her about Perry's opportune arrival.

"Oh, how silly of me. I should have remembered that you would need a partner! How very fortunate that Perry should chance to call upon you. I do not see him here tonight. I sent him an invitation, of course. Do you remember how we plagued him during our London season to escort us to Almacks? I was convinced that if he did not go with us we would both spend the entire evening languishing like wall-flowers!"

"Instead of which, your card was filled within minutes of our entering the place," Valeria reminded her dryly.

Camilla giggled. "That was when I first met Hart. I stood up with him for three dances, and my mama did not know whether to scold me or to praise me!"

They had been good friends, the three of them—herself, Camilla and Perry. But Camilla's memories of their shared season were obviously far happier than her own.

"There's Perry, now. Over by the door," Valeria commented as she saw him walk in. "I think he's seen us."

It took some time for Perry to negotiate the crush of people, but eventually he reached Valeria's side, exclaiming rather ruefully that Camilla appeared to have half Vienna in her drawing room.

"I saw Sir Edward, by the way, Val," he added. "He seems to be enjoying himself."

"He has a good many acquaintances in Vienna," Valeria agreed. "Gentlemen from London who, like himself, have come here to observe the progress of the congress at first-hand. I think he will find Surrey very dull when we return."

Whilst they were chatting, the salon door opened to admit Hart and several other gentlemen. Camilla excused herself and went to join her husband. Valeria became engrossed in the music. It was exceptionally good. She said as much to Perry, and then realized that he wasn't listening. Her earlier feeling that his preoccupation was not entirely due to her unheralded arrival in Vienna returned.

"Perry, something *is* wrong," she said worriedly. "I can tell. What is it?"

"I can't talk now, Val," Perry muttered. "I'm engaged to meet some friends at the Spanish Riding School in the Hofburg Palace, tomorrow morning. Meet me there."

He made no attempt to deny her assertion, and this in itself was sufficient to cause Valeria further anxiety. It was not like Perry to be so subdued and somber. What could have happened? She bit her lip wanting to question him further, but it was too late. Camilla and Hart were bearing down upon them.

"Don't you think Val looks lovely, Hart?" Camilla asked her husband, slipping her hand through his arm. "Vienna obviously agrees with her."

"Vienna agrees with everyone," he commented. "We have all become infected with its gaiety. I have even seen Lady Castlereagh waltzing." His comment provoked general laughter, and Valeria studied him affectionately. William Hartford Devenish, Eighth Marquis of Normanton, or "Hart" as most people knew him, was a gentleman of middle height, amiable countenance, and some ten years older than his butterfly wife. Possessed of a keen sense of humor and a kindly manner, Hart was a firm favorite with both ladies and gentlemen. Valeria had always liked him, and extended her hand readily to greet him; to her surprise, he clasped her lightly in his arms, and kissed her cheek.

"Would you deny a well-married gentleman *all* his privileges, Val?" he teased. "I do believe that of all Camilla's friends you are the one I enjoy kissing the most."

His teasing brought a faint flush of color to Valeria's cheeks, although she managed to retain sufficient composure to acknowledge his introduction to Lord Castlereagh, who greeted her in a more conventional fashion. Valeria had heard that the foreign minister was reputed to be a man of few words and abrupt discomposing silences, but if this were true there was no evidence of it in the faint, but undoubtedly genuine, smile he gave her.

"Miss Fitzmount," he acknowledged, taking her hand in his and shaking it firmly. "I do hope you will enjoy your stay in Vienna. Beautiful young ladies are the one commodity that can never be in too great a supply. I predict that before you return home, you will have danced the soles off more than one pair of slippers!"

So the astute statesman was also capable of turning a very neat compliment, Valeria reflected humorously, as Lord Castlereagh turned aside to talk to her father, who had strolled over to join their small group.

As the foreign minister moved, Valeria was granted an uninterrupted view of the gentleman who had been standing behind him. Wearing the unmistakable uniform of Perry's regiment, he cut a very fine figure in his scarlet jacket with its gold facings and epaulets, immaculate white breeches clinging to his leanly muscled thighs, his thick, dark hair, just brushing the collar of his jacket.

Her heart skipped a beat, as she recognized the features of the tall, dark, officer she had seen in the courtyard of the Minoritzenplatz. As though sensing her regard, his head turned, his eyes resting on her for a fleeting second, their expression— What? Amused? The thought threw her into utter confusion, and to make matters worse, his lips twitched in the merest hint of a comprehending smile as she turned hurriedly away.

The small incident had been observed by Hart, who, following the direction of her gaze, exclaimed affectionately, "Leo! Pray allow me to introduce you to Miss Fitzmount. She and Camilla are old friends!"

"So I saw," came the dry response.

Hart acknowledged the riposte with a smile, taking Valeria by the arm, as though he sensed her desire to flee.

"Valeria, my dear," he announced, "let me make you known to Major Leo Carrington, who has the good fortune to be in the regiment posted to Vienna to act as Lord Castlereagh's escort. As you will soon discover, no rout or ball is complete without its full complement of military gentlemen. The lady who cannot command at least half a dozen officers from each of the allied armies cannot call herself a hostess. If you wish to cut a dashing figure, you must secure yourself a uniformed escort!"

"I am sure Miss Fitzmount is more than capable of doing that, Hart," the major's cool voice rejoined.

Valeria was too stunned to make any response. Never in her wildest imaginings had she dreamed that the recent occupant of so many of her thoughts and Perry's commanding officer would be one and the same person.

Her first thought was that surely the arm of coincidence could not stretch so far. And her second was a profound relief that she had managed to dissuade her father from making his desires known to one whom he had fondly hoped would be an ally in bringing about a match between herself and Perry. It was all she could do to repress a shudder of relief. Imagine if Major Carrington so much as suspected what was in her father's mind! Hadn't she overheard, with her own ears, his views on the subject of matchmaking parents?

She was aware that the major and Hart were conversing. Some discussion about the war in America, and the major's wish that he might have participated in it.

"Oh, come. How can you say so, Leo, when all Vienna is at your feet?"

"Doing it a bit brown, aren't you, Hart?" Valeria heard

him reply dryly. "For myself I prefer the arid plains of the peninsula to the overheated drawing rooms of Vienna."

Valeria was conscious of an odd constriction in her throat, a longing that the Major's cool contempt of her sex would change to respect—and perhaps something even warmer. She could not understand what was happening to her. She looked at the major covertly. His features had a proud, almost arrogant cast. His skin was tanned from being exposed to all weathers, his face faintly lean, as though there had been times when he had had to endure physical hardship. Valeria sensed intuitively that here was a man given to judging himself—and others—harshly. A man who was unlikely to be swayed by sentiment, nor softened by compassion.

"Miss *Fitzmount?*" Major Carrington repeated suddenly, as though the name struck a familiar chord, his attention riveting on Valeria for a second.

As Valeria made a stammered acknowledgment, she saw his earlier amusement give way to icy disdain. Though his eyes were blue, there was nothing warm about them. Rather, they held the color and density of sapphires, coolly stripping away her defenses, until she felt that his probing, dissecting glance had laid bare her every thought. Bravely, she tried to meet his gaze. His expression held a penetrating, freezing intensity that left her emotions raw and vulnerable.

Why was he looking at her like this? The mention of her name seemed to have provoked some deep-seated antagonism within him, some well of bitter dislike, which rendered her anxious and bewildered. What on earth had she done to be the recipient of so much animosity?

Someone claimed Hart's attention, and they were left alone.

"So you are Valeria Fitzmount," the major said softly, at last. "Indeed, I had not thought to meet you so opportunely."

The look in his eyes as he spoke disabused Valeria of any notion she might have entertained that his words were intended to be in any way complimentary. Far from it!

"I am not a man to mince matters, Miss Fitzmount," he added curtly, before she could speak. "Indeed, as a soldier I have grown accustomed to plain speaking, so you must excuse me if my phrases lack the finesse to which you are accustomed." His expression tightened. "Neither do I make a habit of interfering in the lives of my younger officers, but on this

51

occasion, I am moved to protest about your purpose here in Vienna." Valeria was completely taken aback—as much by his incisive manner as by his words. He sounded for all the world like a judge delivering sentence.

"My purpose?" she queried hesitantly. "But—"

"Please do not deny or seek to deny it," the hard voice continued. "Even were I not in possession of incontrovertible evidence in support of your contemptible intentions, your very behavior tonight would betray you."

Valeria was completely lost. She knew she was being insulted as she had never been insulted before in her life—but why? As she struggled for some means of untangling the mystery, he swept on, ruthlessly ignoring all her hesitant attempts to stem the full flood of his wrath.

"Well, let me tell you, here and now, that your shabby scheming will all come to naught. I shall not stand idly by and see you pursue Perry Adaire unchecked, Miss Fitzmount. Even if I were not appalled at the thought of a young woman of good family shamelessly pursuing a husband—indeed I am not such a fool as to suppose such behavior is anything other than common practice with your sex—what I have learned about you would be sufficient to give me the gravest doubts as to your suitability to become *any* gentleman's wife. When a woman pursues a man as blatantly as you are pursuing Perry Adaire, Miss Fitzmount, I consider there is every excuse for that man's peers to do everything in their power to save him from what would undoubtedly be a lifetime of misery."

Valeria was rendered quite literally speechless. For several long seconds she could only stare disbelievingly at her accuser, her brain in utter turmoil. What on earth had she done to merit such a caustic set-down? And as for his accusations concerning Perry! She went pale as she recollected her father's intention of seeking out Perry's commanding officer, knowing that there was no way she could betray her father's foolish hopes to this man!

"What! Nothing to say for yourself?" the major jeered. "It seems that your nature must have suffered a sea change during your journey to Vienna, but I understand that you are not a young lady who is normally behindhand in making her opinions known. Quite the opposite."

Valeria felt the angry color rise in her cheeks. From being struck dumb with mortification, vigorous denials of his accusations now clamored hotly for utterance, creating a turmoil which lent color to her face and a sparkle to her eyes.

"May I know on what grounds I stand indicted?" she challenged proudly. "Surely you cannot claim to know me so thoroughly on the strength of a few minutes' conversation?"

"Possibly not," the major acknowledged, "although unlike most men, I am not easily gulled by a beautiful face or a fine gown. However, in your case, my opinion is but a reinforcement of what I have learned from others, who may, after a lifetime's acquaintanceship, claim to know you rather better than I. I am referring, of course, to your neighbors in Surrey." He then added, ruthlessly ignoring Valeria's startled gasp, "Now the neighbors of my aunt and uncle, Arthur and Euphemia Gervaise."

To say Valeria was taken aback was putting her feelings in their mildest form. Arthur Gervaise and his wife were related to this man! A shudder passed through her as she remembered Euphemia Gervaise's cold, malicious eyes. She was going to pay very dearly indeed for boxing Master Gervaise's ears, if this was a sample of how she was going to be treated in Vienna.

"You do not seek to deny their accusations, I see," the major proclaimed acidly. "But then, you cannot, can you? I own I was a little surprised when my uncle wrote to apprise me of your coming, but now that we have met . . ."

"Your uncle? But that means you must be the Duke of Searle," Valeria murmured stupidly, recalling what Euphemia Gervaise had told her about her husband's family. "But your name is Carrington."

"Leo Alexander Carrington Gervaise, actually," she was told impatiently. "But since, when I first joined up, there was another Gervaise in the same regiment, I elected to use the name Carrington instead. It is indeed your misfortune that I should not only be Arthur Gervaise's nephew, but also Perry Adaire's commanding officer, for I warn you, I fully intend to ensure that you do not succeed in entrapping him into marriage."

Her misfortune, and theirs, Valeria decided bitterly as she stared into his cold eyes. Well, she would not lend weight to his accusations by attempting to deny them. Indeed, it gave her a strange sense of satisfaction to let them lie unchallenged between them. Better by far a gentleman with a plain face and a warm heart, if this was how those possessed of handsome features behaved, she decided wretchedly. And to think she had actually been attracted to the man!

Mingled with her anger was a small ache, that she should be judged so harshly, and on so little evidence. Euphemia Gervaise was well and truly revenged!

Chapter Four

Following her encounter with Leo Carrington, Valeria had little recollection of how she passed the remainder of the evening. That he himself left shortly after their conversation she knew, for she had seen his broad back forcing a path through the crowd by the door. Perry too had disappeared, and although Camilla presented her to a good many charming, young men, she soon discovered that their lighthearted compliments and cheerful banter were not proof against the intrusive memory of Leo Carrington's cold dismissal.

Not even Mr. Haydn's magnificent music could rouse her from the gloom that seemed to have overtaken her earlier good spirits.

Camilla drew her aside as the other guests started to leave. "What were you and Major Carrington talking about for so long?" she hissed. "He has the reputation of being something of a misogynist, although extremely handsome."

"Excessively," Valeria agreed lightly. "What a pity that his manners do not match his face."

Camilla gave her friend a concerned glance. "You did not quarrel with him, did you, Val? I know he can be vastly disagreeable. He has lately inherited his grandfather's title, you know, and it is rumored that he will have to sell out of the army. Hart has known him for ever—they were at school together. I have heard it whispered that he has held our sex in dislike since he was disappointed in love when he first came on the town, but Hart says it is all a hum." She pulled a very wry face. "He will have it that there was never anything more than a boyish attachment, and that the real reason he holds us in aversion is because of his elder brother."

When Valeria looked surprised, she nodded her head. "Oh, yes. Did you not know? Leo never expected to inherit the title, that is why he joined the regiment. Hart says that he wanted to make the army his career, and, indeed, would have done had Philip not died so tragically."

There were times, Valeria decided wrathfully, when her friend's habit of meandering disjointedly around a story before getting to the kernel could be distinctly infuriating—and this was most definitely one of them.

"What happened to his brother?" she asked, trying hard to conceal her impatience.

"Oh, he was betrothed to one of the Ramsey girls. The pretty one—you must remember her, she came out three seasons before us and had the whole town at her feet. The gentlemen were all going mad for her, they say she had over a hundred proposals within a sennight of her coming out. Anyway, she accepted Philip. Of course, all the world knew that he was to inherit the dukedom, and a very handsome fortune into the bargain. The betrothal ball was the talk of London. I distinctly remember my cousin, Cecily Brompton, telling me about it. Her mama had ordered her a pink gown especially for the occasion; only when they arrived, Sara Ramsey was wearing pink too. Her dress quite outshone Cecily's, and she was most wretchedly depressed about it for *weeks* afterwards."

"Camilla!" Valeria muttered direfully.

"Oh, yes. Where was I? Yes, the betrothal. Well, it seems that no sooner had she accepted Philip Gervaise than she ups and decides that she doesn't want to marry him, after all. Instead she elopes with some rakish good-for-nothing she met at Tunbridge Wells, of all places! Can you imagine? However, what must the silly chit do, but send Philip a note telling him what she intended to do. Naturally, Philip went after her. The rest of the story I had from Hart, and you must promise me *never* to repeat it, Val, for it was told to him by Leo Carrington in *strictest* confidence."

Rather guiltily, Valeria gave her word. She knew she should not be encouraging Camilla to betray a confidence, but she had heard too much of the story to be denied the ending now.

"It seems that Philip Gervaise caught up with the miscreants somewhere on the Great North Road. He was a quiet, gentle boy, by all accounts, but he adored Sara. He discovered the inn at which they had stopped to partake of dinner, and challenged his rival to a duel. The outcome was inevitable. The other was an expert shot. Philip didn't even get the chance to fire his gun. He was dying when Leo reached him."

To her consternation, Valeria discovered that her eyes were stinging with tears, and a large lump lodged uncomfortably in her throat.

"That is not the end of it," Camilla told her. "It seems that Leo had learned of his brother's intentions from his valet, an old family servant, and had followed him north. As soon as he realized that Philip was not likely to live, he posted after Sara, and stopped their carriage just outside Carlisle. Hart told me that he begged her to return with him to the inn, so that Philip might see her before he died. Hart says he even promised that he would say nothing of her elopement, if she would only agree, but she would not. 'Let him die' is what she said, or so he told Hart."

"How could she be so hard?" Valeria whispered at last. "A few hours out of her life . . ."

"She was a great beauty and dreadfully spoiled. I dare say she thought it all a great adventure, to have two gentlemen fighting over her. The last I heard of her, she had become Lord Moysten's mistress. It seems the *grande passion* did not last long. However, it served to embitter Leo Carrington. He could have been no more than eighteen at the time—just a boy, really. One only has to recollect oneself at the same age," she sighed, and shook her head. "Never breathe a word of what I have told you, Val. Hart would kill me if he knew, and the only reason I tell you is so that you may be on your guard. Leo Carrington has a heart of stone. I should not wish to see you lose your heart in that direction, especially not when at least half a dozen gentlemen here tonight have asked me who you are," she finished on a note of gaiety.

After that, Valeria had little inclination to participate in the lighthearted conversations going on around her. Camilla's revelations had given her a new insight into Leo Carrington, and the reasons behind his scathing attack upon her. Even so, she told herself, anyone with so low an opinion of another person, prejudging her on so little evidence and so short an acquaintance, was surely not worth concerning herself with. However, she could not deny the small ache in her heart, that she had been so harshly judged.

Camilla had one more piece of matronly advice for her

friend, before Valeria and her father departed, and this time upon a completely different matter. Valeria had been chatting with a gentleman who described himself as one of the czar's aides. He was very attractive, with crisp, dark curls and merry hazel eyes, and he made Valeria laugh with his droll descriptions of his fellow aides and other congress personalities.

"Beware of Count Polinsky," Camilla warned her, when he had left. "His gossip often has a sting in its tail, and he is reputed to be one of the czar's spies. You look surprised! I assure you it is quite true. Hart told me so himself. The count is also the most shocking flirt!"

"I shall be on my guard," Valeria promised her, a teasing smile in her eyes. "Dearest Camilla, I am not quite so green as to be taken in by a charming manner, you know. I had already conjectured that the count was something of a ladies' man, although he can scarce hope to discover any important secrets from me!"

"Oh, as to that. In Vienna everyone spies upon everyone else. It has become the national pastime. As long as you do not take him too seriously, the count will make an excellent acquaintance. He waltzes magnificently."

She pouted a little when Valeria laughed, but was soon sharing her friend's amusement.

"You still have to show the modiste your emeralds," she pointed out to Valeria. "I have tomorrow afternoon free. Should we go, then?"

Valeria thought quickly. With any luck she should have returned from the Imperial Riding School in time to accompany Camilla.

"That will be fine," she agreed. "Here comes Papa. I must tell him that I will need the emeralds."

Sir Edward was in the greatest of good spirits. He had spent a most convivial evening in good company; had consumed exactly the right amount of excellent port; had seen his daughter for once apparently bearing all his strictures in mind; and felt in a very indulgent frame of mind, indeed.

He would have been dismayed had he been privy to Valeria's thoughts. Whilst it was true that Perry featured largely amongst them, it was not for the reason that Sir Edward would have wished. Her earlier conviction that Perry was worried about something had returned. Perhaps tomorrow he would have the opportunity to tell her what ailed him. She certainly hoped so.

On their return journey Sir Edward repeated at great length several conversations he had had during the course of the evening, but Valeria found it impossible to pay the attention she knew she ought. Time and time again, her thoughts kept returning to Leo Carrington, even though she tried to school them into less emotive channels. Was it *her* fault that the major's brother had chosen to fall in love so unwisely? Of course not!

Her maid was waiting up for her, but Valeria dismissed her. She did not feel in the mood to satisfy Hester's obvious interest in how the evening had gone. Rather than risk hurting her feelings, she sent her to bed, explaining that she would want to be up early in the morning, as she had arranged to meet Perry.

Next morning, by the time Valeria had eaten her breakfast and dressed for the street, she discovered that the day was well advanced. She elected to walk to the Hofburg Palace, much to the city-bred Hester's dismay, and discovered it to be an imposing edifice, with some magnificent formal gardens through which she strolled on her way to the stables.

Several groups of officers in varying uniforms were already gathered in the gallery, which ran right around the indoor show-ring, when Valeria arrived. Amongst them were half a dozen members of the czar's Imperial Guard, watching one of the grooms putting two of the stallions through their paces. One of them hailed her, much to Valeria's astonishment, and as he drew nearer, she recognized the feaures of Count Polinsky.

He was every bit as entertaining as he had been the previous evening, introducing Valeria to his companions with a mock reluctance, claiming that he wanted no rivals for her affections. As Camilla had stated, Valeria discovered that each and every one of the Russian officers was a good deal taller than she was. So much so, in fact, that she found herself having to tilt her chin to look up at them. This was a grave mistake, for it reminded her of Leo Carrington's imposing height, and Leo Carrington himself!

In the practice ring below them, the grooms exercised their charges tirelessly.

"The czar is determined to take a stallion and some mares back to Russia with him," the count confided as Valeria turned to watch, but when she would have questioned him a little more closely about how the animals were trained, he murmured some ridiculous comment about wishing his fellow officers a thousand miles away in the wastes of Siberia, and naturally they replied in kind.

Indeed, as the gentlemen chatted to her, passing outrageous compliments, for the first time in her life she knew what it was to feel deliciously helpless and feminine. Count Polinsky would not even allow her to carry the dainty parasol, whose purpose was merely one of adornment, and insisted on walking solicitously at her side, as she searched the crowd for Perry.

"Perhaps we could ride together, one morning," he murmured softly in her ear. "I should like to steal a march on all my rivals, Miss Fitzmount, and have you all to myself. I have never seen such coloring as yours," he added admiringly. "You are delightful! An enchantress, who has me fast in her spell. Will you ride with me?"

"I might," Valeria teased. "And then again, I might not."

"When a gentleman flirts, he expects you to respond in the same vein," Camilla had cautioned her. "Only gentlemen who are not serious flirt."

"And when they are?" Valeria had mocked, but Camilla was determined to answer seriously. "That is when they are at their most awkward, poor things," she said wisely. "When a gentleman is awkward and clumsy, unable to speak often more than a single word in one's presence, that is a sure sign his feelings are truly engaged!"

Obviously, from this description, Count Polinsky's feelings were not, and so Valeria felt quite justified in gently escaping from him, when she eventually espied Perry with a group of his fellow officers. He hailed her with his normal, cheery smile. She was wearing the first of the finished dresses from Madame Bertine. A simple slip of jonquil muslin over an underdress of matching, embroidered batiste. It was both fresh and eye-catching. Her parasol was covered in the same fabric, and a delightful straw bonnet, tied with jonquil ribbons, drew attention to her sparkling eyes and lovely face. No one at home would have recognized this ravishing creature as the same Miss Fitzmount who used to trudge to the village in a pair of faded half boots in beige kid, wearing a shabby, striped muslin, her hair severely restrained in old-fashioned plaits. Even Perry did a double take as she advanced, and judging by the amicable squabbling going on amongst his companions as to whom should be introduced to her first, Camilla had not been so far out, after all, in her declaration that she could turn Valeria into a toast.

With Hester discreetly in attendance, Valeria listened to the gentlemen, discoursing upon the various merits of the horses being paraded round the sawdust-strewn practice ring. Faint strains of music reached her, and she gasped in amazement as the horses reared on their hind legs, pirouetting gracefully in time to the sound.

"Surely it cannot be good for them," Valeria protested, fascinated despite her doubts, by the animals' expertise.

"They are bred for it," one of Perry's companions assured her, "and pampered like royal children. They are better fed and better housed than many a minor noble."

Valeria was not the only lady present. As she stared about her she realized that a morning spent watching the royal horses—and discreetly displaying one's new gown—was a favorite pastime among the ton.

Most of the ladies favored elegant walking dresses, some topped by toning striped spencers, others favoring fur-lined pelisses; but whatever the style, the quality and elegance of the outfit was unmistakable. Someone kindly pointed out to her the Princess de Lieven, and her attendants, and Valeria was reminded of the conversation she had overheard at the Minoritzenplatz. Although there were a good many officers present, all jovially vying for the ladies' attention, she did not recognize anyone from the courtyard.

Very few of the gentlemen were in civilian dress. Everywhere one looked, the eye was caught by uniformed figures: gentlemen who were proud for the world to know of their part in Bonaparte's defeat. Some Prussian grenadiers sauntered past, their backs stiff as ramrods, followed by another small group of the czar's personal guard in their gold and white. It was no wonder that most of the ladies favored sweetpea colors, Valeria reflected, for they could not hope to vie with the richness of the gentlemen's uniforms.

Valeria's own presence did not go unremarked, and before too long, she was exchanging nods and smiles with at least half a dozen persons, including the lady-in-waiting to whom Camilla had introduced her at the musical evening. Valeria found it very heartwarming to be the recipient of so much goodwill, and as the gentlemen chivied one another in a jocular fashion, she reflected that in other circumstances, she could have found herself thoroughly enjoying her stay in Vienna.

Perry, as Valeria noticed, was becoming increasingly impatient at his companions' reluctance to allow them to take their leave, and constantly referred to his fob watch, frowning as he did so. At length, however, he was able to draw Valeria apart to a quiet part of the amphitheater, away from the bustle and noise of the crowds, where they could talk uninterrupted. Hester was dismissed to await her mistress at a discreet distance, whilst Valeria settled herself on the chair which Perry had procured.

"Perry, what is wrong?" she asked with some concern, when they were alone. "And do not, I beg, seek to convince me that all is well, for anyone with half an eye can see that it is not!"

"You're right," Perry agreed gloomily, a fresh frown creasing his forehead. He ran a hand through his hair in a distracted fashion, looking absurdly youthful, and causing Valeria's heart to contract in sympathy.

"I'm in the devil of a fix, Val," he admitted at length, without preamble. "God knows I ought not to burden you with my problems, but to be honest with you, I just don't know where to turn."

He sounded so serious that Valeria could only stare. This wasn't the gay young man whom she knew. "Don't keep me on tenterhooks," she begged. "Tell me, at once. What ails you? Surely you can confide in *me*, Perry," she pressed when he seemed about to demur. "I'm sure we're far closer than many a brother and sister, even if we do not have a blood tie."

"That's true," Perry admitted, sighing heavily. He hesitated for a second, plainly torn between inclination and convention, chewing his bottom lip in a distracted fashion. And then, to Valeria's dismay, he buried his face in his hands, his shoulders trembling with the pent-up force of his inner turmoil.

"Dear God, Val, if only I could offer you some feasible excuse for my behavior, but I cannot."

His voice broke on the words, and Valeria was left to exclaim worriedly, "What behavior, Perry? You *must* tell me what is wrong," she stressed urgently.

He looked down at her, his face no longer youthful, but drawn and shadowed. "God knows, Val, I hate myself for involving you in this mess, but I must tell *someone*." He looked away from her and then, making a heroic effort to pull himself together, carried on.

"I don't need to tell you the sort of conditions the regiment experienced in the peninsula. Hard campaigning, poor food, fighting, never knowing if one would be alive from one day to the next. When we heard we were to be posted to Vienna, the men went wild with joy."

Unable to see where these disclosures were leading, Valeria waited in some trepidation.

"When we arrived here we were told that any man found gaming or fighting would be court-martialed instantly and——"

"You have not been gaming, have you, Perry?" Valeria interrupted in considerable alarm.

He shook his head decisively. "Worse," he admitted bluntly. "Some of the other fellows from the regiment discovered a gaming hall in one of the poorer quarters of the city. They persuaded me to go there with them—just for a lark, they said—and I could hardly refuse. You know how it is? The outcome was that I got involved with a . . . a female there —the daughter of the woman who runs the establishment." He broke off, grimacing with distaste. "What must you be thinking of me? This is not a tale for delicate female ears, I—"

"Having told me so much, you must give me the whole," Valeria persisted firmly. "I am not such a ninnyhammer that I do not know of these liaisons."

Perry blushed, about to demur, and muttered something to the effect that had they not been so long in the peninsula, he doubted that he would ever have been foolish enough to become involved.

"This 'female' is not a lady, I take it?" Valeria inquired delicately.

"A lady! Anything but," Perry admitted bitterly, shuddering slightly. "The fact is, Val, that it was but a momentary foolishness. Lisle was there, and the other fellows . . . Well, you know how it is," he added lamely, avoiding Valeria's eyes. "I had been drinking pretty heavily and was in no condition for sensible thought. By the time I realized what I had got myself into, and brought the association to an end, Lisle was creating all hell—and her mother, too."

This was not the time to lecture Perry on the irresponsibility of his behavior, Valeria decided wisely. It was becoming

63

more and more obvious that he had been egged on by his companions, who had probably drunken as deeply as he had himself. She knew better, of course, than to inquire why Perry had not simply ignored them. She knew enough about gentlemen to realize that, no matter how deep in his cups he might have been, Perry could never have ignored what she suspected had been a challenge from his companions with regard to the girl, Lisle.

There was nothing to be gained from chiding Perry for what was past, Valeria admitted to herself. However, one part of his story *did* puzzle her.

"If you have brought the liaison to an end, I cannot see your problem," she commented practically. "To be sure, you have behaved a trifle foolishly. But then, you are not the first gentleman to do so, and I doubt you will be the last."

Far from reassuring Perry, her comments seemed to throw him into even deeper despair.

"I haven't told you the whole, yet, Val," he admitted. "The fact is that I have fallen in love! Oh, not with anyone at all unsuitable," he hastened to reassure her, seeing her expression. "Far from it! She is the most enchanting creature! We met at a ball and her mama allowed me to waltz with her. I fell in love, there and then. Her name is Maria Schubraum. Her family is an old one. Her father, the present baron, is a close friend of the empress." He grimaced slightly. "You can see how much it would go against me if it came out that I had been visiting that wretched establishment. Not to mention my involvement with Lisle."

"And Miss Schubraum?" Valeria inquired cautiously. "Does she return your regard?"

Perry's eyes shone. "I believe so. Or at least, I was beginning to hope that she might . . . but now . . . Oh, Val if only this had not happened. I had fully intended to approach Baron Schubraum for Maria's hand before the month was out."

"If she does return your feelings, I am sure she will overlook what was, after all, a very brief lapse, which occurred before you had met her," Valeria soothed. "Of course, it would be too sanguine of you to expect her to be complacent about it. But need she know? What is in the past—"

"But that's just it, Val," Perry protested drearily. "It isn't. In the past, I mean."

He fished in his pocket and withdrew a crumpled missive, written on vulgarly colorful notepaper.

"Here—read this," he commanded her.

Quickly, Valeria perused the violet-hued sheets:

Captain Adaire,

>   *This note is to remind you of yr obligation to one who thought she held yr hart, but is now suplanted by Another! If you do not come to the house that you know of in the Schaltplatz the grievious affliction which has come upon me since yr own deceetful desertion will cause me to warn yr new young lady for her own sake of your cruel treatment of a girl who has no father to protect her. I look to see you before the week is out.*

>   *Yr own Lisle*

The letter was misspelled, but its meaning was plain, and the ugly threat it contained brought a worried frown to Valeria's eyes.

"But why do you suppose this Lisle wishes you to call on her?" Valeria asked, referring to the demand contained in the note. "Surely, she must realize that you have given her her *congé*, and that the liaison is at an end?"

"You would think so," Perry agreed. "But I detect her mother's hand in this. Depend upon it, she has learned of my title, and hopes perhaps, to persuade me to make some financial provision for Lisle."

"Surely not," Valeria objected. "From what you have told me, the relationship was of a most casual nature."

"Casual, or not, 'tis plain that I must give way to their demands, whatever they might be," Perry said gloomily. "If they fulfill their threat to expose the liaison to Maria, there will not be the slightest chance of the baron agreeing to my suit, and—quite apart from that—the mere fact that I was present in there would be sufficient to warrant my being court-martialed, even though I never played at the tables. Can you imagine what it would do to Gramps, if I were forced to leave the regiment, in disgrace? You know how proud he is of the family name."

Valeria could only agree that Lord Adaire would be bitterly hurt and disappointed—and just when Perry would need his approval and goodwill.

"I had hoped to persuade him to accept my marriage to Maria, notwithstanding his hopes in regard to you, but now . . ."

"But surely there must be *some* way of preventing them from carrying out their threat?" Valeria protested.

"Yes. I must accede to their demands," agreed Perry bitterly. "This meeting will be but the first of many, and all the time I will fall deeper into their toils. I wish to God I had never set eyes on Lisle!"

"Could you not seek out Major Carrington, and lay the whole before him? He is your commanding officer, and you seem to be good friends."

"Oh, Val, you do not understand," Perry groaned. "Friendship is one thing. Duty is another. I was there, and if I told Leo as much, he would be obliged to make an example of me, for breaking the rules. He could not turn a blind eye. You *must* see that!"

"But what about the other officers who were with you? The ones who *took* you there? Surely, it is not right that you should be punished whilst they, who are in my view far more guilty, get off scot-free."

"Val, you do not understand. To admit that I was not there alone would reflect adversely upon my honor," he sighed. "You must take my word that this is so." Perry persisted when Valeria looked doubtful: "Before God, Val, you would not wish me to appear lacking in honor, as well as common sense?"

Valeria knew him too well to persist with her original line of reasoning. Gentlemen, she knew, accounted honor of primary importance, and unlike wealth or station, once gone, it could never be regained.

"There is nothing else for it," Perry announced firmly, squaring his shoulders. "I shall just have to accede to their demands, whatever they might be. But one thing is for sure, I cannot approach the baron whilst Lisle and her mother cling to me like damned leeches! I can only hope that by the time Maria and her parents return to Vienna, I shall have quitted it!"

"Return?" Valeria queried, an idea forming.

"Maria's godfather is sick of a fever. He has a chateau

66

some miles from Vienna, and they have gone there so that Maria's mother might oversee his recovery, for he has no wife to care for him. It is a mercy that they are not here."

"A mercy, indeed," agreed Valeria warmly. "For it gives us the opportunity to remove your 'leeches' before she returns."

"Remove them? But how? They are stuck fast, and intend to suck me dry, I fancy."

"From their letter, I judge that they think their hold over you strong enough to force you to give way. But that hold is merely a threat to betray your liaison with Lisle to Maria. They dare not risk making your presence in their establishment known," Valeria said practically. "For if they did, *no* officers would patronize it for fear of being discovered, and they would lose their means of livelihood. What *we* must do, Perry, is outwit them, and I believe I know how this might be achieved."

"How?" Perry asked eagerly.

"Quite simple," Valeria replied with a smile. "I shall pretend to be Maria Schubraum and call upon Mistress Lisle and her mother, and inform them that not only have you apprised me of your regrettable association, but also that I have *completely* forgiven you, and have come in your stead to tell them as much. That should draw the venom from their sting."

"I think it might work," Perry breathed. "Oh, but Val, I could not allow you to do this for me. The place is in a most unsalubrious part of the town, and Lisle and her mother are not fit company for you to consort with."

"*You* consorted with them!" Valeria reminded him unanswerably, relenting enough to give him a reassuring smile.

"Come, it is not quite the thing, I know, but no one shall know I have been, and I am sure that it will work. When Lisle and her mother see that you cannot be coerced or threatened, they will gladly cease to harass you, I am sure."

At the back of her mind, but undisclosed to Perry, was the intention of playing Lisle and her parent at their own game, threatening to reveal to the commanding officer of the regiment the existence of their place. This countermove, she was convinced, would reinforce her allegations that their threats would afford them naught!

"No wonder you seemed so dismayed when Papa and I

arrived," Valeria commented sympathetically. "Eventually, we shall have to tell Papa about your love for Maria, but that can wait upon Lisle and her mother."

"I don't know how to thank you, Val," Perry said sombrely. "I feel as though you have lifted an unbearable weight from my mind. I am sure I shall be able to make Gramps see reason. If he is as pleased with me as you say, he might become disposed to see my point of view."

"He *is* pleased with you, Perry," Valeria reiterated. "Dr. Chadburn is convinced that your achievements with the regiment have done much to aid his recovery. So," she continued briskly, "all is decided. All that remains is for you to give me the direction of this gaming hall, and the name of the woman who owns it. I cannot go out there today because I have an appointment with Madame Bertine for a fitting, but I am free tomorrow morning." She frowned, a fresh problem occurring to her. "How shall I let you know how I have gone on? It would not do for you to call upon me, for that would only reinforce Papa's desire to see you as his son-in-law. What about the empress's ball?"

Perry shook his head. "I cannot wait until then to discover how you have fared. We could meet in the Woods tomorrow afternoon. There are some very pleasant rides there, which we often use for exercising our mounts, and there are constant picnics, and the like. No one will think anything of it should we meet there."

"That sounds excellent," Valeria approved. "By the way," she added lightly, not wanting to depress him even further. "The most shocking coincidence—your Major Carrington is none other than the nephew of the couple who have rented the house from Papa. I was obliged to endure a most uncomfortable interview with him, for what must his aunt do but write him a lengthy and descriptive letter denouncing my character. You know it is all about the neighborhood at home, that Papa and Lord Adaire wish us to marry? I have never bothered to deny it, and in some roundabout fashion, Euphemia Gervaise has the tale wrong, and repeated that it is *I* who wish for the match and am come to Vienna for no other purpose than to pursue you quite relentlessly!"

Perry was shocked. "Of course! I had forgotten that Leo was connected there, otherwise I might have warned you. The old cat! But surely you set him right?"

"I was not granted the opportunity," Valeria answered lightly, unwilling to confess exactly what had ensued.

"Would you like me to speak with Leo?" Perry asked. "It is unforgivable that he should have such a low opinion of you."

"There is no need," Valeria said, with an assurance she was far from feeling. "If he wishes to account his aunt's words as gospel, who am I to stop him? No, Perry. He had made up his mind that I am at least twice as black as I am painted. Even if you were to tell him the truth, I am quite sure he would discover some ulterior reason for your doing so!" Seeing that she was not to be swayed, Perry escorted her back to where Hester was waiting, with a final injunction to her not to forget their appointment for the following day.

"You are sure you wish to go ahead with our plan?" he asked anxiously.

"Quite sure," Valeria reassured him. "Now I must return home before any of your friends start to comment on the length of time we have been closeted together."

Chapter Five

Valeria was not given much opportunity to dwell upon Perry's confidences nor her promise to help him. Their talk had lasted longer than she had anticipated, and upon her return to the apartment, there was scarcely time for her to change her gown before Camilla arrived to accompany her to the modiste.

Asking Hester to bring her pelisse, Valeria hurried to join her friend. As the day was so fine, Camilla had elected to use her open barouche, and she proudly called Valeria's attention to this smart equipage as they stepped out into the street. Painted in cream, with the Normanton Arms discreetly displayed on the door panels, its interior lined with pale blue velvet, the carriage was, indeed, a fine sight.

"Isn't it gorgeous?" Camilla exclaimed, inviting Valeria to admire her latest acquisition. "Hart bought it for me—the darling."

"And you could not wait to use it," Valeria teased, as her friend unfurled a dainty parasol against the dangerous rays of the sun.

"You have an unfair advantage," Camilla complained, as her groom opened the door and assisted both ladies into the barouche, before taking his seat on the box. "You never freckle, Val. Whilst I am positively plagued with the wretched things."

"You should try placing slices of cucumber on your face," Valeria replied absently, as the carriage set off. "I have heard it is most effective."

It was true that her own skin was not subject to this unfashionable affliction, but nevertheless she listened patiently whilst Camilla commented upon the ineffectiveness of the various remedies she had tried thus far.

"I purchased some Denmark lotion advertised in the *Ladies Journal*, but it had not the slightest effect. I do believe it is high time some of these advertisements were more closely examined. I have yet to find a single product that fulfills its maker's claims. Indeed, I am sure that half of those persons who purport to be the sole possessors of some ancient Egyptian beauty secret are nothing but charlatans. Oh, now you are laughing at me, Val," she protested crossly.

"Not really," Valeria assured her. "Indeed, I concur with all you have said. But as long as our sex is foolish and vain enough to pay heed to their claims, I am afraid that the rogues will flourish."

"Hart is of the same mind," Camilla agreed on a sigh. "Have you remembered to bring the emeralds?"

"I have them in my reticule," Valeria assured her. "Goodness, aren't the streets busy!"

"Oh, it is always like this," Camilla agreed. "Whereas, at home in London, all the fashionable notables will parade in the park between five and six o'clock, showing off their horses and person, here in Vienna the ton may be constantly seen in the squares and streets, and, of course, with the congress, the town is positively bursting at the seams."

When the barouche was obliged to stop to allow a small group of hussars to cross the road, Camilla made good use of the time to point out to Valeria several members of the Austrian nobility, chatting and laughing outside an elegant coffeehouse whilst they waited for their carriage.

"You will soon discover that the Viennese frequent their coffeehouses much more than we do at home. During the summer, the ladies often gather on their terraces to drink chocolate and exchange gossip. Indeed, it is a most pleasurable pastime.

The hussars had gone, and they were free to move off through a square hung with flags and bunting, representing all the allied armies.

"Every ballroom this season is hung with the colors of the victorious armies," Camilla commented knowledgeably. "Pink silk and fresh flowers are quite démodé, although I attended a ball a sennight ago, where the hostess had had manufactured, from flower heads, the arms of all the royal houses. It was most effective!"

At last the coachman set them down outside the modiste's

establishment. The fitting for the ballgown seemed to drag on interminably. For a start, Madame Bertine had to give the emeralds a thorough inspection.

"These are excellent," she approved at length. "I have never seen finer. You are, indeed, fortunate to possess them, Miss Fitzmount. Having seen them, for myself I suggest that we keep your gown as simple as possible. Indeed, it would be difficult, even for me, to design a dress that would outshine jewels such as these," she admitted frankly.

Camilla had, of course, seen the Fitzmount emeralds before, but, like the modiste, she was plainly impressed by them. Huge stones of a cabochon cut were set in an ornate gold necklace of very antique and intricate design.

There was a story in the family that the necklace had originated from the Aztec gold mines pillaged by the Spanish, although how true it was, Valeria could not say. She only knew that the family records showed it to have come into Fitzmount possession during the time of Elizabeth I.

It was Valeria's grandmother who had had the original necklace shortened, and the spare stones and filigree work reset into a pair of matching bracelets and earrings.

With the modiste to advise her, she eventually settled upon a very fine silk fabric, in a shade currently very fashionable, known as "nile green" and which toned exactly with the emeralds.

The modiste suggested a severely classical style for the gown, entirely in keeping with the vogue for Greek Revival, and although at first Valeria was a little concerned that this might be rather outré, by the time the seamstresses had finished tucking and pinning, she had to allow that the gown had an elegance which far surpassed anything she had visualized.

Camilla, whose own gown was a pretty confection of rose pink tulle, trimmed with bunches of flowers, made a small moue as the seamstresses bore away the uncompleted gown.

"It is not fair," she mourned. "You will quite eclipse me, Val. You will quite eclipse *everyone!*"

Valeria could not allow this to be so, and was telling Camilla so when they left the shop.

"I must procure some new slippers. It won't take long," Camilla promised, turning aside.

Valeria moved to follow her, and almost cannoned into a couple walking past. She started to apologize, and then broke off as she realized that the gentleman was none other than

Leo Carrington. On his arm was one of the most beautiful women Valeria had ever seen. Whilst not in her first youth—Valeria judged her to be somewhere around Leo Carrington's own age, of one and thirty—her skin still had the perfection of camellia petals, eyes of a warm, velvet brown, turning meltingly in the direction of her handsome companion whose shoulder she barely reached.

Leo Carrington gave no indication of having recognized them; the incident was over in seconds, and he and his companion were swallowed up by the crowd. But Valeria had a most vivid and unforgettable picture of the two of them. The beautiful woman; the handsome man; the way the woman had raised her face to his; the corresponding smile he had bestowed upon her.

"Well! if I hadn't seen it with my own eyes I should never have believed it," Camilla breathed, staring after them. "Leo Carrington with a woman, and that woman in particular. She was Metternich's mistress for a time," she explained knowledgeably, and has been casting out lures for Leo ever since the regiment arrived in Vienna. I never thought to see him fall into her trap, though. If she entertains any hopes that he will make her his duchess, she will be sadly disappointed. He must marry one day, of course, to safeguard the title—but never to a woman of that order. It is rumored that when the czar arrived in Vienna he besieged her with gifts and entreaties, but she spurned him."

"She is very beautiful," Valeria acknowledged.

"But hard," Camilla chimed in. "I cannot wait to tell Hart that his idol has feet of clay. He will never believe me. I shall call upon you as a witness, Val. Leo Carrington, of *all* people! I never thought to see the day."

"Even Homer nods," Valeria interrupted wryly. She should have felt satisfaction that Leo Carrington was as susceptible to female blandishment as any other male, but she did not. Indeed, she could not have said *what* she felt, save that added to everything else she had on her mind, it served to make her feel exceedingly dolorous.

She barely listened to Camilla when she rattled on about all the gentlemen she might expect to meet at the empress's ball. Nor did her spirits lift when, after saying goodbye to Camilla and returning to the apartment, she discovered that she was the recipient of a delightful floral tribute sent by Count Polinsky.

74

• • •

Later that evening, as she prepared for bed, Valeria found her forthcoming interview with Perry's harpy weighing heavily upon her mind. She slept fitfully, her sleep broken by a succession of vivid nightmares, and was glad when the first, tentative fingers of morning sunshine stretched across her pillow, heralding the new day.

Naturally, Valeria had been obliged to take Hester into her confidence, regarding her proposed visit to the gaming establishment. At first the maid had been inclined to complain that Master Perry should not impose so, but when Valeria gently reminded her that the decision was hers and hers alone, Hester subsided into a chastened silence, although sticking very closely to her mistress's heels when Valeria eventually set out upon her mission.

Valeria herself, was far from feeling the confident she pretended. Of course she wanted to do all she could to help Perry, and yet, she could not help reflecting that she might have bitten off more than she could chew.

This time, she did not pause to admire her surroundings, and, indeed, as the elegant homes of the ton gave way to cluttered shops and grimy houses, it was hard not to allow her thoughts to be overshadowed by the shabby neighborhood.

The streets grew meaner as the safety of the wide fauborgs was left behind, but Valeria refused to allow her apprehension to break her resolution. Perry had not wanted her to venture here alone, she reminded herself, but she had insisted. After all, it *was* broad daylight, and it was only her wretched imagination that painted the shabby houses with dark cavernous mouths and sinister shuttered windows.

Perry's description of the area as "unsalubrious" had been no exaggeration of the truth, and Valeria shivered a little, despite the warmth of the sun. There was something alien, and not a little daunting, about the labyrinth of narrow streets, and she wished that they had had the foresight to bring one of the footmen with her. However, it was too late to think of that now!

Perry's instructions had been clear and concise, and she found the square in which the gaming hall was situated without too much difficulty. The square itself was small, bounded by a row of three-story houses whose height obliterated the friendly

75

sunshine, and whose windows gaped blindly onto the dusty cobbles.

Immediately opposite the hall was an inn, its patrons arguing loudly over the rival merits of two fighting cocks. The birds were in a small, wicker cage on the floor, and Valeria averted her eyes as she skirted the alehouse.

"Cock fighting!" Hester exclaimed in shocked tones, eyes clutching nervously at her cloak. "Oh, Miss Valeria, we didn't ought to be here. It isn't the place for a lady!"

"Don't fuss, Hester," Valeria commanded with a calm she was far from feeling. Fortunately, the patrons of the inn were too engrossed in their noisy quarrel to pay much attention to the two hooded and cloaked females who had encroached upon their territory.

She had told her maid nothing, save that she was carrying out a small commission for Perry, and she was now trying to conceal her trepidation. It was one thing to tell Perry that he could leave all safely in her hands, but, as she was now discovering, it was a different matter altogether to put that boast into practice. At first he had wanted to escort her, but she had dissuaded him, conscious that he might not approve of her intention of playing Lisle and her mother at their own game.

A slatternly maid, wearing a filthy apron, opened the door to Valeria's knock.

"Well, what do you want?" she asked in a surly manner.

"I wish to see your mistress," Valeria announced firmly. "Mrs. Noakes, I believe?"

"Huh! The 'mistress' is it? Hoity-toity, ain't we?" she jeered unpleasantly. "And who shall I say is calling? The empress herself?"

"Oh!" Hester gasped in outrage.

"You may tell Mrs. Noakes that my name is Maria Schubraum," Valeria replied coldly, ignoring both the girl's incivility and her maid's disapproval. Leaving Valeria standing on the doorstep, the girl disappeared down a long passage. Wine fumes and the smell of stale tobacco floated on the air, causing Valeria to wrinkle her nose in fastidious revulsion. Somewhere a door opened, and a woman emerged in the passage.

Small and frankly buxom, she peered at Valeria with sharp, black eyes. Wearing a purple wrapper, which looked none too clean, her hennaed hair partially concealed by a be-

76

ribboned cap, she gestured to Valeria to follow her back down the corridor, and into a room which was obviously used as a gaming salon during the evenings.

Having subjected Valeria to an intense and suspicious scrutiny, she motioned to a chair.

"Well, Miss Maria," she asked in an overly familiar fashion. "And what brings you here? I'll wager it isn't for the pleasure of gaming in my salons."

"Then, you would wager correctly," Valeria agreed, resolving to remain as cool as she could.

Perry had warned her that she would find Mrs. Noakes and her place extremely vulgar, but he had not prepared her for the garish effect of purple and satin chairs, embellished with a quantity of gold tassels, strategically placed around half a dozen baize-covered tables.

"I see you're admiring my salon," Mrs. Noakes smirked complacently. "Only the best is good enough for my gentlemen clients, that's what I always say."

"I don't doubt that you do," Valeria agreed coolly. "Nor that you make them pay for it—one way or another."

The small black eyes narrowed, the air of assumed gentility swiftly banished.

"All right then, miss. Let's lay our cards on the table, shall we? What brings you here?"

"I think you already know," Valeria replied calmly drawing off her gloves. "I have in my reticule the letter your daughter sent to Captain Adaire. In that letter she made several threats, not unconnected with my own relationship with Captain Adaire."

"Well! Here's a cool one," Mrs. Noakes declared in mock admiration. "But you won't do for the captain, my dear. I tell you that straight."

"I have not come here for your opinion on our suitability, Mrs. Noakes."

"No? Then why have you come, if it ain't impolite to ask?" the other said sarcastically.

Valeria was beginning to understand why Perry had been so worried by the letter. He had told her that Mrs. Noakes had first come to Vienna in the wake of the French Army, or so she had said. Although Irish by birth, she had been calling herself Madame Noilles, but had apparently strategically reverted to her original nationality following Bonaparte's defeat.

77

Beneath the raddled skin and painted face, Valeria suspected there lay a very shrewd mind indeed—shrewd and cunning!

"I have come to prove to you that neither yourself nor your daughter has any hold on Perry Adaire."

The black eyes flashed dangerously

"No? We shall see about that!" She pulled angrily on the bell rope, and within seconds the slatternly maid was back.

"Find Miss Lisle!" Mrs. Noakes commanded.

What was she planning to do? Valeria wondered. She soon knew. The door was opened and a plump brunette bounced in, her high color and snapping eyes instantly betraying her relationship to the older woman.

"What do you want me for, Ma?" she asked crossly. "Jack's promised to take me out."

"Never mind Jack. He can wait. This *LADY* here has come on behalf of Captain Adaire. It seems the gentleman don't want to visit with us no longer!"

"Oh, yes? And who's she, then?" Lisle asked rudely.

"My name is Maria Schubraum," Valeria began, but the other girl cut her off, arms planted firmly on her hips. She turned to her mother.

"She's lying, Ma," she announced firmly. "She ain't the Maria I saw Captain Adaire with. You know, I told you about it. Curious about her, I was, seeing as how he had just cast me off without a by-your-leave, and me having turned down a good many offers to stay true to him. Refused a carriage and pair, I did, from a Russian gentleman," she said to Valeria, in aggrieved accents.

"Well now, here's a pretty kettle of fish!" Mrs. Noakes announced complacently. "It seems to me that Captain Adaire is going to have to change his tune. Thought you'd fool us nicely, I'll be bound. Well, we ain't so easily fooled, miss. I wasn't born yesterday! You can tell that fine handsome captain that me and Lisle still have some unfinished business with him."

"But what do you want of him?" Valeria asked. "The liaison with your daughter, such as it was, is over!"

"Never you mind what we wants with him. You just give him that message, and if he don't come this time, it will be the worse for him. It won't just be Miss Maria who gets to hear about his junketings, but that major of his, as well!"

"You cannot do that," Valeria declared authoritatively. "If you do, you will destroy your own livelihood, for you may be sure that no officer will patronize your tables once it gets about that you have deliberately exposed one of their number to a court-martial."

"Well, that's where you're wrong, miss. Major Carrington might not allow his men to frequent our tables. Oh yes, I know all about the proud major, you may be sure that precious little happens in this town that I do not get to hear of. But not all the officers in this city are British. Only the other night, a Prussian general was sat down right over there. Lost a pretty sum, he did. And as for the Russians!" She laughed mirthlessly. "Why, gaming's like their mother's milk to them! They'll bet on anything! So you see, Miss—whatever your name is—you can't threaten me that way. Now you go and tell him what I've told you. If he don't take heed, it will be the worse for him!"

"Miss Valeria, whatever was all that about?" Hester asked in scandalized accents, when they had left. "Why are you masquerading under a false name?"

"Hester, you must say nothing of what has happened here, to anyone. Do you understand me?"

"Well, if you say so, miss. But it don't seem right to me, a young lady of your class subjected to such insults and familiarity. I can tell you that more than once, the palm of my 'and itched to smack that woman right—"

"That will do, Hester," Valeria reproved, hiding a small smile. Dear Hester, always staunch in her mistress's defense. Her visit had been a complete waste of time, Valeria admitted, and she was now no nearer to aiding Perry—far from it. Mrs. Noakes was a veritable bulldog, and Valeria suspected that she would not give up until she had achieved her aim, whatever that might be. Poor Perry. He would be so cast down by the failure of her mission.

The men and the fighting cocks were gone from the inn, Valeria noted thankfully, as they crossed the square. A soldier in Austrian uniform lounged against the wall in front of them, obviously the worse for drink. Valeria moved to one side to avoid him, but he lurched directly across her path, blocking it.

Even as Hester mouthed an anxious warning, one large hand was imprisoning Valeria's arm. Coming on top of her unsuccessful interview with Mrs. Noakes, his action frightened her more than it would normally have done, and she gave an involuntary cry of alarm. Plainly it was the wrong thing to do, for the soldier grinned hugely, lunging with his free hand for Valeria's other arm, obviously intent on pinning her to the wall.

"Please, release me," she begged, struggling to free herself. His face was unshaven, his eyes bloodshot and bleary, the smell of gin easily perceptible on his breath. Nauseated, Valeria jerked away, wincing with pain, as his grip on her arm tightened.

"Let me go!"

"I believe the lady gave you an order?" A cool, male voice announced from Valeria's shoulder. "Release her instantly!"

Recognizing the voice of authority the soldier let her go, muttering under his breath as he shuffled off down one of the many alleys leading off the square.

"Thank you, so much. If you had not chanced by I do not know how I would have gone on." Valeria began impulsively, turning to thank her rescuer, but the rest of the sentence died before she could voice it, as she found herself staring into the impassive face of Major Carrington.

"M-m-major!" she stammered nervously. "It is you! Oh . . ." His unexpected presence threw her into complete confusion. Despising herself for her lack of composure, Valeria reminded herself that the major's chivalric behavior could have nothing to do with any partiality for her personally. Quite the contrary. His eyes seemed to bore through her, missing nothing, so that she herself was immediately conscious of her flushed cheeks and trembling limbs. If only her rescuer had been anyone but this man.

What must he be thinking, coming across her like this in this unpleasant part of the city? Mortification took the place of her earlier gratitude, and Valeria longed only for him to absent himself so that she might continue on her way. How very stern and unrelenting he looked. Gone was the gentleman who had so roughly upbraided her, but in his place was a courteously aloof stranger, whose formality was, if anything, even more intimidating than his earlier, unleashed fury. His air of frigid civility, accentuated by the barrier of cool disdain he had erected between them, brought home more acutely to Valeria than anything else, exactly how he intended any future relations to be conducted. And the frail, barely admitted hope she had cherished that he might have thought better of his previous aspersions, shriveled in the icy blast of his hauteur.

It was, of course, unthinkable that he might have left her to her fate, but he was making it abundantly plain that it was duty, and not personal inclination, that dictated his actions.

Such was the effect of his reserved mien and cool composure, that Valeria's already overstretched nerve threatened to dissolve altogether, and she found herself floundering helplessly in a vain attempt to be both conciliating and grateful.

With the shock of meeting him so unexpectedly—and coming as it did on top of two already unpleasant encounters —Valeria found herself close to tears. Aghast at this reaction to his presence, she struggled desperately to regain some modicum of equanimity.

"If you are quite recovered, I suggest that you permit me to escort you to a less hazardous part of the city," he said distantly, taking her arm and propelling her inexorably away from the square. Valeria knew she ought to be grateful for his timely interference, and of course she was. But the mask of politeness he had assumed to disguise his undoubted contempt threw her into utter confusion when she tried to thank him.

When Valeria did manage to stammer a rather hesitant acknowledgment, he brushed it aside with a cool shrug.

"I could hardly have left you to your fate, deserved though it undoubtedly was. What were you about? To frequent such a part of the town—and without a male escort?"

Just for a second his control slipped, and Valeria glimpsed the anger in his eyes, before it was firmly banished.

"I was exploring, and lost my way," she prevaricated in low tones, hating herself for the lie. "It was, indeed, fortunate that you chanced by, otherwise I fear I could well have lost my purse."

Her companion's dark eyebrows rose in sardonic disbelief. "My dear Miss Fitzmount," he exclaimed in mocking accents, "your purse should have been the *last* thing that concerned you. Unless I mistook the matter, your assailant was more taken with your person than your purse."

Frank speaking indeed! Valeria's cheek burned with fresh mortification, so shocked was she by what the major inferred.

"I should not have said that. Pray forgive me," he said formally. "But I would have thought you had the wit to realize that wandering unescorted in such a squalid part of the town would lay you open to all manner of insults and importunings."

"I was not alone," Valeria whispered, dangerously close to tears. "I had my maid—"

"Your maid!" Hester's presence was dismissed with a contemptuous smile. "My dear girl, you cannot really be so naive. Have you no comprehension of what manner of rogues frequent these alleys?" Valeria shrank a little, under the rough anger she sensed, for instead of rebuking her further for her folly, he explained that only the merest chance had necessitated his own presence in the square. One of his soldiers had taken "French leave" and he had heard that the offender was outside the inn.

"I could not prevent him from being court-martialed, of course, but it could be that there were extenuating circumstances. However, the innkeeper is either a liar or a fool, for he denied all knowledge of the man."

"Could there not be some acceptable reason for his absence?" Valeria asked timorously, thinking of Perry's plight.

Her companion shook his head firmly. "There is *never* any adequate 'reason' for breaking the rules, Miss Fitzmount. However, it might have been that we could have mitigated the punishment somewhat."

So much for her hopes that he might be persuaded to take a lenient view of Perry's misadventure. A fresh wave of despondency assailed her. The high hopes with which she had set out had been totally vanquished by the unfortunate chain of events which had overtaken her. She had done nothing to aid Perry, quite the contrary. And worse, she had been discovered in embarrassing circumstances by a gentleman who considered that he already had every reason to see her in a bad light. No wonder she felt depressed.

It seemed that every contact she had with the major only served to lower his opinion of her still further.

He insisted on escorting her right to the door, in a silence so stiff with formality that Valeria was heartily relieved for it to be over. Matters were not improved when Count Polinsky hailed them just as Valeria set foot upon the steps.

"So, Major," he declared in a bantering tone. "You are a dark horse indeed. I thought you scorned the fair sex, and yet here you are escorting the loveliest young lady in Vienna."

"Quite by chance, I assure you," the major replied with an inflection which was not lost upon Valeria.

The Count turned toward her. "I had hoped that you might ride out with me," he explained, "and was just about to call upon you to suggest as much, or do you have a prior engagement?"

Valeria did not need to look at the major to guess what he was thinking. Another string to her bow.

She could have cried with vexation. Count Polinsky's comments could only reinforce his opinion that she was a determined flirt, on capturing the attention of any male who chanced to cross her path. She refused the count's invitation, but sensed that the damage was already done.

Why should *she* care what Leo Carrington thought of her? she asked herself furiously. Had he not already proved that he was both bigoted and blind? Surely his own perception should tell him that she was not the sort of female described by his aunt. The fact that he continued to think that she was was somehow more hurtful than all the rest put together.

It was with a curious ache in the region of her heart that she took her leave of him, blessing the formalities of convention which allowed her to take refuge in the trite leave-taking ritual demanded by society. The hand she proffered was taken for the briefest second, the dark head bent toward her from her vantage point on the steps. Then, with a curt bow, the major was gone, striding down the street, no doubt removing her as firmly from his mind as he hoped to do from Perry's life.

Chapter Six

Naturally, Valeria was in a fever of impatience to relate to Perry the outcome of her interview with Mrs. Noakes, and wished there might be some way she could get in touch with him before their appointed meeting in the Park.

The rest of the day stretched emptily ahead of her. She was, indeed, becoming spoiled, she chided herself, if she could not occupy herself for a handful of hours. Why, at home she was accustomed to only her own company for days at a time.

She would not allow herself to think of Leo Carrington, she told herself firmly; yet his features kept imposing themselves upon her mind, coming between her and her thoughts.

Following her debut at Camilla's party she had been besieged with a positive avalanche of invitations, ranging from impromptu breakfasts held al fresco in the cool and fragrant gardens adjacent to the many palaces, to full-scale formal balls; there were picnics, firework displays, masked routs, river parties, riding parties, and a whole host of other entertainments. Why, had Valeria accepted one third of them, she would not have had a free minute of the day to call her own. However, upon this occasion she found herself wishing that she did have an engagement, if only to give her thoughts a less depressing direction. A quiet dinner with her father did nothing to raise Valeria's spirits. Sir Edward had no engagement for the evening, and suggested that Valeria partner him in a game of chess to while away the time after the covers had been removed.

Unwillingly, Valeria agreed, knowing that her mind would not be on the game. Normally a gifted player, she found herself making more than one foolish move. When he had won three games in succession, Sir Edward shook his head chidingly.

"All this gaiety must be tiring you, Val," he complained. "I have never known you so lacking in concentration."

She was tired, Valeria admitted when she retired shortly after supper, but it was some time before her turbulent thoughts would allow her to rest properly.

The moment she opened her eyes on another sunny, cloudless day, the problems Valeria had managed to banish in sleep returned to prey on her mind.

Hester entered with her chocolate, but Valeria was unable to take more than a few sips of the rich, sweet beverage. Somehow or other she must contrive to be in the woods to meet Perry as arranged. But how? If only all this subterfuge were not necessary.

Over breakfast, Sir Edward commented on his daughter's preoccupied air. Valeria debated the wisdom of suggesting that they hire a couple of hacks so that they could ride in the woods and enjoy the morning, but just as she was about to propound this suggestion, Sir Edward announced that he had arranged to meet some friends in one of the coffeehouses. She could hardly ride alone, Valeria thought fretfully, but she must see Perry.

Fortunately, Camilla arrived before she was forced to tax her already overburdened brain any further.

On learning that her friend intended to ride, she expressed doubtful concern. "I have no wish to be a wet blanket, my love, but only consider. Neither of us is an experienced judge of horseflesh, and unfortunately Hart is engaged with Lord Castlereagh, otherwise we could have sought his advice."

"But Camilla, I must have some fresh air," Valeria expostulated desperately, unable to refute the logic of her friend's words.

"Well, if fresh air is all you want, we could take my barouche," Camilla said practically. "I was in two minds as to whether I should attend Countess Sauterre's luncheon party, and had come to see if you wished to accompany me, but if you would prefer to ride through the woods . . ." It was not quite what Valeria had hoped for, but it was better than nothing, and Camilla dispatched a footman to her home to instruct her coachman to collect them, dismissing her maid at the same time.

86

"What do you think of this gown?" she asked Valeria critically. "I had thought to wear my lilac, but I realized it would clash horridly with your hair."

By the time Valeria had managed to reassure her friend that the celestial blue carriage dress was quite delightful, the barouche was outside. Half an hour later they were bowling merrily out of the city and through leafy lanes toward the famous Vienna Woods.

Valeria had elected to wear a walking dress of softest peach, scattered with embroidered flowers and tied with satin ribbons of a deeper hue. Her hair had been dressed in soft ringlets, which peeped enchantingly under the deep brim of her chip-straw hat.

"Very fetching, my love," Camilla approved, when she had had time to study her. "Hester is managing to cope very well with your hair, I see."

"Indeed she is," Valeria agreed, a smile lurking in her eyes, for Hester had steadfastly refused to return to the old days of neatly plaited braids, even for the times when Valeria was merely dining quietly with her father.

The first signs of autumn were already creeping over the woods, green leaves giving way to a multitude of shades varying from palest lemon to deepest ochre. Bird song and the muffled beat of the horses' hooves were the only sounds to break the silence.

"How lovely it is," Valeria sighed, craning her neck to examine the scenery a little better.

"Enchanting," Camilla agreed. "I must persuade Hart to arrange a picnic one evening. We could have fireworks. They are vastly popular here, and some of the tableaux, quite extraordinarily lifelike. When the congress started there was one depicting Prince Metternich and the czar. I didn't see it, but Hart said it was truly marvelous. Did you wish to visit the woods for any particular reason?" she asked curiously, when Valeria continued to glance about her.

She was saved the need to reply as two gentlemen rode out of the forest toward them, plainly oblivious to their presence. One of them was quite definitely Perry, but Valeria's heart sank as she recognized the aloof countenance of the other.

"Isn't that Perry and Leo Carrington?" Camilla asked her, raising her hand to summon them over before Valeria could stop her. "Oh, look, they have seen us, and are riding this way. How fortunate that you should be wearing one of your new gowns, and looking so attractive. It will all be wasted on Perry, of course, who still sees you as the tomboy he used to know, but there is still Leo." She darted Valeria an assessing glance as she spoke, but Valeria refused to be flurried.

"I doubt my appearance will have any effect upon him. You yourself told me that he is immune to feminine wiles," she pointed out.

"That was before I realized that there was a chink in his armor. A duke! My dear, if—"

"If nothing," Valeria interrupted firmly. "Leo Carrington and I have nothing in common save that we are both English and both unwed, and that is how I wish it to remain, Camilla. Please do not embarrass me by encouraging him to think otherwise."

She would have been seriously alarmed had she seen the extremely speculative look her friend gave her. But she was concentrating all her attention on the riders, and Camilla's docile "No, no, of course not" soothed her fears that Camilla meant to embark on some madcap scheme for throwing her and Leo Carrington together. As the gentlemen approached, Valeria could not help noticing that the major sat upon his horse with all the masculine grace of a natural rider, far outshining Perry, who was slouched in his saddle, his expression withdrawn and preoccupied.

Both gentlemen were in uniform, and doffed their hats as they approached the carriage.

"Major Carrington and Captain Adaire," Camilla exclaimed with pleasure. "When Valeria persuaded me to come out driving I never suspected that we should meet two such handsome gentlemen!"

Valeria discovered that she was mesmerized by the major's dark blue eyes. Not only did they register every word Camilla had said in sardonic comprehension, but they also reflected quite clearly their owner's views upon them.

Camilla could not know, of course, that she had just reinforced Leo Carrington's poor opinion of her, Valeria admitted. But it was unfortunate that he should chance to look up just at the very moment when Perry was mouthing urgent instructions to her to draw away from Camilla. In helpless dismay, Valeria saw disdain give way to instant comprehension, anger smoldering in the hard, dark eyes, as they raked her from head to toe. She had only to make some polite acknowledgment of Perry's presence and beg Camilla to command her man to drive on to banish that look. But great though the temptation was, Valeria resisted.

In a voice which she felt sure must sound as unnatural to the others as it did to herself, Valeria asked Perry if he could spare the time to walk a little way with her in the woods.

"I hope you will not mind, Camilla," she said to her startled friend. "But I know that you detest walking, and I should very much like to penetrate the beauty of our surroundings a little more deeply than a ride permits."

"If that is what you wish," Camilla agreed, giving her a curious look. To the best of her knowledge she had never vouchsafed any opinion to Valeria on the subject of walking, far less expressed an aversion to it, and it occurred to her that this meeting with Perry was no mere chance. But why should Valeria go to the trouble of meeting Perry Adaire in the Vienna Woods when he was perfectly capable of calling round to the apartment? The problem creased her forehead in a perplexed frown. Surely it couldn't be that Sir Edward's dreams were about to be realized and Valeria was falling in love with Perry? A swift glance at her friend's countenance banished this suspicion.

"If you will excuse me then, Camilla," Valeria murmured, breaking her companion's train of thought, as she made to step down from the carriage, extending her hand for Perry to assist her safely to the ground. However, it was Major Carrington who clasped hard fingers about her wrist, his eyes so dark and contemptuous, that she all but lost her balance.

"I had no idea that you were such an ardent student of nature, Miss Fitzmount," he commented curtly, as she stepped downward. "Indeed, you are a source of continual surprise to me. One never knows where one will discover you next."

His words held such an undercurrent of meaning that Camilla stared anew at her friend. There was something about her with which she was not cognizant, and to judge by Valeria's set face, it was not something she was likely to discuss.

Valeria herself had been shaken by the major's comment, but soon had herself under control. With a brittle smile, she thanked him for his assistance.

"Where is Sir Edward?" the major enquired coolly. "I

should have thought he too would have enjoyed the woods. I understand he has a fondness for the country."

"So he has," Valeria agreed, "but today he is engaged with some friends at Junglings Coffeehouse."

"To discuss politics and the progress of the congress," the major commented knowledgably. "It is one of the best coffeehouses in Vienna."

"And it admits ladies as well as gentlemen," Camilla added. "We must go there one morning, Val. I promise you, you will see all the world and his wife, and in such congenial surroundings."

"Personally, I prefer to stand on the Jaegerzeile at five o'clock in the afternoon and watch the townspeople pouring down toward the Rothen Turm, in the direction of the Prater Park. It is one of Vienna's virtues that she provides so many pleasure grounds for her people," Leo Carrington said.

"Indeed, with so many fine parks, it is not hard to understand why the Viennese are so very gay," Valeria agreed lightly, as she made to follow Perry, more than a little surprised by the major's concern for the ordinary people of the city.

The moment they were out of sight and earshot, hidden from the carriage by a fine grove of birches, Valeria turned to Perry.

"I'm afraid my visit was not in the least successful," she began.

"I know," Perry cut in. "There was another letter waiting for me at my lodgings last night."

"Do you know, yet, what they want?"

Perry nodded his head. "Yes, indeed. In return for their silence on the subject of my liaison and visits to their place, I am to pay them £20,000."

He ignored Valeria's shocked gasp of protest and continued bitterly, "And if I do not comply with their demands, they intend to make sure that Leo Carrington knows exactly where I have been spending my spare time." This time Valeria knew better than to urge Perry to confide in the major.

"You said you were selling out," she reminded Perry, but he shook his head, forstalling her.

"That wouldn't make any difference. Even if I handed my papers in tomorrow, it would be a couple of months before my resignation became official. I cannot hope to hold off the Noakeses for that length of time. If they went to Leo with their tale after I had told him I intended to sell out, he would be bound to place the gravest interpretation upon my actions. Can't you see, Val?" he exclaimed. "At the moment, I am merely guilty of being a fool. If I were to try and escape punishment by selling out, I would be branded a coward, as well."

"And is there no way you can raise the money?"

"None at all. I don't come into my full inheritance for another four years. I have a generous allowance, but there is no way I can raise £20,000. No. I must just prepare myself for the inevitable. When I think of my lovely Maria!" He dropped his head in his hands. "Dear God, call me what you will, but if I did have the money I would pay it and gladly, to be rid of those bloodsucking creatures. If Maria only knew! She would shrink from me in horror."

"Of course she would not," Valeria told him bracingly. "She loves you, Perry, and I am sure she would understand."

"Her *father* certainly would not," Perry insisted bitterly. "He would have me drummed out of town if he ever heard. God! Val, what am I to do?"

"I don't know," she admitted. "Perhaps if I were to approach Papa?"

"And have him lecture me like some Dutch uncle, as though I were still in short petticoats," Perry exclaimed in revulsion. "No, Val. I must find some way out of this mess by myself. I am only sorry that I dragged you into it in the first place. I should never have confided in you. It was the act of a coward, a man not fit to be called a gentleman."

He was plainly working himself up into a state of self-hatred, and Valeria shook her head in denial of his accusations.

"It could have happened to anyone, Perry," she pointed out quietly. "You are not to blame. Mrs. Noakes obviously intended to make what capital she could out of your association with her daughter. I am convinced that *money* was what she wanted all along. She just wanted to ensure that you would take her threats seriously!"

"Well, she certainly succeeded in that," Perry admitted ruefully. "Damn it all, Val. It is most ungentlemanly for me to say this, but I'd as lief end up in the poorhouse than recommence my association with Lisle."

"A fact which her mother is well aware of," Valeria warned him. "She will stop at nothing to achieve her ends,

Perry. I believe she would see your reputation ruined, and your career in shreds, before she ceased her demands."

"Aye, I shall have to find some way round the problem, but now I'd best get you back to Camilla, or she'll be thinking I've eloped with you."

"Has . . . has the major mentioned me to you at all?" Valeria asked hesitantly, as Perry stood up and took her arm.

He answered her vaguely, brushing fallen leaves and twigs off his uniform.

"He may have done so. Asking how long we had known one another and so forth, you know the kind of thing. Why?"

"Oh, it's nothing." They were in sight of the carriage, and Valeria did not want to add to his problems.

Leo Carrington had plainly grown impatient, waiting for them to return. A deep scowl marred his handsome features, and his eyes were as cold as winter skies when they rested on Valeria's face.

"Goodness, we were just about to send out a search party," Camilla exclaimed. "I was just telling the major that he will have to try and secure you as his partner for the waltz, Valeria. My teacher tells me that you have an exceptional aptitude for it."

This was news to Valeria, but she bore it stoically, wishing she might think of some clever retort to assure Leo Carrington that there was nothing she would like less than waltzing with him, but since none came to mind, she was left in the embarrassing position of having been practically thrust upon him, by her enthusiastic friend. He made no attempt to rescue her. Indeed, Valeria had the distinct impression that he was enjoying her discomfiture.

"Oh, Val won't lack partners for the waltz," Perry intervened at last. "That Count what's his name—the Russian fellow —will make sure of that."

As the gentlemen were mounting their horses and preparing to ride off, Camilla had to be satisfied with this unsuccessful result to her attempt at matchmaking.

"Major Carrington is attending the ball, at any rate," she exclaimed triumphantly to Valeria when they were alone again. "Only think of it, my love. A duchess!"

"Pray do *not* think of it," Valeria replied firmly. "For I can assure you that I shall not. I would as soon marry Perry."

Camilla looked at her in consternation. "You have not fallen in love with him, have you? I cannot conceive why the two of you are so keen to be alone, all of a sudden. Major Carrington was curious too, do you know," she confided. "He was on tenterhooks the whole time you were gone. I promise you, he all but bit my head off when I spoke to him. What do you make of that?" she finished on a speculative note.

"Not a single thing," Valeria answered firmly. "I suspect the major was displeased because we interrupted his ride. If you are entertaining any romantic notions in connection with the major and myself, I beg that you cease to do so. I am quite convinced that we should not suit."

"That is what you said about Perry," Camilla interrupted slyly. "And yet, 'twas plain that this morning's meeting was no mere chance."

Valeria's eyes clouded, her forehead puckering in a concerned frown, and instantly Camilla wished the words unsaid.

"To be sure it is no business of mine, if you choose to meet Perry," she added, hurriedly. "I was but teasing you, Val."

"No, you are in the right of it," Valeria admitted. "I did have certain matters to discuss with Perry and—"

"I understand exactly how it was," Camilla interposed smoothly. "I collect the two of you wanted to discuss how best to convince Sir Edward that you have no wish to marry. You may leave all that safely to me, Val. I have already pointed out to your papa that when you become a reigning toast, you will have your pick of the gentlemen. Gentlemen with for more exalted titles and positions than Perry Adaire. I promise you he was quite taken with the notion. After all, what does a young boy of one-and-twenty years know about the management of two vast estates? Your papa quite took my point. He confided to me that one of the reasons Lord Adaire is so keen for Perry to return home is so that he may *learn* how to run the estate. Having heard that, it was but a simple matter for me to point out to your papa the advantages of a match between yourself and an older gentleman. Preferably one who already has some experience in these matters."

"Camilla, you are a scheming wretch," Valeria protested, torn between amusement and concern. "If you have managed to dissuade Papa from this notion of marriage to Perry, then I shall be eternally grateful to you. But I cannot conceive how you have managed to achieve in a few days what I have not been able to bring about in four years!"

"That is because you do not know how to handle gentlemen, Val!" Camilla announced smugly.

This was probably quite true, Valeria reflected, ruefully. Camilla, with her artless chatter, was far more likely to get round Sir Edward than Valeria herself.

"Having spoken to your papa, I can quite see why he does wish to have you safely married, Val," Camilla continued, on a more serious note. "The estate is not entailed, and besides the house and land there is a sizable fortune, all of which will pass into your husband's hands, once you marry. One hears so many dreadful tales . . ."

"You cannot be suggesting I would marry some scheming fortune hunter, Camilla," Valeria protested in shocked accents. "Besides, Papa is not precisely in his dotage!"

"No, indeed, but accidents can happen. Obviously one would expect Sir Edward to make every provision to ensure your future is secured with properly drawn-up marriage settlements, when you marry, but one cannot overlook the fact that, were he to fall victim of some accident, you would be left an exceedingly rich young lady."

"I am not quite sure who has been convincing whom," Valeria said dryly. "It seems to me that Papa has a very firm advocate in you, Camilla, to judge by the unpleasant picture you are drawing. Plainly, I should lose no time in securing myself a husband, instanter!"

Despite her droll smile, Camilla knew that Valeria was displeased. "Come, don't let us quarrel," she begged cajolingly. "I am sure that both your father and I have only your best interest at heart, Val. Surely, out of all the gentlemen in Vienna, there must be *one* with whom you could fall in love?"

For a moment, Valeria dwelt on Major Carrington's handsome features, a rather wistful smile playing round her lips. And then, chiding herself for her folly, she smiled at her friend.

"You are right, Camilla, and I am being foolish. It is just that I have no wish to be forced upon some gentleman!"

Camilla was plainly shocked. "Forced! Val, how could you think so? Just you wait," she said. "I predict that, following the empress's ball, you will be besieged by admirers!"

But it was one admirer in particular of whom Camilla was thinking, having had her coachman put Valeria down outside her apartment. Perhaps it would be worthwhile her having another little talk with Sir Edward. Despite the assurance she had given Valeria, Camilla had found him surprising obdurate over the matter of Valeria's marriage. "No wretched foreigner, no matter what his title, is ever going to set foot on Fitzmount land," he had told her roundly.

It was a pity that Valeria appeared to have taken Major Carrington into such dislike. Of all the gentlemen present at the congress, in Camilla's opinion, he would make an ideal husband for her friend, and not even Sir Edward would cavil at the thought of having a duke for a son-in-law. Somehow she would have to contrive a way to make sure that Valeria and the major were thrown more frequently into one another's company. It was a great pity that she could not enlist Hart's aid in this venture, but he was sure to disapprove of such meddling, no matter how well meant! And of course, Valeria must not know! How cross she would be! But it would all be for the best, Camilla told herself virtuously. To be sure, the major had not yet expressed interest in her friend, but all the world knew that he would have to take a wife to ensure the succession. And who better to fill that demanding role that Valeria—newly emerged from her confining chrysalis, transformed into a dazzling, beautiful butterfly.

It was a challenge Camilla could not resist.

Chapter Seven

Happily unaware of Camilla's ambitions, Valeria prepared for the empress's ball. This would be the first time she had attended such a grand event since the year of her coming out, and even that had been nothing to compare with the magnificent function the ball promised to be. To be sure, there had been evenings at Almacks, and her presentation, but shy and awkward as she had been then, Valeria had refused to attend many of the glittering receptions to which she had been invited.

Now, of course, things were vastly different. For one thing the intervening years had brought a certain measure of self-confidence; for another, her initial fears that the humiliating events of her first season would be repeated in Vienna had faded into insignificance when compared with her concern for Perry.

Hester had filled the hipbath, which was set before the bedchamber fire, with rose-scented water, and as Valeria luxuriated in the sensation of its perfumed softness against her skin, she could not repress a small frission of excitement. Indeed, she was hard put to remember when she had last prepared for anything with so great an expectation of enjoyment. For tonight all her anxieties and concern were submerged beneath a new mood of gaiety such as she had never experienced before—as though a fairy godmother had waved her wand and decreed that, for tonight, the old sensible Valeria was banished, and a new, frivolous creature, bent on enjoying all that the evening had to offer, had taken her place.

Indeed, it was as though everything conspired to complete this illusion.

Simple though her gown undoubtedly was, when Hester

had slipped it over her mistress's head and fastened the minute buttons, there was no doubting that it had come from a master hand. Clever draping emphasized the slender elegance of Valeria's body, giving her an exquisite delicacy.

At Hester's breathless, "Oh, Miss, you look like a princess, you really do!" she stared critically in the mirror at her reflection, amazed by the transformation wrought by a mere gown.

Was this ethereal, sugar-spun creature, who looked as though she might blow away on a puff of wind, really herself? Happiness bubbled up inside her, the glow in her eyes matching the soft light diffused by the candles on the dresser.

As Hester fastened the emeralds around her neck, it seemed to Valeria that her eyes were darker and larger than normal, their color reflected in the stones glittering against the alabaster skin of her throat.

Just discernible above the square-cut neckline of her dress, the pearly outline of her breasts caused her to frown momentarily and wonder whether to add a fichu to the gown. As though divining her thoughts, Hester shook her head. "It is only you that aren't used to such low-cut necklines, Miss Valeria, but it won't be in any way out of the ordinary. Why I've seen young ladies walking out in broad daylight showing far more of themselves!"

"I suspect we've become too countrified, Hester," Valeria sighed in agreement, wishing that the green satin ribbons crisscrossing her breasts did not outline her figure quite so plainly. The sheer silk floated as she moved, enhancing the air of fragility she possessed, her diamanté-studded slippers catching the light as she walked. A last anxious look at her hair, its color and texture revealed by her new hairstyle, a final check that she had her wrap and her reticule, and it was time to leave.

Sir Edward was awaiting his daughter in the hall, and his expression as she descended the stairs put the final seal upon her pleasure. "Upon my word, Val," he exclaimed heartily, "I have never seen you looking so fine. I shall be the envy of every gentleman at the ball."

"Oh, Papa, you exaggerate," Valeria chided, but his words brought a delicate flush of pleasure to her cheeks.

The gates of the main courtyard of the Hofburg Palace had been opened wide to admit the unending stream of carriages, each pausing before the impressive flight of stone steps to permit its passengers to alight before passing on to allow the next to stop.

Valeria and her father had traveled to the palace with Camilla and Hart to avoid using two carriages unnecessarily. Two footmen sprang forward when it was their own turn to halt before the stairs, one opening the carriage door, whilst the second unhooked the steps assisting first Camilla, and then Valeria down to the ground.

Although the night was fine, a canopy had been erected over the entrance to protect the guests' finery, and looking upward Valeria realized that the crimson silk covering had the Hapsburg arms wrought upon it in gold and black.

Because of the press of people in the main reception hall it was impossible to pick out the finer details of the decor. Tall columns of a pink-veined marble supported an arched ceiling, painted and gilded in the style so fashionable in Paris before the revolution. The floor of the hall was covered in the same marble as the columns, the smooth, polished stone giving off a distinct chill, despite its impressive appearance.

On the walls hung silk banners representing the arms of all those who had participated in the exhausting struggle against Napoleon Bonaparte, a mute testimony to the valor of those who had fought so hard and so long.

An elegant flight of stairs led upward to massive double doors which Valeria presumed opened into the ballroom, the stairs themselves a cool white marble inlaid with onyx and picked out with gilt paint.

On either side of the doors stood a footman resplendent in the Hapsburg livery.

A huge chandelier lit the hall, and even as Valeria stared admiringly at it, there was a sudden brash clarion call of trumpets and the ballroom doors were flung open to reveal the empress in a rich golden gown, her diamonds sparkling in the lights from the room behind her.

Very slowly the long procession made its way up the stairs, pausing whilst a servant announced each guest in mellifluous tones until, at last, it was the turn of Valeria and her father.

"Sir Edward Fitzmount and Miss Valeria Fitzmount!" the servant boomed out. Sir Edward bowed and Valeria curtseyed.

The empress acknowledged them both, giving Valeria a

particularly sweet smile. Despite her beautiful gown and fabulous jewels, she looked tired and drawn, frail almost, beneath the brilliant light of the chandelier.

"All the entertaining for the congress has fallen upon the empress's shoulders," Hart told them as he and Camilla joined Sir Edward and Valeria in the ballroom. "It is no wonder she looks so tired; she is no longer young."

Valeria had never seen anything to rival the Hofburg's ballroom. Although her father claimed that it was not as fine as the Salon des Glaces at Versailles, it was all Valeria could do not to stare openmouthed at the magnificence before her. The room was so vast that it was impossible to make out the features of the people at its furthermost end. From the intricately plastered and painted ceiling hung twelve enormous chandeliers, each one large enough on its own to illuminate an entire room at Fitzmount Place.

Along one wall of the ballroom were arched windows looking out onto gardens which had been decorated for the evening with thousands of colored lanterns, and opposite these windows on the other wall hung gilded mirrors, reflecting the guests in all their finery. For the occasion the ballroom had been decorated in the colors of the victorious armies, blue and gold, scarlet and gold, green and gold and white and gold—a rich profusion of color dazzled the eye.

Bunches of ribbons in these colors, cunningly wrought in the shape of roses adorned a gallery at one end of the ballroom where the musicians had been positioned. Whilst the assembled guests waited for the empress to finish receiving the last arrivals, the room, which not so long ago had echoed to the strains of the *Marseillaise*, filled with the resounding marching tunes to which the allied armies had rallied.

With perfect timing, the last notes of an English air were just dying away as the footmen closed the double doors behind the last guests.

The musicians struck up the first dance, a waltz. The emperor and empress circled the floor decorously, keeping perfect time to the music and then, one by one, the other guests joined them. Valeria danced with her papa, a little surprised by his unexpected talent for the new dance. "Wish it had been in fashion in my day," Sir Edward commented when the music stopped. "Can't think of a better way to get acquainted with one's partner."

Valeria's card was filled faster than she would have

thought possible. In no time at all Count Polinsky had claimed two dances, and Perry three; the remainder were hotly contested by a variety of young men—most of them officers known to Perry—who had begged to be introduced.

The young officers were all in the gayest of moods and it was impossible not to be infected with their high spirits. A good-natured rivalry broke out amongst them over who was to have the last dance left on Valeria's card, each one producing a cast-iron reason why he should be preferred to his fellows. Their bantering forced Valeria to declare breathlessly that she could not choose between them, and that anyway she must save one dance for her papa.

It was as though she had never attended a ball before, and in truth she had not—at least not one like this.

Partner after partner whirled her onto the floor, her feet seeming to follow the lilting rhythm of the music without any instructions from herself. "You waltz like an angel," more than one partner whispered to her as his arm curved about her waist; and although she knew that many persons at home considered the dance to be shockingly indecorous and liable to lead to all manner of licentious behavior, Valeria knew that no matter how many balls she attended in the future there would never be one to compare with this, nor a dance to compare with the waltz.

It only needed one thing to complete her happiness. "It is no use hoping," she said to herself. "He will not ask you to dance, for he holds you in the greatest aversion as well you know." And yet she could not stop herself from searching the crowd, whilst willing herself not to let her foolish hopes run away with her.

As it happened it was Camilla who spotted him first. "Isn't that Major Carrington over there with the empress and her lady-in-waiting?" she commented as she and Valeria sipped delicious, cooling glasses of ratafia.

"I believe it is," Valeria agreed noncommittally, wishing that her heart would not beat in such a very erratic manner.

In his full dress uniform the major seemed to stand apart from the other guests, despite the fact that most of the gentlemen were similarly attired. However, there was something about the set of his scarlet jacket; the way it emphasized the breadth of his shoulders, the gold buttons catching the light of the chandeliers. A ceremonial sword hung at his right side, and unlike some of the other officers, he appeared to be unhampered by this purely formal addition to his attire. As Valeria knew to her cost some of the younger officers had difficulty with this particular piece of equipment when dancing, but as she saw the major leading the Princess de Lieven onto the floor, it was obvious that he suffered from no such handicap. As she watched him her heart twisted with pain. "Forget him," she urged herself, but this was easier said than done. There was no sign of the beautiful woman Valeria had seen him with outside the modiste's and she could only presume that his companion was not well-born enough to merit an invitation.

Perry came up to claim one of his dances. He was looking decidedly worn down, Valeria noticed. As he led her onto the floor he confided to her that he dreaded waking up each morning lest some fresh disaster might have overtaken him.

"You have not been able to raise the £20,000 then?" Valeria asked him sympathetically.

He shook his head. "Nor am I likely to."

"I only wish there was some way I could help. Are you sure you don't want me to talk to Papa?"

"No, I must find my own way out, Val. By the way," he added, "I see that Count Polinsky is bearing down on us. It isn't serious between you, is it?" Valeria shook her head. "I don't think the count could be serious about any woman. He is an excellent dancer though."

"Umm, well just make sure it is only as a dancing partner that you see him," Perry reproved in a brotherly fashion. "He is something of a rake, and I shouldn't like to see you break your heart over such a man."

By the time Valeria had assured him that this would never happen the music had ceased and Perry was leading her off the floor.

A lavish supper had been laid out in the antechamber, but Valeria found she had little appetite for the delicacies provided. Camilla commented upon her restraint, adding knowledgeably that she herself had often suffered exactly the same disinclination for food at balls. "But that was before I married Hart. I have often remarked," she added teasingly, "how falling in love can rob one of one's desire for food. Have you not found it so?"

Valeria ignored her remarks. In love, what nonsense! But was it? Her heart gave an uncomfortable jolt.

She danced twice more with Count Polinsky, resisting all his attempts to persuade her to take a turn in the gardens. "Oh cruel Beauty," he whispered after her second refusal, "have you no heart? Or is it as cold as those jewels you wear about your neck. They must be worth a king's ransom," he finished, dropping his pose of romantic lover. "I swear I have never seen their like."

The words stuck in Valeria's mind, repeating themselves in an insinuating refrain. A king's ransom—Perry only needed £20,000. Perhaps if she were to suggest . . . But no, Perry would never allow her to sell the emeralds. But if Perry were not to know until the deed was accomplished? Once born, the thought would not be denied. The emeralds were hers, after all. Papa had told her so more than once. But to sell them when they had been in the family for so long? What was more important, she asked herself ruthlessly, a handful of green stones or Perry's happiness? But how to go about effecting a sale? It was Camilla who all unwittingly supplied the answer. She and Valeria were standing watching the other dancers, Camilla chattering on in her normal fashion, commenting on this and that, whilst Valeria listened with half an ear.

"Just look over there," Camilla exclaimed suddenly. "The woman with Prince Metternich. She is supposed to be his mistress and they say he has lavished thousands upon her. She is still wearing paste diamonds though, all Vienna is talking about her."

"Paste! How can you tell from here?" Valeria asked her curiously.

"Because the whole world knows that she pawned the real ones to finance her stay in Vienna. They say that twice a week she visits the court jewelers to assure herself that no one else has bought them, and that the jewelers have advanced her fifty thousand pounds against them. It is all very shocking. I am surprised the emperor believes her!"

Fifty thousand pounds, and she only wanted twenty! They had passed the jewelers in question on their way to the modiste's. Of course, it was a very shocking thing to do, but if it would save Perry! If she was discreet, no one was likely to find out, Valeria assured herself. Valeria's heart began to pound with nervous trepidation, and it was only Camilla's fingers pinching her arm that brought her back to reality. "Look, Major Carrington is coming this way," Camilla hissed. "What a blessing that you still have that waltz left." There was no time for Valeria to reply that the major was hardly likely to dance with her, for he was upon them, his expression grimly forbidding; so forbidding, in fact, that she shrank back a little, earning herself a faintly sardonic grimace as he asked politely for the pleasure of the next dance. It was with mingled disappointment and relief that Valeria was able to refuse him. A quick glance at her card showed her that the next waltz was Perry's.

The musicians struck up the first strains of the music. Several couples drifted out onto the floor, but there was no sign of Perry. "It seems as though your partner is somewhat forgetful of his obligations," the major commented coolly.

Camilla glanced at her friend's card. "Oh Val," she exclaimed, "it was one of those you promised to Perry. I expect he is in the card room with Hart. I'm sure he won't mind you partnering the major." It seemed she had no choice.

The major's arm rested firmly on her waist as he swept her expertly onto the floor, and it seemed to Valeria that her body tingled slightly under his impersonal touch. He did not speak as they circled the room and Valeria had to tilt her head upward to see his face. It was set in an expression of cold fury. Perturbed, she almost missed her step, but her small lapse was expertly covered by her partner's expertise.

"Do you like the waltz?" she ventured shyly into the silence. The major's eyebrows rose in sardonic amusement. "What man would not?" he drawled softly. Although his expression was hidden from her, Valeria felt his sudden tension, a tension that spoke of emotions vigorously held in check.

"Oh come" he mocked bitterly, "isn't that what you expected me to say? To tell the truth I am not over fond of dancing but, in this case, it was a necessary evil. A means to an end one might say," he added as he swept her out through the French windows and onto the deserted terrace beyond before she could protest. "For it gives me the opportunity to talk to you undisturbed." No sooner had he finished speaking than his hand was disengaged from her waist to clamp firmly under her elbow, preventing any chance of escape as he propelled her in the direction of a flight of stone stairs leading down into the gardens.

A full moon cast its benign glow over the landscape, faint strains of music reaching them from the ballroom. The night air was full of the scent of late roses, with just a hint of crispness to show that autumn was almost upon them. As she looked upward questioningly into her companion's grim features, Valeria realized with a small tremor of dread that his rage had burst through the stringent control he had placed upon it. The arrogantly aloof gentleman who had rescued her from her assailant in the square was gone, and in his place was a man plainly in the grip of an intense emotion. Indeed, it seemed to Valeria that his fury was all the more terrifying for having previously been banked down. She shrank from him automatically, turning to flee to the crowded security of the ballroom, but the major was too quick for her. His grip on her arm tightened as he hurried her down the steps, damp with dew, which penetrated her flimsy slippers. Once they were alone in the shadowy darkness he abandoned all pretense of politeness, scrutinizing her face in the pale light of the moon.

"So very beautiful," he murmured harshly, "and so very heartless."

Valeria shivered nervously, unaware of the picture she made. Her pale green gown, rendered almost colorless in the moonlight, its draperies wafting about her in the slight breeze —she might have been a piece of statuary come to life, so robbed of color and form was she by the moon's magic glow. Only her hair retained its warmth, proving that she was indeed human and not some beautiful muse sent by the gods to torment mankind.

She glanced up and saw the major regarding her with an expression she could not read. His jaw clenched as though he were fighting for self-control, his voice harsh in the silken silence of the night as he said suddenly, "Before God, Miss Fitzmount, I wish you had never come to Vienna."

He didn't need to tell her that, Valeria thought miserably. All his actions had made his views quite plain. The excitement which had kept her buoyed up with anticipation all evening had fled, leaving her drained and tired. What had she expected, she asked herself mockingly. That somehow the sight of her in a new gown would banish all his prejudices? How ridiculous! Suppressing a tremulous sigh she addressed the major. "Why have you brought me here?" she asked feebly in protest at his behavior. In the darkness she caught the faint grimace he gave before answering.

"Not so that I can make love to you in the privacy of some secluded Gothic temple," he assured her, ignoring her shocked gasp. "I wanted to talk to you and this seemed to be the best way of ensuring that I could do so uninterruptedly.

"Have you no pity?" he asked suddenly, his voice, for once, not quite under control. "Can't you see what you are doing to young Adaire, or is it that you just don't care? The boy looks positively haunted. Surely you must know that he doesn't care for you, and yet you constantly pursue him." His sudden attack had caught her completely off guard, and before she could muster her defense he was speaking again. "I have already seen one young man's life destroyed because of a vain and greedy woman, Miss Fitzmount. I shall not stand idly by and see it happen to another."

Too stunned to retaliate, Valeria could only stare at him. The early autumn scents of the garden hung heavily on the air, perfuming it with intoxicating fragrances, but she was in no mood to appreciate the splendor of the evening.

"You will not succeed in your intentions," her persecutor swept on ruthlessly. "I shall put every stumbling block in your way that I can. Adaire has confided to me that his grandfather desires this match—God knows why—but I warn you now that I shall do everything within my power to prevent your coldhearted scheming from coming to fruition."

Anger lent her the courage to retort boldly. "Indeed, major. Pray tell me, do you take such a personal interest in all your junior officers? Are none of them free to make their own decisions, live their own lives without your interference?" She thought she detected a faint hardening of the well-shaped mouth, a disturbing glimpse of a warning muscle pulsing angrily in one lean cheek, but it was too dark for her to be sure.

"Fortunately, all my junior officers do not commit the folly of becoming entrapped by female predators."

It was too much. Valeria opened her mouth to protest, but the words just would not come. Then to her own horror she heard herself saying in a high, unfamiliar voice, which held more than a hint of challenge, "And pray just what do you intend to do about it, Major?" It was plain that her adversary had also detected the betraying tone, but his own voice hardened, leaving her in no doubt that it would not go unanswered—or unpunished.

"For a start I shall make sure that young Perry is kept fully occupied with regimental business over the next few weeks—too occupied to be lured into any of your schemes. Furthermore, I shall advise him that he is a fool if he allows the wishes of his grandfather to overrule his own feelings. Do I make myself plain, or must you have it spelled out for you, Miss Fitzmount? I will not have Perry Adaire forced into a betrothal to satisfy your own vain craving to fulfill your boast that he will become your husband. Permit me to tell you that, for all your beauty, I have never met a young lady who is less deserving of him!"

His words pricked the bubble of her anger, bursting it like a fool's bladder. Wrenching her hand from his constraining grasp Valeria pulled herself free, almost stumbling in her anxiety to be gone from the shadowed garden and all that it held. Shivering, she hurried back to the palace, twigs snatching at her gown and hair in her efforts to regain the comparative sanctuary it offered. When she did manage to regain the ballroom she went straight to the room set aside for the use of ladies, and what she saw there in the mirror appalled her. Was this really her face, so white and drained, her hair all but tumbling about her shoulders, her gown muddied, and her eyes wild with misery? She closed them, willing herself not to give way, and when she opened them again Camilla was at her side.

"I saw you come in from the gardens. Whatever happened? Valeria, are you all right?" she asked anxiously.

"I cannot speak of it, please do not ask me," Valeria begged, pressing her hands to her cheeks which were now as hectically flushed as they had been frighteningly pale. "I must go home, Camilla. I am sorry to spoil your evening. If you could just summon the coachman, and tell Papa that I have a bad megrim."

"Nonsense," Camilla declared stoutly. "We shall all leave together when you are feeling a little more the thing. I will go and find Hart and bring you a glass of negus. You wait here."

She would not disgrace herself by crying here, Valeria told herself fiercely. The evening, begun in such high hopes, now lay shattered about her, and she felt her humiliation must be writ clear on her forehead for all to see.

Camilla returned with a glass of negus, her forehead furrowed in a worried frown. Valeria drank as her friend instructed her, as docilely as a small child obeying its nurse. "My love, can't you tell me what is wrong?" Camilla urged gently. "I hate to see you like this."

"There's nothing wrong," Valeria persisted stubbornly. "I just have a megrim, that is all."

Camilla opened her mouth to say that megrims did not bring such shadows to one's eyes or the sheen of held-back tears, but then closed it again, judging it wisest not to tease her friend with questions.

On the drive back to the apartment, Valeria sat in silence whilst the others discussed the evening. If she had once cherished foolish dreams that Leo Carrington might come, in time, to see how she really was, those dreams were now crushed forever, buried beneath the cruel words he had heaped upon her. From now on, Valeria decided numbly, she would treat the major as he treated her, with cold contempt and icy politeness.

Even at night Vienna did not rest. Some workmen were busily engaged in erecting wooden platforms at one end of one of the squares they drove through.

"They're building stands for the army commanders and their guests to view the tattoo from," Hart commented, referring to the military tattoo which was being planned as part of the celebrations. "Camilla and I are hoping that you and Valeria will attend as our guests, Sir Edward."

Sir Edward accepted his invitation enthusiastically, but it was as much as Valeria could do to manage a wan smile.

"I hope you aren't going down with something, Val," Sir Edward commented, eyeing her pale face with concern.

"It was just the noise and heat in the ballroom," Valeria assured him. "You forget I am not used to such a hectic social life."

"Aye, that's probably it," Sir Edward agreed with relief, turning to question Hart more closely about the tattoo.

Valeria let their voices flow over her. All at once she longed for the placid life she had left behind in England. There, there was no Leo Carrington to hurl unwarranted accusations at her and destroy her peace of mind.

Chapter
Eight

Not unnaturally, after a night of broken sleep and harrowing, but unremembered, dreams, Valeria awoke the following morning with a throbbing headache.

As she washed and dressed, the events of the previous evening kept intruding upon her thoughts, and on more than one occasion something suspiciously like a sob had to be stifled behind tightly closed lips.

Of course, it was inconceivable that there should be any *particular* reason why the major's attitude should affect her like this. It was but the natural reaction of anyone finding themselves held in such great aversion.

However, Valeria was an intelligent girl and her brain told her what her heart refused to admit. Namely, that it was more than the major's patent dislike that made her feel so wretchedly low. It was pointless cherishing unrealistic dreams, she chided herself. The major was blinded by his own prejudices and misconceptions. Instead of anger and pain, she should feel pity for a man so plainly lacking in perception.

Sensible though these conclusions were, they did little to raise her spirits and when she eventually took her seat at the breakfast table, it was as much as she could do to eat a single slice of bread and butter.

"Feeling any better?" Sir Edward asked solicitously, as he prepared to quit the table. He had business of his own to occupy the morning, and had an appointment to interview his agent.

"A little," Valeria agreed wanly. "I might take a walk a little later and get some fresh air."

"Aye, you do that," Sir Edward agreed heartily. "Nothing like fresh air for banishing a megrim. Damned stuffy in that ballroom last night.

"Saw you dancing with Leo Carrington," he added casually. "Seems a well set-up fellow. More than just bone between his ears, which is more than you can say for a lot of army men, although my guess is that he won't be staying in the army long. He'll want to get home and put his house in order. They say the old duke didn't have too tight a hand on the reins in his last years and the estate needs some sorting out."

"Whatever sorting out needs to be done, Papa, I am sure one may rely upon Major Carrington to see that it is done," Valeria said crisply. "Now if you will excuse me, I must go and reply to all these invitations." She gestured to the small pile of cards beside her plate.

In addition she had received another posy of flowers from Count Polinsky and a plea to allow him to drive her in the Prater Park.

"Seems to me that young Perry is looking rather down in the mouth," Sir Edward announced abruptly. "Nothing wrong there, is there, Val?"

If only she had Perry's permission to confide in her father.

"Perhaps he's tired of being pursued, Papa," she said mildly instead, and was surprised to see Sir Edward looking a trifle uncomfortable.

"As to that, Val, perhaps I was somewhat precipitate. Only wanted to do my best for you, my dear. Wouldn't want to see you married to some jackanapes who would run through your fortune and make you unhappy, and you and young Adaire always seemed to get along so well."

"We do, Papa," Valeria agreed, placing her hand on her father's arm, touched by this new, softer mood. "And I hope we shall always be good friends and that I may always turn to Perry for advice when I need it. But we are too much like brother and sister to ever contemplate marriage."

"Aye, I see that now," Sir Edward admitted. "Been having a long talk with Camilla about you. Seems to me that young lady's got her head screwed on right."

How on earth had Camilla managed to convince her father that she and Perry were not perfect marriage partners in a few short days, when she herself had not been able to achieve as much in several years, Valeria wondered. However, she had too much on her mind to dwell on the perversity of human nature.

Shortly after luncheon, when the throbbing in her temples had dimmed to a nagging ache, she set out for the jewelers, the case containing the emeralds carefully hidden in her reticule. She would not allow herself to dwell on the impropriety of what she was contemplating, she told herself firmly, as she headed in the direction of the shopping arcade. None of the expensive and elegant fashions displayed in the windows of the fashionable modistes drew so much as a passing glance from her, and Hester, walking dutifully at her heels, cast worried looks at her mistress's straight back. Something was troubling Miss Valeria, that was as plain as the nose on your face, but what?

As always the fashionable streets were crowded with people; window-shopping, laughing and talking, whilst all about them workmen in the uniform of the emperor worked busily decorating the buildings with fresh bunting and flags in preparation for the military tattoo Hart had been discussing with Valeria's father the previous evening.

From the snatches of conversation she overheard as she hurried in search of the jewelers, Valeria realized that the tattoo was to be an occasion of glittering pageantry. In addition to a parade by all the allied regiments stationed in Vienna, there was to be a huge fair in the nearby Prater Park, and several prominent hostesses had seized upon the occasion as an excuse to throw a lavish ball. Valeria had received invitations for three of these affairs, but, as yet, had not accepted any of them, preferring to await Camilla's guidance before committing herself.

Whatever other criticisms could be leveled at Camilla, no one could accuse her of not being punctilious in the extreme about matters of good ton. Despite her friend's predilection for matchmaking, Valeria knew she was fortunate to have her as a mentor. However, upon this occasion her thoughts were far from the pleasures of her many social engagements.

Even the new gown she was wearing had done nothing to raise her depressed spirits. It was one of the latest walking dresses, a pale blue dimity embroidered with knots of flowers

111

and embellished with a triple flounce at the hem. It could have looked insipid, but instead, the modiste's sure touch had ensured that it was the epitome of chic elegance. A bonnet with the fashionable small brim, tied with satin ribbons, completed the ensemble, and a matching silk parasol opened to shield Valeria's complexion from the sun.

The court jeweler occupied a double-fronted, low-windowed shop in the Wipplingerstrasse; a tall, handsome building, with two storys of living accommodation above the shop.

Now that she had reached her goal, Valeria was attacked by fluttering tremors of uncertainty, her fingers tightening involuntarily upon the handle of her reticule. Blind to the magnificent display of jewels adorning the windows, she hesitated uncertainly before the door.

Heavens, what on earth was the matter with her? she scolded herself. She had never cared for the emeralds, thinking them far too ostentatious. Surely she was not so feeble-minded as to abort her mission having come this far?

The interior of the shop was dark and gloomy after the bright sunlit flagway. A gentleman in a neatly tailored outfit in some dark fabric hovered helpfully behind a counter set out with a mouthwatering display of gems.

Dismissing Hester to wait outside for her, Valeria hurried forward before her courage could desert her.

"Can I help you?" the gentleman asked pleasantly, coming forward from behind the counter and summing up the girl standing in front of him with one experienced glance.

His family had been jewelers to the royal family for six generations and he knew a lady of quality when he saw one. He also recognized nervous uncertainty when he saw it, and another discreet glance assured him that his would-be customer was elegantly and expensively dressed, and unmarried.

"Do you— That is—" Fumbling nervously with the clasp of her reticule, Valeria tipped the emeralds out onto the wooden counter oblivious to the faint widening of her companion's eyes as he saw the magnificence of the jewels thus displayed. "I need £20,000," she told him baldly, "and I thought— That is—"

If only the shop was not so public. She looked unhappily about her as the jeweler fixed a glass to his eye the better to

112

examine the emeralds, whilst assuring her that he understood the matter perfectly.

"£20,000," he murmured thoughtfully, after what to Valeria seemed an interminable length of time. "Will you excuse me for a second?"

Left to her own devices, Valeria stared vaguely around the shop. Her heart beat painfully fast and her cheeks were unusually warm, as though she had been running fast. What if he were to refuse her the money? What if the emeralds weren't as much as she supposed?

The rattle of curtain rings along a pole warned her that she was no longer alone. This time she was not merely confronted by the young man who had originally served her but an older man as well.

"You wish to raise £20,000 against these emeralds, my son tells me?"

Speechless, Valeria nodded her head. Please, please let them agree, she prayed. She could barely bring herself to meet the old man's eyes, so shrewd and assessing they were. What must he be thinking?

"I need the money for a most particular reason," she heard herself saying breathlessly. "For a friend. It is imperative that I have it."

Scarlet-cheeked, she bit her lip. What had possessed her to speak so impetuously? It could not matter to the jeweler why she wanted the money.

"I quite understand," he answered gravely, "but these jewels— Perhaps you would care to leave them with me for a few days so that I might give the matter my consideration."

A few days! Valeria's heart sank.

"Oh, but surely—" She began to protest but swallowed her words as she realized the speculative looks the jewelers were exchanging. "Very well then," she agreed with a valiant attempt at indifference, "but I must have your decision by the end of the week." Surely Mrs. Noakes would give Perry a few days' grace to raise the money? She could only pray so.

"By the end of the week," the old man agreed courteously. "My son will give you a receipt, Miss . . .?"

"Miss Fitzmount," Valeria supplied automatically.

"And your direction? A formality, nothing more," he assured her smoothly when Valeria would have protested.

She heard the warning bell on the door and, anxious

to be gone before she was subjected to any further embarrassment, Valeria told them hurriedly where she might be found, adding that she would call in three days' time for their decision.

"That will be quite in order," the older man assured her. He had adroitly swept the emeralds from the counter into their case the moment the door opened, but not before a pale beam of sunlight had lit upon them, turning the dark stones the color of green fire in the somberness of the shop's gloomy interior.

The younger man handed her a receipt, neatly folded, and Valeria placed it in her reticule, turning quickly and all but stumbling as she collided with the couple who had just entered.

Her breath left her lungs in a dismayed gasp. A hand reached out to steady her, lean and tanned, with neatly manicured nails. "Stupid girl, you all but knocked me over," a high-pitched female voice protested acidly. Mumbling an apology, Valeria felt her face flame. The younger jeweler had rushed round to open the door, full of apologies for the stygian darkness of the shop. The hand on her arm fell away, and as she darted a look upward the words of thanks died on her lips as she stared into Leo Carrington's saturnine face. Had he overheard anything? No, he could not have done so. A quick glance at his companion confirmed that she was the dark-haired woman Camilla had said was his mistress. Her hand was tucked possessively round his arm, her eyes flashing warning signals at Valeria, who mustered what was left of her shattered composure.

"Do you know this—this person, Leo?" the woman asked coldly, with what to Valeria seemed to be a staggering amount of self-possession.

"I do," he agreed, without making any attempt to introduce them, and Valeria was not sure whether this was because he considered her of insufficient importance to make her known to his companion, or because he was aware of the breach of good manners it would be to introduce her to his mistress.

His companion plainly labored under no such uncertainties. The look she gave Valeria was both contemptuous and amused. "Poor little thing," Valeria heard her say quite clearly, as she stepped out into the sunshine. "She looked quite overwhelmed. Now, about that bracelet—rubies I think."

There was no reason why she should feel shocked, Valeria told herself firmly as she walked away. She was not some silly little chit with no knowledge of the ways of the world. How often had her papa deplored the folly of one of his peers, inveigled into bestowing expensive items of jewelery upon his lastest ladybird?

"Miss Valeria, are you alright?" Hester's anxious voice penetrated her thoughts.

"I'm fine," she reassured her. Three whole days before she knew whether she would have the money. How could she endure it?

Back in the jewelers', father and son reexamined the emeralds in the privacy of a small back room. In view of the immediacy of the situation a second cousin, who was normally only allowed to run errands, had been dispatched to mind the shop whilst they decided upon a course of action.

"There can be no question of the young lady's having acquired these stones in some unorthodox fashion, I suppose?" Wilhelm senior murmured.

His son shook his head. "Oh no, they're hers right enough, but 'tis plain she has never done anything of this sort before."

"Umm, if she had, she would have known to take them to a pawnbroker instead of us. What do you suggest we do?"

"£20,000—we could find that easily enough, Father. She seemed an intelligent young lady to me—and pretty. With careful handling this could bring us a good deal of business."

"Exactly what I thought," his father approved. "But first we need to make a few discreet enquiries about Miss Fitzmount. I've no objection to lending a lady £20,000 against emeralds like these, but it strikes me that we ought to make sure that the stones are hers to dispose of. Not that I'm suggesting that she'd come by them dishonestly—not a lady like that. But there's no accounting for what young ladies will get up to when they fancy themselves in love."

"You mean she might want the money to finance an elopement?" Wilhelm junior asked his father nervously. "Major Carrington seemed to know her, perhaps if we were to enlist his aid."

115

"Major Carrington, you say. Umm, well there's no doubt that he's a gentleman whose word may be relied upon. Did he buy anything by the way?"

His son shook his head. "The lady tried hard but he wasn't having any. She looked ready to throw a fit of hysterics when they left. Called in especially yesterday she did, to ask me to put aside that ruby and diamond bracelet she wanted. The only thing he bought was that Sèvres snuffbox we got in the other day. It seems he collects them. He asked me to have it sent round to his lodgings."

"There's a piece of luck. You must take it yourself and see if you can't find out a little bit more about Miss Fitzmount."

"You mean ask him outright about the emeralds?"

"If you have to," Wilhelm senior agreed, giving his son a searching look. It was just as well he was here to keep an eye on the boy. The sight of a pretty face was enough to drive out what little sense he had in his head. No doubt he would have given Miss Fitzmount the money without demur.

"Why don't you go instead, Pa?" the younger son suggested, eyeing his father hopefully, but the latter shook his head purposefully. "No, we've got to tread warily here. We don't want to cause any offense—to anyone! There's no sense in having the major think we don't trust our customers. No, a few casual questions as you hand him the snuffbox, that's all that's needed. And provided we get the right answers Miss Fitzmount can have her £20,000."

It wasn't until she returned to the apartment that Valeria realized that she and her father promised to spend the evening at a reception to be held by Lord and Lady Castlereagh.

The occasion was the Castlereaghs' first official function of the congress, and Valeria was aware that it was a great honor to be invited. She would be mixing with the cream of Viennese society. Several heads of state were invited and the evening promised to be an exceptionally high standard of entertainment. Even so, Valeria found it hard to raise any enthusiasm. She was becoming every bit as bad as the bored London belles whose languid airs she had found so affected during her short season, she scolded herself.

If only the jewelers had been able to give her an answer there and then. Her insides felt as though they were tied in knots, but she could find no way of alleviating her growing tension.

Camilla was supposed to be chaperoning her at Lady Castlereagh's reception, but during the afternoon one of her footmen delivered a note, written in hurried scrawl, explaining that she was not, after all, going to be able to accompany her friend. Valeria frowned as she read it. It seemed that Lucy, the baby, had broken out in a rash of spots, and Camilla, quite naturally, was beside herself with concern. The note ended with profuse apologies for letting Valeria down, and a plea for understanding, which was readily forthcoming.

Bidding the footman to wait, Valeria swiftly penned a response, assuring her friend that she quite understood that her role as mother must come before that of chaperone.

Sir Edward tut-tutted a little when Valeria explained the position but assured her that since he himself was accompanying her she need not fear anyone would look askance at her. "Make sure you wear one of your finest gowns, Val," he abjured.

"Why? Has Perry received an invitation too?" Valeria asked rather acidly.

"I believe several members of the regiment have been invited," Sir Edward replied, oblivious to her sarcasm.

Valeria shook her head chidingly, but before she could comment they were interrupted by a footman bearing an invitation for Valeria and her father to join Lord Charles Stuart, the English ambassador, for dinner before the reception. Rather unwillingly Valeria agreed to go. She was not overfond of Sir Charles who was as different from his austere half brother, Lord Castlereagh, as it was possible for a man to be. In fact, it was rumored in the salons that Sir Charles considered himself something of a ladies' man and devoted far more time to their pursuit than ambassadorial affairs. It was with this in mind that Valeria elected to wear one of her plainer gowns. She had no desire to arouse Sir Charles's interest, or for him to make her the object of his rather heavy-handed gallantry, as he was wont to attempt to do with any unfortunate young woman who came within his orbit.

The gown was lemon silk, the bodice and scalloped hemline embroidered with matching beads. A Norwich silk shawl with a knotted fringe and a reticule barely large enough to hold a tiny lace-edged handkerchief completed her ensemble.

As the evening was so fine, Sir Edward insisted that they walk to the embassy, which was only a step away, although they were to be conveyed from the embassy to Lord and Lady Castlereagh's reception in Sir Charles's private chaise. Although the evening air was balmy, the flagway felt uncomfortably hard beneath Valeria's thin slippers, and she was glad the walk was but a short one. Despite his advancing years Sir Edward was still a very well set-up gentleman, and he and Valeria attracted more than one admiring glance as they walked through the shadowy tree-lined streets.

Ridiculous to think how she had always made such a bogey of her extra inches, Valeria thought wryly. Now, when she was confronted by real problems, she scarcely gave her height a second thought. Of course the admiration she had received since coming to Vienna could have had something to do with that, she allowed. There was hardly a day when she did not receive an attractive posy or a note requesting the pleasure of her company at this or that entertainment.

Surrey would seem sadly flat when she returned home she admitted, but was it only the balls and gaiety she would miss? Valeria refused to admit such traitorous thoughts. What else should she miss? Fortunately before she was forced to dwell upon this question the gates of the embassy hove into view.

A manservant bowed them into Sir Charles's private apartments. A small group of people were already gathered there. The Prince and Princess du Liechtenstein; a Viennese baronet of middle years, whose name Valeria did not catch, but who smiled admiringly at her; an English couple who had just arrived in the town and looked rather dazed and tired; and several other persons of varying rank and nationality. In all, they were thirty at dinner and Valeria discovered that she was partnered with the middle-aged Viennese whose presence she had remarked earlier.

"I come only lastly," he explained to her in stilted English. "The English major, he could not come."

Valeria's heartbeat accelerated. There must surely be more than one English major in Vienna, she told herself; but still the thought that the major had been Leo Carrington, and that he had refused to attend the dinner because he knew of her presence would not be denied. In fact, Valeria was both right and wrong in her assumptions. She was right that Leo

Carrington had been invited to dine with Sir Charles, but wrong about the reasons for his absence.

Upon leaving the jewelers he had escorted his dark-haired mistress back to her apartments in a silence that smoldered with unspoken resentment on her part, and crackled with icy disdain on his. As he lost no time in telling her when she vented her frustrated wrath upon him, he had not the slightest intention of bestowing any costly items of jewelry upon her, either now or in the future.

"Why not?" she flared angrily. "It is not that you cannot afford it. You are now a duke and—"

"And I never pay for my pleasures in cash or kind, my sweet," he told her coolly. "You made the running and you knew the score."

One slightly raised eyebrow invited her to deny his words and for a moment it seemed she would, but then she turned on her heel, storming up the flight of stone steps leading to her front door which banged angrily behind her, leaving her companion standing outside.

With an expression that betrayed nothing of his feelings, the major turned his steps in the direction of his own lodgings. These were situated in the same building as Lord and Lady Castlereagh. His mistress would have been affronted had she known how far from his thoughts she was. She had openly pursued him from the moment the regiment had arrived in Vienna. A woman who took male homage as her due, she had attributed his brief capitulation to the efficacy of her charms, acknowledging it merely with a triumphant smile and an inviting pout.

Disillusionment had been swift to follow. The fish she thought she had netted so cleverly showed an alarming tendency to wriggle. The jewelry ploy was one she had used to good advantage in the past: a discreet maneuvering of her escort; a soft smile; entreating eyes; and the jewelers well-primed to produce the article she had in mind—always some ruinously expensive piece of jewelry which could later be converted into hard cash. This was the first time it hadn't worked. A rather cynical smile curved the major's firm mouth as he entered the foyer of his apartment. He had few illusions about the fair sex, and had no doubt that the countess would make a rapid recovery from her sulks. On this occasion, though, she would find that her tantrum had cost her dear. The only difference between women of her sort and the young ladies so eagerly paraded around the marriage marts by their mamas, he thought sardonically, was that wives were generally less expensive to keep once one had overcome the initial discomfort obligatory to taking a wife.

A footman relieved him of his hat and gloves before clearing his throat and exclaiming discreetly, "There is a . . . person waiting for you in the library, Your Grace. I did tell him that you were dining out but he insisted upon waiting."

"Did he so? Well I had best see him then."

Thinking to find one of his men in the salon, he threw open the door, stopping short when Wilhelm, the young jeweler, rose clumsily to his feet from the chair he had taken by the window. Frowning for a moment as he tried to place him, the major snapped his fingers as realization dawned.

"Of course, the snuffbox. But you could have left it with my man. There was no need for you to wait for me."

"No, no, you mistake the matter, Your Grace," Wilhelm stammered uncomfortably.

Having been made aware of the major's elevated rank by his haughty footman, he was miserably aware of how the Englishman might construe the questions his father had told him to ask. The Wilhelms were proud of their reputation as fine jewelers. Vulgar activities such as pawnbroking had never formed part of their trade and he swallowed convulsively as the major's blue eyes rested imperiously on his face.

"Well, man, what is it?" His altercation with the countess must have frayed his temper more than he had suspected, Leo Carrington reflected wryly, but there was no need for him to take it out on this poor devil standing in front of him. In fact, it occurred to him that of late his temper had been unusually uncertain—indeed, ever since Miss Valeria Fitzmount had arrived in Vienna. His eyes grew darker as his eyebrows drew together in a heavy frown.

"If it pleases Your Grace, it's Miss Fitzmount." He checked as the major gave a curt exclamation. "You may have noticed . . . That is, Your Grace was in our shop this afternoon as Miss Fitzmount was leaving. May I ask, does Your Grace know Miss Fitzmount?"

"Yes I know her. What of it?"

The interview was not going as smoothly as Wilhelm junior had hoped. He wished his father was at his side to explain the quandary they found themselves in. "It is just that . . ." He was twisting his hat miserably between fingers that seemed to grow stickier with every passing second.

The major suddenly dropped into a chair and pulled a bell rope. When a servant appeared, he commanded, "Bring us two glasses and a bottle of port will you, Peters?

"You'll join me in a drink I hope?" he asked, turning to a startled Wilhelm. A shrewd judge of men, it had suddenly struck him that his visitor bore all the signs of a man laboring under a burden of indecision. Quite what had caused this he did not know, save that somehow it concerned Miss Fitzmount. When they were both served with a glass of port and the servant had been dismissed, Leo Carrington turned back to his visitor.

"So, let us recap. Miss Fitzmount visited your premises this afternoon. I saw her there, from which you deduced that she is known to me, which indeed she is. And now you are in my apartment, presumably on some errand connected with Miss Fitzmount?"

Wilhelm allowed that this was so. "It's the emeralds, you see." he burst out. "What Pa and I want to know is, are they hers?"

"The Fitzmount emeralds, you mean? Certainly they belong to her family."

"But are they hers to dispose of as she wishes?" Wilhelm persisted.

The major's alert mind picked out the salient word. "Dispose of? Is that what Miss Fitzmount was doing in your shop? Selling her jewelry?"

"Well, not exactly," Wilhelm hedged.

"Not exactly? What the devil does that mean? Come on, man, having come thus far, you may as well tell me the whole. Plainly you must have thought there was something suspicious about the whole thing, otherwise you would not be here."

"Not suspicious exactly," Wilhelm protested. "Never that. No it was just that the young lady—Miss Fitzmount—well, anyone with half an eye could see that she hadn't the first notion of how to go about things. Just showed me the stones, she did, and asked straight out if we'd advance her £20,000 against them. They're worth at least ten times that amount. I didn't know what to do so I went and got Pa."

"Very wise of you," Leo Carrington said dryly, his eyes never leaving the other's face. "Go on."

"Well, Pa told her to come back in three days. It was as plain as the nose on your face that she was all overset like, my heart went right out to her, but Pa said we had best just check to make sure things was all aboveboard before advancing the money."

"Did he so? By 'all aboveboard' I presume you mean that he wanted to be sure Miss Fitzmount has the right to dispose of her jewelry in such a cavalier fashion."

"Well there was that, but Pa wanted to make sure that she wasn't going to use the money for any rum business—eloping or such like," he explained miserably.

"Eloping?" the major queried in a voice suddenly sharp and hard. "Did Miss Fitzmount give you the impression that this was what she had in mind?"

"She didn't tell us anything, save that she wanted the money—urgent like. Pa said she didn't have the look of a gaming type, and besides, she wasn't knowing enough. If that was the way of things she would have gone straight to the Jews."

"And yet, despite the obvious doubts you and your father held concerning Miss Fitzmount's right to dispose of the emeralds, you did not think to question her a little more closely on her need for this £20,000. I find that rather strange."

The jeweler gulped nervously at his critical tone, trying to explain that jewelers who valued their business did not question their clients as though they were in a court of law. "We thought —that is Pa thought with Miss Fitzmount so plainly being known to you . . ."

"That I might provide you with the means of discovering the answers to your questions?" the major supplied grimly.

Inwardly his mind was assembling the information like so many jigsaw pieces. As though by divine intervention he now had the means of forcing Valeria Fitzmount to accede to his wishes. For Perry Adaire's sake, he must advise the jeweler to refuse the loan. But should he wish it, he could do so much more—such as destroying Valeria's reputation by putting the tale of what she had tried to do all about the city. It only needed the merest hint dropped in the ears of Vienna's most notorious gossips, and like poison the news would spread fast

122

throughout society. And yet he knew he could not do it. Such an action would not be honorable, but when had Valeria Fitzmount ever considered honor in her own machinations, he asked himself angrily. No matter, it would be enough for him to put a stop to this marriage, without tarring himself with the same brush as Valeria had adopted.

Another thought occurred to him: already the jewelers had put two and two together, and were they to spread the rumor of an elopement. . . with the added embellishment that the bride had sold her jewelry to finance it. There was no reason why he should lift a finger to prevent Miss Fitzmount from becoming the subject of malicious gossip and a laughingstock amongst society, he told himself, and certainly no need for him to take any steps to ensure that this should not be so.

His mouth compressed. Perhaps he was being a fool, but she was after all a lady, a member of his own class, no matter how much he privately despised her. *Noblesse oblige*—call it what you would—he had a certain duty. At length he turned to the jeweler.

"My apologies, my last comment was uncalled for. Naturally you would wish to assure yourself that everything was aboveboard. Well, you need have no doubt on that score. However, Miss Fitzmount's family is known to me and I should not like to think of her being obliged to part with family heirlooms for the sake of such a very modest sum."

"We may lend her the money then?"

"I think not." the brief utterance was softened by a slight smile. "I know, of course, that I may rely upon your discretion, but these matters have an unpleasant way of becoming public. I should not want that to happen to Miss Fitzmount."

The jeweler was shocked and allowed his expression to betray as much.

"I am not suggesting for one moment that you personally would be responsible for such gossip," Leo Carrington assured him, reading his thoughts correctly. "It is just that on this occasion I think it would be wiser were you to decline Miss Fitzmount's request, and then forget that she ever visited you. Do you agree?"

The jeweler assured him hastily that he did. Here was a pretty kettle of fish! What Pa would have to say about it he just did not know. Did the duke intend to lend Miss Fitzmount the money himself? His mind boggled at the thought of asking such a question. However, there was still one point to be finalized.

"And the emeralds, Your Grace?" he asked hesitantly. "Will you return them to Miss Fitzmount?"

The major frowned. He had no taste for melodrama and had no desire to face Valeria with the emeralds like some avenging fury. However, there was no mistaking the pleading look in the other man's face.

"I shall leave that up to you," he replied, checking as the jeweler's consternation grew. "What is the matter?"

"It is just that ladies . . . that is . . . if you . . ."

As he listened to the nervous stammering, comprehension dawned. "You fear an unpleasant scene when the lady learns that her loan is to be refused, is that it? Very well then, have the emeralds sent to me and I shall return them to Miss Fitzmount, but I warn you if I hear so much as a whisper about Miss Fitzmount's presence in your shop you may count your position as official court jewelers well and truly lost."

Not for one moment did the jeweler doubt that he meant what he said. Hurriedly assuring the major that he had already totally forgotten Miss Fitzmount, he bowed his way out of the room, leaving Leo Carrington frowning rather heavily into the empty hearth. Someone had placed an embroidered fire screen across it, but he barely noticed the colorful peacocks with their glittering tails. All he could see was Valeria's face the last time he saw it.

"Ahem! You haven't forgotten that you are engaged to dine with Sir Charles Stuart, have you, Your Grace?" a manservant enquired respectfully, breaking the silence of the room.

He had forgotten; the events of the last hour had completely driven his engagements from his mind. He needed time to think. "I shall have to cancel. Send a message to the sergeant on duty, will you? And have him ask Captain Adaire to report to me as quickly as possible."

Thank goodness his position as Adaire's commanding officer gave him the right to question his junior officers as closely as he liked on their private lives.

Twenty minutes later, he was wishing he had not been so generous to Valeria. A poker-backed soldier had just finished informing him that Captain Adaire had already left their headquarters, and what was more, the sergeant wasn't sure how

124

he could get in touch with him as he had said he was intending to take several days of the leave he had owing to him. The decision had obviously been a sudden one. Leo Carrington swore suddenly, an angry light springing to his eyes.

"You may go," he instructed the soldier," but tell the sergeant to let me know at once if Captain Adaire cannot be reached at his lodgings. I need to speak to him on a matter of urgency—leave or no leave. Tell him he may reach me at Lord and Lady Castlereagh's. I am engaged there tonight."

For several moments after the soldier had gone he continued to stare into the empty hearth, his brow furrowed. Deep in thought he paced the room, the intensity of his fury such that he could barely contain it. An elopement, the jeweler had said, but that did not ring true. With both families wanting the marriage there could be no reason for a hasty, secret service, nor would it be likely that the bride would need to convert the family heirlooms into hard cash to finance the wedding. No, the answer must lie elsewhere.

He thought for a moment and then tugged impatiently on the bell rope. When the servant answered he said curtly, "Send a message to the officers' mess. I want to see Captain Somers and Lieutenant Merriman—at once."

He intended to stop this marriage at all costs! His mouth thinned, giving his face a look of hard determination. Had anyone asked him why he was set on preventing a match between Perry Adaire and Valeria, he would have told them shortly that it was because he had once seen the effect of a spoiled, ruthless woman on a man, and he had no desire to see it again.

The two gentlemen he had summoned arrived together, faintly apprehensive and wary.

"What I have to ask you concerns Captain Adaire," he told them briskly, "and should a distorted sense of loyalty incline you to giving answers that are less than truthful, you will please resist it. I do not ask merely as an idle exercise, nor will your answers reflect adversely on Adaire. Now, do either of you know if he has been gaming heavily since he came to Vienna?"

The two gentlemen exchanged despairing looks. Both of them had been privy to Perry's visits to the gaming hall and both were loath to get him into trouble by admitting as much. "Your expressions give you away," Leo Carrington advised them dryly, "and since neither of you deny it, I take it that my suspicions are correct."

"He has been visiting one of the halls," the captain admitted, "but as to whether he was badly dipped I could not say." He glanced at his companion for corroboration, which was instantly forthcoming, and having assured them that what had been said would go no further than the four walls of the room, Leo Carrington dismissed them.

What he had learned had confirmed his own thoughts. It was the usual story. A young man with good prospects but possibly a small income; tempted into betting more heavily than he could afford; then finding himself dunned by his creditors. Indeed, it was not unknown for them to offer their victims physical violence in the absence of prompt payment. He sighed, frowning again. Gambling was strictly forbidden by the regiment and could lead to court-martialing should the circumstances warrant it. He could quite understand how Perry had been desperate enough to turn to any source of aid to rescue him from the consequence of his folly.

Miss Fitzmount was getting her viscount cheap indeed, he thought sardonically. When Perry's grandfather died he would be worth a pretty fortune. Perry, no doubt, had gone to earth, hiding from his creditors until Valeria produced the money to buy them off, which he suspected she would not do until the ring was safely on her finger. Strangely enough this irrefutable evidence that his conjectures had been right all along did little to alleviate the savagery of his fury and indeed seemed only to serve to fuel the violence of his emotions. He passed a highly satisfactory interlude pacing the floor and imagining exactly what he would say to Miss Fitzmount when he eventually confronted her, but even this was not sufficient to appease him for very long. Miss Fitzmount would rue the day she decided to pursue Perry Adaire, he told himself at the height of his rage.

For the first time in his life he found himself in the unique position of being beset by two conflicting desires. The first was to see Miss Valeria Fitzmount, at his feet, admitting all her many and varied faults, whilst begging for his mercy—a scenario so unfamiliar and disturbing that it alone accounted for a good deal of his impotent fury. And the second, of far more concern to a gentleman of acute perception, and as yet

126

scarcely admitted, had a great deal to do with what might have occurred had he not received his relatives' damning letters; sensations so revolutionary that he ruthlessly squashed them before they had time to cause further dissension amongst his hitherto orderly and well-regulated thoughts.

Chapter Nine

It was a little after ten o'clock when Sir Charles Stuart's party arrived at Lord and Lady Castlereagh's apartment in the Minoritzenplatz. Sir Charles, who was a little high flown with wine, confided to them as they stepped over the threshold that his half brother was none too pleased about the excessive rent he was being charged for the twenty-odd rooms he was leasing.

"It's costing the government £500 per month," he told Sir Edward, "and apparently half the rooms are too small to be of much use anyway. He's already complained about it, but to no avail."

Privately Valeria could find nothing to cavil at in the spacious entrance hall hung with panels of Chinese silk embroidered with birds of paradise. A double row of onyx columns, their bases embellished with gilt paint marched down the room toward a huge pair of mahogany doors.

These were thrown open by a couple of footmen wearing royal livery, "because Lord Castlereagh is representing the throne" one of the ladies whispered to Valeria by way of explanation.

A third footman announced them. The large double drawing room was already crowded, the buzz of conversation making it almost impossible for the footman to be heard above the din.

Lady Castlereagh came forward to welcome them, a lady of ample girth and stately manner with no pretensions to following fashion. Valeria liked her although she found Lord Castlereagh's manner a little overwhelming upon occasions. He had the reputation of a rapierlike mind, cold and shrewd, and Valeria could well believe it. Another member of their party nudged Valeria as the Empress Maria Ludovica walked past, but Valeria already knew the empress from her ball. All the leading Viennese families were represented—the Schwarzenbergs, Esterhazys and Liechtensteins—and before too long Valeria's head was whirling with names.

It wasn't long before Sir Edward was drawn into a circle of acquaintances leaving Valeria alone and feeling extremely self-conscious. Lady Castlereagh, who had taken a liking to her, caught sight of her out of the corner of her eye and hurried toward her rather like a ship in full sail.

Several unkind persons had been disposed to make mock of Lady Castlereagh behind her back upon her initial arrival in Vienna, but their amusement had given way; first to surprise and then respect as they perceived the efficient manner in which she directed her household; most were envious of the unaccountable ease with which she smoothed over the domestic upheavals so prevalent in their own homes.

"My dear, I must introduce you to the czar and Prince Metternich. Such a pity Camilla could not come, she rushed round here in a panic this morning asking if I could give her the direction of a reputable doctor. As luck would have it the czar was here and insisted upon sending his own physician to attend the child. He is like that, of course, such a charming person, although if one were to believe all one hears about him . . ." She left the sentence unfinished but Valeria knew she was referring to the czar's reputation with women.

Only the previous evening Camilla had repeated to her a rumor that the Princess Bagration, whose wild exploits had set Vienna by the ears only weeks before, was now out of favor with the czar and kept to her private apartments in the Palais Palm, shunned by those who once flocked to her salons.

"Not at all the thing," Camilla had said wisely. "She is not accepted by the ton at all and will have to pay dearly for her association with the czar. They say her debts are phenomenal!"

Gossip about the various personalities involved in the congress abounded. If one believed every rumor one heard about the debaucheries and high living that went on, it was a wonder that any business was conducted at all.

Since the purpose of the reception was to make the czar

and Prince Metternich known to as many of their guests as possible, the Castlereaghs were kept busy and it wasn't long before Valeria found herself quite alone again. Where her father had gone, she did not know, but she suspected that he and several other gentlemen had probably repaired to another room to play cards.

There was a small French contingent present, including the new French foreign minister, Talleyrand. Lady Castlereagh had been a little vexed at the unexpected arrival of this reputedly brilliant statesman and his entourage, for he had not received an official invitation but, as she said to Valeria, she could hardly turn him away.

"Talleyrand has turned his coat so many times it is a wonder he remembers which side he is on," she had murmured waspishly to Valeria as she swept forward to greet the French minister.

The night was very close and Valeria's head still throbbed uncomfortably, the combination of heat, noise and perfumes making her long for a breath of fresh air. Unwilling to seem impolite or draw attention to herself, she edged her way round the room hoping to find a less oppressive spot to recuperate for a few seconds without being missed. As it happened it was a relatively easy task to slip out of the crowded, overheated drawing room. The foyer was deserted, all the footmen apparently on duty in the main salon, so there was no one Valeria could approach to ask where she might sit for a few moments in privacy. Several doors led off the foyer. All of them were closed. From behind one Valeria caught the indistinct hum of male voices and guessed that it was there that the gentlemen had repaired for their game of cards. Choosing a door at random and hoping that Lady Castlereagh would not think her guilty of prying, Valeria turned the handle and stepped inside.

She found herself in a rather gloomy library with a single candelabrum standing on a small drum table near the window. The room smelled faintly musty and Valeria wrinkled her nose a little wondering if she would not have been better slipping out into the gardens behind the house.

She had not the energy for further exploration, she told herself, and sinking into a chair, luxuriated in the cessation of the constant noise and chatter. A faded Turkey carpet covered the floor, and despite the framed family portraits on the desk, the room had the resigned faded atmosphere of a dwelling long accustomed to transience and impermanence.

Valeria lay back and closed her eyes, trying to relax her tense muscles. A faint creak as the door opened warned her that her privacy was about to be invaded. Half expecting to come face to face with her hostess she sprang up, apologies falling from her lips. As the intruder turned toward her she gave a small gasp. It was not Lady Castlereagh but a gentleman who, although a complete stranger to her, was obviously not as surprised to see her as she was to see him.

With every evidence of satisfaction he swaggered across the carpet, his eyes lingering on Valeria's person with greedy anticipation. Glancing swiftly at the door, Valeria got to her feet, hoping to quit the room before the gentleman could detain her.

"Come, *chérie*, surely you do not wish to leave me," he declared, his accent betraying his nationality. "When I saw you slip from the *chambre* I thought that at last the gods were smiling upon me."

So he had deliberately followed her into the library! Valeria's heart beat a little faster. Had anyone else seen her leave? A servant or, better still, Lady Castlereagh perhaps? The Frenchman continued to advance, swaying a little as he did so. He was more than a little high flown with wine, Valeria decided astutely, and this was probably the reason he was so intent upon accosting her. She stepped backward, intent on avoiding his outstretched hand, and stumbled against a leather footstool, losing her balance. The Frenchman moved swiftly, capturing her in his arms as she fell, a look in his eyes that made her blanch with fear.

"Please release me," Valeria stammered, trying not to let her fear show.

"*Mais non*," her captor responded, cursing suddenly as the library door was pushed open. Relief washed over Valeria. Embarrassing as it was to be discovered in the Frenchman's arms, embarrassment was infinitely preferable to the consequences of her remaining his prisoner. Or, at least, that was what she had thought until she realized the identity of the newcomer, for it was none other than Leo Carrington.

"So, it seems you number infidelity amongst your other failings, Miss Fitzmount," the major commented contemptuously, ignoring the Frenchman's threatening stance. "Forgive me for the intrusion," he drawled to her captor, making a small bow and turning to leave. "I had not realized the room was occupied."

He was going to leave! Terror lent Valeria the courage to protest.

"No! Please!" she begged. "You don't understand! This gentleman . . . that is . . . this gentleman followed me here and forced his attentions upon me," she managed to whisper.

"Indeed." The word and the look which accompanied it made it plain that the major did not believe her.

"She lies!" the Frenchman burst out, his fingers biting warningly into Valeria's flesh. The major's eyes narrowed as his eyes went from Valeria's strained face to the Frenchman's truculent one. Fear all but drowned out Valeria's initial embarrassment and her eyes clung to the major's face, mutely pleading for him to intervene.

"Whatever her initial desire, it seems the young lady has now had a change of heart. You will oblige me by releasing her at once," he said at last.

At first it seemed as though the Frenchman would ignore the deceptively mild command, and then, to Valeria's intense relief, he removed his hands from her arms allowing her to move to the other side of the fire. She suspected that having measured the major's cool determination and breadth of shoulder he had decided that they constituted a far more formidable obstacle than that presented by a young, defenseless female.

"Very well then," he announced truculently, moving toward the door. "I wish you joy of her, monsieur, a cold piece I judge."

Valeria thought her dismayed gasp had gone unnoticed, but when her attacker had quitted the room and she made to follow him, the major stopped her. "There is no need to play the part of the innocent for my benefit," he told her in a silky voice. "I don't doubt for one moment that you encouraged that young fool, although plainly you bit off more than you could chew."

"Encouraged him!" Valeria protested indignantly. "How dare you say so. I came in here merely for a few minutes' respite. I had no idea he would follow me or that he would think—"

"Think that you were not averse to some idle moments of flirtation," the major supplied softly. "Come, you cannot expect me to believe that you were not to blame. A woman

133

as beautiful as you are must know the effect she has on susceptible males, especially those as easily inflamed as our French friend. What did you hope to gain? Jealousy from young Adaire? That is always a useful spur to drive a jaded horse, isn't it?" he goaded concealing his thoughts from her.

If Miss Fitzmount found it necessary to give Perry a rival it could only mean that she was still not entirely sure of him. He was overcome by a desire to denounce her there and then, to tell her what he knew, but for Perry's sake he had to keep silent. Until the younger man had been found and assured that his sins did not necessitate the drastic step of marriage to Miss Fitzmount, his hands were tied. All he could do was to make clear his own contempt and hope that somehow he could find Perry Adaire before it was too late. If only he might have half an hour alone with Miss Fitzmount, he thought grimly, he would soon discover Perry's whereabouts but he could do nothing at this crowded reception, with people liable to interrupt them at any moment—as the Frenchman had discovered to his cost.

"Please allow me to pass," Valeria said faintly, her throat tight with the effort of controlling her emotions. She would not respond to his unkind gibes; she would not give him that satisfaction.

As he moved to one side, with a brief bow, Valeria swept past him, head held high, ignoring the tumult his presence always wrought within her.

It wasn't until she emerged into the foyer that she realized he was immediately behind her. The Frenchman was leaning sulkily against the wall and a wave of faintness threatened to overcome her as she was forced to inch past him. There was a burst of hurried conversation and Lady Castlereagh appeared through the open salon door.

"I wonder if you could procure Miss Fitzmount a glass of wine," Leo Carrington asked her, immediately taking charge, before Valeria could protest that she had no need of any wine, nor any need of his mock solicitude either. "I have just rescued her from the drunken attentions of one of Talleyrand's aides."

Valeria heard the irony underlying his words, but it was plain that Lady Castlereagh had taken them at face value, for she instantly exclaimed in shocked accents, "My poor child, really it is too bad of Talleyrand. He will insist on surrounding himself with these young men, and most of them have not the slightest notion of how to go on. Shall I call your father? Would you like to go upstairs and rest? I could send my maid to you."

Valeria assured her hostess that she was suffering from nothing more than a bad shock, admitting that it was probably her own fault for wandering off into the library unescorted.

"No such thing," Lady Castlereagh exclaimed heatedly. "If one cannot seek a few minutes' peace in private apartments without being accosted, it is a very poor thing indeed. This would never happen at home of course. The French really do not have the faintest idea of how to conduct themselves!"

"I shall leave you to Lady Castlereagh's ministrations," the major interrupted dryly. "Plainly they are more to your taste than mine." Whilst Lady Castlereagh was still trying to understand his meaning, he added casually, "By the way, have you seen anything of Perry Adaire lately? It seems that he is missing from his lodgings."

Valeria felt as though all the breath had been driven out of her lungs. She was powerless to prevent herself from changing color—Perry missing! What could this mean? she wondered in dismay.

Her father had strolled out of the card room just in time to catch the major's question and it was he who answered. "Haven't seen young Perry in days," he told the other man. "Not at his lodgings you say!"

"The duty sergeant tells me that he returned to our headquarters at the Minoritzenplatz today and informed him that he intended to take a few days' leave which were owing to him."

"Umm, ain't got himself into any trouble, has he?" Sir Edward asked perspicaciously. "Levelheaded enough young fellow normally, but it strikes me he's been looking down in the mouth of late."

"As family friends, I am sure you are far better able to answer that question than I," the major responded smoothly, his eyes lingering on Valeria's pale face for a second.

What was he insinuating? That *she* was responsible for Perry's absence? If only he knew, Valeria thought half hysterically. He was the one Perry was unable to face, not her. Why, oh why, hadn't she told Perry what she intended

135

to do? No matter how hard he had objected, she would at least have set his mind at rest upon the question of the money. What should she do now? Continue as planned.

Eventually the major took his leave of them.

"Seems to have taken quite a shine to you, Val," Sir Edward commented jovially when he had gone. "Danced with you at the empress's ball, and now this."

"He was but behaving as any gentleman would do, Papa," Valeria said tiredly. "Pray do not go reading anything else into it."

There had been something in the look Leo Carrington gave her when he mentioned Perry, an added degree of contempt, but she refused to allow herself to dwell on it now. All her thoughts were concentrated on Perry, and where he might be. What misery had driven him to this course? And how unlike him it was too. The Perry she knew was a fighter, but upon this occasion, she admitted, the forces ranged against him were formidable. Perhaps, if he only had himself to consider, he could risk the worst that the Noakeses could do to him, but he had his grandfather to consider, and Maria too. It all seemed too unfair, Valeria reflected impotently. It wasn't even as though Perry had been gaming. But then, of course, Leo Carrington would never believe that; he would take one look at the facts and condemn him out of hand!

Valeria and Sir Robert were amongst the first to leave the reception. Valeria's headache had grown worse rather than better, and she had prevailed upon her father to take her home. Just as they were on the point of departing, Leo Carrington waylaid them. The draught from the open door set the tapers flickering wildly, throwing dancing shadows across his face. Nevertheless, Valeria was well able to discern the hard purposefulness in his eyes. Sir Edward was talking to Lord Castlereagh and thus Valeria had no means of defense when the major's fingers tightened about her arm. He smiled mirthlessly at Valeria's assumed disdain. What would she say if he told her he knew about the emeralds? For a moment he was tempted but, as he reminded himself, he could not afford to risk alerting her to the fact that he was aware of her plans.

For Perry Adaire's sake he must hold his peace—for the time being at least. Even so, he could not resist a parting thrust, driven to it by the cool control Valeria was exhibiting, for all the world as though she were the injured party. Indeed, so powerfully did her pose work upon his already short temper that he would love to have thrown his accusations in her face. But he was convinced that to do so would only have the effect of hardening her resolve to marry Perry. The strain of smothering this desire showed in his face and eyes, but Valeria, unaware of his train of thought, could only shrink away from him as he started to speak.

"You may think you have deceived me, but I know full well what you are about," he told Valeria acidly, "and it will not work. I shall make sure of that. I have left a message at Adaire's lodgings and I must tell you here and now that I intend to dissuade him from this reckless folly. Indeed, in normal circumstances I would look to your father to pull rein on you, but from my conversations with him I recollect that he is as eager to see you married as you are to achieve that state yourself. It is plain to see why, of course," he added, looking her over with insulting thoroughness. "Had I such an ungainly bean pole of a daughter, I doubt not that I too would be anxious to be rid of her!"

The handsome face swam mistily above her for a few seconds, as Valeria battled against a rush of tears, and then he was gone, turning abruptly on his heel and leaving her staring after him, pale and trembling from the shock of his attack. Numbly she followed her father out to the waiting carriage. Could it have been only an hour earlier that the major had accused her of using her beauty to ensnare her victims? If so, he must have been mocking her, for with one short cruel sentence he had robbed her of all her newly emergent self-confidence.

His parting words throbbed mercilessly through her aching head as they drove home. She had not been able to make any sense of the major's accusations. Had he somehow discovered Perry's folly? She did not know what to think. Indeed, it required an unbearable effort merely to lift her aching head and descend from the carriage.

A sleepless night spent worrying about Perry did little to restore Valeria's complexion to its normal color. Indeed, as she observed the dark smudges beneath her eyes, she reflected that an observer might be forgiven for thinking her grown positively haggard.

She was engaged to ride in the woods with Count Polinsky and, little though she relished the prospect, it was too late to cancel the arrangement now.

She had chosen to wear a carriage dress in heavy silk of a dusky pink shade, normally quite unwearable by anyone with her coloring, but as Hester fastened the tiny buttons on the sleeves, Valeria admitted that this particular shade of pink looked extraordinarily attractive. A band of sable fur edged the hem and also the short cape that matched the dress, and the count exclaimed admiringly as she descended the stairs just in time to see him admitted by the butler. He himself was wearing biscuit-colored pantaloons, his cravat tied in a crisp waterfall of white muslin, an elegant jacket of blue superfine clinging to his broad shoulders.

Outside, a groom wearing his livery walked the pair of matched grays drawing a bright yellow racing curricle.

"Forgive me if I appear to rush to be on our way," the count apologized charmingly as he assisted Valeria into the curricle, "but it would not do to leave my horses standing.

"This is a relatively new sport for me," he added as he pulled a capped riding coat round his shoulders. "In Russia we are more used to sledges than curricles, but I must own I find myself becoming an enthusiast."

"It is very much the fashion amongst the London bloods," Valeria agreed knowledgeably. "There is a club to which only the very best drivers are allowed to belong. It is called the 'Four Horse Club' and those gentlemen fortunate enough to be members have regular meetings to see which amongst them can race his horses the fastest."

"Then Major Carrington must surely be a member," the count told her, expertly flicking his long whip above the team's ears, "for it was he who was kind enough to help me choose this team and give me a few pointers on how to handle them. It is said that the English are kinder to their horses and dogs than they are to their wives."

"I suspect Englishmen are no worse than any others," Valeria replied dryly. "It is just that they are less adept at concealing it." The count threw back his head and laughed. "A woman with a sense of humor! You look particularly delightful this morning, Valeria—may I call you that?" Without waiting for a reply he added seriously, "There are times when having the reputation for being a flirt is a decided disadvantage. I believe this is one of them. You are not disposed to take me at all seriously, are you?"

"I have no desire to take anyone seriously," Valeria responded firmly. "How can I? When I am in Vienna?"

"You are quite right," the count agreed. "Vienna casts her spell over us all, making us dance to her bidding, and bidding us commit all manner of foolish things."

Relieved that the awkward moment had passed, Valeria devoted her attentions to being an entertaining companion. The count was very easy to get along with, seeming to know instinctively that she had no wish to indulge in any serious conversation, and he kept her so well amused that she was surprised to find how quickly the time flew. There were many girls, she knew, whose hearts would have been put in a flutter by the count's polished manners and teasing charm, but like him though she did, *her* heart remained soberly steady.

"A very pleasant outing," he said as he assisted her down from the curricle outside her apartment. "I hope we may repeat it upon another occasion, perhaps when you have less on your mind." He bowed over her hand, raising her fingers to his lips in a fleeting gesture. Wishing he were a little less perceptive, Valeria took her leave of him.

The fresh air had brought color to her cheeks, banishing the headache that had plagued her, but as she entered the apartment all her thoughts were on Perry and where he might be.

Thus it came something of a shock to discover that the hallway was occupied—by Leo Carrington. Having been unable to discover any hint of Perry's whereabouts he had decided, against his better judgment, to make a final appeal to Valeria to abandon her plans and tell him where he might find the younger man—not a decision he had found easy to reach.

He stood up as Valeria entered, towering over her. This morning he was not in uniform. He greeted her curtly, glancing at the footman hovering protectively by the stairs.

"I want to talk with you," he began without preamble, "and unless you wish your servants to be privy to what I have to say, I suggest you dismiss your man."

Valeria glanced helplessly from her visitor to the footman. It would be quite improper for her to receive an unmarried gentleman without a chaperon, but it was equally plain that Leo Carrington did not intend to leave until he had had his say and so, dismissing the servant, she ushered him into her father's library.

"If you would care for a glass of wine," she began uncertainly, indicating the silver coaster containing a decanter of wine and several glasses. The smile she received was completely devoid of warmth. "This is not a social visit, Miss Fitzmount," she was told coldly. "Indeed, let me tell you that it is only my concern for Perry Adaire that prompts me to seek you out in this fashion."

He walked toward the fire and stood with his back to it, surveying her so intently that Valeria could not contain the color flooding her face. "Strange how beauty can be so corrupt," her tormentor mused, "but then that is ever nature's way to trick and deceive.

"Where is Perry Adaire?" he flung at her without warning, abandoning his pose by the fire to stand by the desk, his hands placed firmly on the leather top as his eyes bored into hers.

Valeria could not repress a small quiver of apprehension. If only he did not look so dark and forbidding. If only she could correct all his misconceptions and plead Perry's case.

"Very well then, if you will not tell me, I suppose it is no more than I should have expected. It is plain that you do not possess a single shred of remorse or pity. I was a fool to even think that you might be constrained upon to abandon your course—"

"I do not know where Perry is," Valeria protested, not understanding why his eyes had darkened so suddenly. Why would he not believe her?

"I have thought you many things, Miss Fitzmount," he said contemptuously, "but until this moment I had not considered you to be cowardly enough to take refuge behind a lie. Or do you perhaps excuse yourself on the grounds of expediency? Any weakening now could lead to the loss of your prize, is that it? Any diplomatic silence on your part until the knot is safely tied. What are your plans? A triumphant return to England and a fashionable wedding at St. George's, or daren't you wait that long? Did you know that before you came on the scene young Adaire was halfway to falling in love with a young Viennese girl and she with him?

140

I can guess what means you have used to force him to his present pitch."

Valeria had closed her ears against his insults after the first few words. Like someone in a trance she heard the sound of his voice, without comprehending the meaning of what he was saying. All she knew was that each word seemed to pierce her heart like a tiny sliver of ice, inflicting dreadful pain.

The major was finished speaking and appeared to be waiting for her to say something. What? Was she supposed to break down and admit she knew where Perry was. If only she did! "Please go, Major," she said quietly. "We can have nothing further to say to each other. Quite plainly you believe me incapable of speaking the truth, so I shall not waste my time reiterating that I do not know where Perry is, nor do I intend to lower myself by refuting your other accusations."

"Lower yourself!" Leo Carrington gave a disbelieving laugh. "I should have thought that was impossible, and as for your other remark, allow me to congratulate you on your acting abilities. For a moment there I was almost convinced, despite the fact that I have concrete evidence to prove your guilt."

In all her life no one had ever accused Valeria of such vileness, and she felt scorched by the insults that had been thrown at her, undeserved though they were. There was much she could have said in her own defense but pride prevented her. Indeed, she felt that the very effort of speech would choke her, so paralyzing was the hard lump of despair in her chest. How could he be so blind? By what right did he sit in judgment over her?

"I warn you now," Leo was saying. "Abandon the course you have set yourself, otherwise I shall be forced to make you do so."

He was gone before Valeria could respond, striding through the door and out of her life. She was not to know that as the front door slammed behind him, he was cursing himself as much as he was her. For a moment he had almost believed her, almost hoped that . . . That what? he asked himself angrily. Valeria Fitzmount was a classic example of the duplicity for which her sex was notorious; and if he could find no other way of dissuading her from marrying Perry Adaire he might be forced to threaten her with the disclosure of the means she had used to force Perry to the match. He grimaced distastefully, hearing again her cool voice saying that she would not lower herself to his level. For a moment he was tempted to go back and break her pride by telling her what he knew, but he abandoned the notion as not one befitting a gentleman.

Alone in the salon, Valeria sank down into a chair, her body trembling with shock and rage. The tiny lace-edged handkerchief she was holding in her hand was methodically shredded into pieces as she relived their interview. How could he think so ill of her? How could he?

And Perry? Where was he? Her heart gave an uncomfortable lurch as she remembered how distressed he had been. Surely he could not have done anything foolish, such as . . . But her mind refused to contemplate what in her heart she was beginning to dread.

Plainly the major believed that a marriage between herself and Perry was imminent—and further, ascribed it to some sort of conniving on her own part. But on what he based his assumptions, save for sheer determination to see her in the worst possible light, she did not know. Nothing could have underlined his dislike of her more sharply. Valeria sighed, firmly banishing the major, and his prejudices, from her mind, If only she knew where Perry was!

Chapter Ten

Far from planning his elopement, as Leo Carrington suspected, or his early demise, as envisaged by Valeria in her deepest moments of despair, Perry was actually comfortably seated in the window seat of a small salon, in a fairy-tale castle perched over the Danube. His fair head was close to the smooth dark one of Maria Schubraum—now Lady Adaire.

On her hand glistened the diamond ring lent to him for the occasion by Baron Schubraum and next to it nestled the plain gold band that was all he had been able to purchase in the neighboring town.

Perry Adaire had been taught as a child to face his problems squarely, without taking cowardly refuge in deceit. Lord Adaire had been a strict disciplinarian, placing honor and courage amongst the highest requirements for a gentleman, and Perry could not now find it in himself to turn his back on his grandfather's teachings.

For the entire length of one long night, duty warred with inclination, but when he rose the following morning his mind was made up. Having informed the duty sergeant of his intention to take the leave owing to him, he had saddled up his horse and ridden out of Vienna to the small village where his love's parents were staying.

Many times during the journey he had cursed himself for an impetuous fool but he knew that, even if Maria were to refuse him, he would at least have told her the truth. Better that, by far, than a marriage founded upon lies.

To his own surprise the baron received him most cordially. His sick relative was mending fast and when they had exhausted all small talk, Perry begged his host's indulgence for his unheralded arrival and without further ado launched into an explanation of his visit.

The baron heard him out in a silence that had him sinking to the very depths of despair, but having set his foot to the path, he was determined not to turn aside until every single piece of his folly was revealed. When at last he came to a halting silence, the baron regarded him thoughtfully. Although some fifteen years his junior, he reminded Perry very much of his grandfather.

"I won't pretend to be surprised by what you have told me," Baron Schubraum said at last. "You have been truthful with me and I should wish to return the compliment. Your association with this female was already known to me— please, say nothing. I admit I was unhappy about the thought of an alliance between yourself and my daughter. After all, what did we know of you? You have a title and comparative wealth, but to a caring father, these are not the things that matter. What I have learned today has shown me that you have other, more important, qualities." His stern expression gave way to a vagrant smile.

"We are all guilty of committing follies when we are young, Perry. You will not be the last young man to be caught in such a trap. Indeed, I myself when I was your age . . . But there I will not bore you with old stories. You have my permission to pay your addresses to Maria, if that is what you wish."

When he had finished wringing his hand and thanking him, Perry hurried toward the door. "A moment," the baron called after him. "Will you tell Maria what you have told me?"

"I must," Perry replied firmly, squaring his shoulders. "Otherwise I could not live with myself."

His prospective father-in-law nodded his head as though well satisfied with his reply, and when the door had closed behind him, he gave a faint sigh and picked up the miniature of his daughter from his desk. "He has proved himself worthy of you," he said to the smiling portrait. "All that remains to be seen is whether you are worthy of him."

Perry found Maria in the small round room at the top of one of castle's many towers, staring idly out at the vista below, a tambour frame at her side. She flushed shyly when he entered and, remembering Mama's lecture, begged him very prettily to be seated. Perry shook his head, unable to restrain himself from prowling restlessly about the room until he realized that the soft brown eyes raised to his were full of gentle encouragement, not to say breathless anticipation.

Taking his courage in both hands, he launched into a muddled confession, breaking off with a groan of despair when he realized that Maria did not comprehend his meaning. Good resolutions fled when he perceived the bewildered trembling of the warm red lips and before he could stop himself he had taken her into his arms, murmuring his proposal between kisses. But finally, a recollection of what he had not told her brought him to a standstill, and he wrenched himself away from her to stare blindly out of the narrow slit window.

A gentle hand on his shoulder reminded him of his duty, and haltingly he explained to her just why he was worse than the lowest vermin in the land for proposing to her before he had detailed the full extent of his iniquity. To his surprise she was less startled than her father.

"I know all about the girl," she told him, placing a silencing finger against his lips. "Did you think that amongst such a large circle of acquaintances as mine that there would not be one girl jealous and spiteful enough to tell me?" She blushed again, giving her head an admonishing shake. "Oh Perry, you had no need to distress yourself with this. I am glad you did though," she added softly, "for now I need have no fears that I shall have to share you with anyone else. Mama has always told me . . . that is . . . I know that gentlemen may sometimes show a preference for . . . other women."

Perry brought her unsteady explanations to a halt by the simple device of taking her back into his arms and showing her very thoroughly indeed that she made up his entire universe.

"I want us to be married as soon as possible," he told her. "I am selling out of the army and would like you to return to England with me. But if you prefer to wait . . . ? Of course I should have liked Gramps to be here—he will love you as much as I do. But I am not disposed to delay our wedding for the length of time it would take to write to England and have him come out here for the ceremony. He will be disappointed at not being present, but I believe he will appreciate my motives. After all, he himself married my grandmother without so much as a by-your-leave, and she was all but betrothed to another man. You must get him to tell you the story, it is very romantic. I don't think he ever fully recovered from her death. That is why I am sure he will forgive me my impetuous actions."

His grandfather would accept Maria, Perry was sure of that, especially when he got to know her, and perhaps, after all, this was the best way, for it would show Gramps that he was fully adult, capable of making his own decisions and standing by them. Indeed, Perry felt that he had matured immeasurably in the last few weeks.

He took Maria's hand and pressed a gentle kiss in the palm. "Well, my love," he asked huskily, "what is it to be?"

Miss Maria was as sensible as she was pretty. No one was going to get the chance to snatch her Perry from beneath her nose. With a smile she told him that they could be married from the family chapel, and, she added ingeniously, that way they would not have to endure a tedious wait whilst both families were informed what was afoot.

Perry was ready to fall in with whatever she suggested. Maria's mama, at first inclined to demur, gave way to her daughter's importunings, and within three days of his arrival at the castle, Perry was a married man.

No sooner had the knot been tied than Perry reluctantly informed his bride that it would be necessary for them to return to Vienna. His commanding officer would have to be advised of his marriage; there were formalities to be attended to relevant to his withdrawal from the regiment; and, of course, he wanted to apprise Valeria of his newfound happiness.

The baron offered to put his Viennese residence at the disposal of the newly married pair for as long as proved necessary. And feeling happier than he could ever have believed possible, Perry stepped into the carriage his in-laws had loaned him, never dreaming what construction had been put upon his sudden disappearance.

For two days following upon Leo Carrington's visit, Valeria could not bring herself to set foot outside the apartment lest a message arrive from Perry. The third morning after his departure brought her two items of correspondence. The first was a note from Camilla, informing her that the baby's spots—the cause of so much maternal anxiety—had proved to be nothing more than a slight heat rash. The doctor had assured her that they were neither contagious nor sympto-

146

matic of a more serious illness, and this being the case she hoped to call upon her friend at the earliest opportunity. Valeria could muster very little interest in the letter. Indeed, her altercation with Leo Carrington had had such a lowering effect upon her spirits that she could take no pleasure in anything. Just when she thought she had successfully banished her black mood, the major's unkind words would slip unchecked into her mind and she would be swept by a feeling of such desolation that tears would prick her eyes and pain make her heart ache with misery.

The second letter was delivered whilst she was sitting alone in the salon. It bore a neat gold crest proclaiming Messrs. Wilhelm and Wilhelm were the official jewelers to the Imperial Court. Valeria's fingers trembled as she broke the seal, conscious of a nervous fluttering in her stomach. If only Perry had not disappeared before she had had the chance to tell him of her intentions. She perused the note quickly, disbelief and dismay flooding through her as the purpose of the letter became plain. Regretfully, politely, but plainly nonetheless, the jewelers were refusing the loan, and she had been so sure that they would agree. What was she to do now? Everything had gone so dreadfully wrong. First Perry's disappearance and now this! The letter made no mention of returning the jewelry and Valeria surmised that they expected she would rather collect the emeralds herself than risk their being entrusted to the post. That meant she would have to visit their shop yet again. How could she face them? Her cheeks burned. Why had they refused her? If only there was someone she could turn to. Someone in whom she might confide all her doubts and fears. It came to her with sickening clarity that even were Perry, by some miracle, not missing as Leo Carrington had said, but merely engaged on some business which had taken him out of town, she could now do nothing to help him. Her private thoughts were that Perry, in his present mood of deep depression, was in the gravest danger and, this being the case, she was forced to contemplate a course which in any other circumstances would have been totally repugnant to her.

If Lord Adaire had been more easily accessible she would have gone straight to him, or even elicited the aid of her own father had she thought he would be able to achieve anything. However, Perry was not a free individual in that he

147

had a duty to the army—a duty which he had already made plain he considered of great importance.

Valeria was forced to admit that there was really only one person who could help her friend; only one person with the power to nullify Mrs. Noakes's threat, and mount a discreet search for Perry before the burdens he was carrying became too heavy for him to bear.

Trembling with nervous dread, Valeria tried to marshal her thoughts. How could she go to Leo Carrington? Indeed, he held her in such contempt that he would probably refuse to receive her, and then, if he did, she still had to overcome the stumbling block of his rigid interpretation of the rules. She had no guarantee that he would listen to Perry's story sympathetically, much less do anything to aid him, but there was no one else.

Valeria contemplated the alternatives soberly. She herself could now do nothing to aid Perry, Leo Carrington could do a great deal. Did her pride matter more than her old friend? If she was honest with herself, wasn't the thought of pleading with the major nearly as daunting as having to explain Perry's folly?

All afternoon Valeria debated the matter inwardly, veering first this way and then that, but then as she heard the clock in the hallway striking four, she made up her mind. She would go. She must go, for Perry's sake.

At about the same time that Valeria was perusing her letter, a small package was delivered to Leo Carrington, wrapped in sturdy brown paper and sealed with red wax. He guessed immediately what the parcel contained.

Once revealed to the light of day, the emeralds were even more magnificent than he remembered. He smiled bitterly as he looked at them. It was a very determined lady indeed who could bring herself to dispose of these, purely to make good a boast. But then he had never doubted that Valeria Fitzmount was anything other than single-minded.

Despite the fact that he had his own personal batman discreetly scouring the town, he had still not managed to discover Perry's whereabouts, and he cursed himself for not forcing Valeria to reveal the truth. Now that the emeralds were in his possession he could confront her with the evidence that he had it in his power to prevent her from marrying Perry. And yet, for some unfathomable reason, he found himself strangely reluctant to use the weapon fate had so conveniently placed in his hands. He had been hoping to discover where Perry had gone to ground, and had intended offering to lend him whatever money was needed to buy off his creditors. Such an action would be strictly against the rules, he knew, but he refused to allow Perry to sacrifice himself for the sake of a paltry £20,000. He considered himself a good judge of men and believed that the shock he had been given would keep Perry away from the gambling tables for the rest of his life.

Now, with Perry's whereabouts still undiscovered, he cursed himself for allowing his gentlemanly instincts to sway his judgment. A young lady of Valeria Fitzmount's calibre would surely hardly balk at hearing that her loan had been refused, he reminded himself. Indeed, she was more than capable of bluffing the whole thing out, he decided bitterly, and then hoping that her father's generosity would buy off her new husband's creditors.

There was another way of coercing her, of course. He could threaten to reveal her visit to the jewelers and its purpose. He glanced bleakly at the emeralds. What was he sunk to? Had she turned him into a blackguard as well as a fool?

Valeria felt no braver when she eventually stepped out into the street, hurrying toward the Minoritzenplatz, and urging Hester not to dawdle. Today she was in no mood to appreciate the good humor of the Viennese, or to waste time admiring their fine buildings.

The entrance hall to the palace was every bit as busy as it had been upon the occasion of her first visit, but this time a liveried flunky bore down upon her the moment they entered the foyer. On requesting to see Major Carrington, she was escorted to his office and asked to wait inside while the footman went in search of him.

Valeria stood by the window so that she might have the advantage of facing the major the moment he entered the room. He did not keep her waiting very long, although she had to admit that she had never known a handful of minutes stretch to such a nerve-wracking infinity. Over and over again she repeated to herself what she intended to say, but the moment the door was pushed open all her carefully rehearsed speeches fled, leaving her tongue-tied and desperately afraid.

"Miss Fitzmount!" The major made no attempt to hide his surprise. Indeed, for a moment Valeria had the impression that he was almost relieved to see her. The reason for this quickly became apparent. Before she could so much as utter a word, the major was seating himself behind his desk, indicating that she take a chair opposite him and saying briskly, "So, you have come to your senses. I thank God for it. Where is Adaire?"

Valeria checked. She had completely overlooked this outcome to her mission. Plainly the major still believed her to be deliberately concealing Perry's whereabouts.

"I cannot tell you." Indeed, she would have given much to know the answer to that question herself, she thought, shrinking a little under the disbelieving fury she saw in the major's eyes. If only he did not make her feel so wretchedly nervous, so very conscious of him. This thought lent her the courage to lift her head and say bravely, "I have come here to enlist your aid, Major. Indeed, I have to enlist your aid, for there is no one else—"

"You dare to beg *my* aid?" the major interrupted in astounded accents before she could finish. "This is coolness indeed! I did not realize I was dealing with a young lady of such iron nerve! What made you think I would so much as lift my little finger to help you, when I have made my views more than plain?"

For a moment Valeria was confused. Surely the major was not going to refuse to help Perry, purely because he did not approve of her? And she had not even fully explained her errand yet.

"Ah, I see what it is," the major continued bitterly, before she could enlarge on the reason for her visit. "You think because I have been lenient toward you once, because I was foolish enough to show a momentary weakness, that I will turn a blind eye to what you are doing now. Well, let me tell you that I will not."

Surely that could not be contempt and disgust she saw in his eyes, Valeria thought wretchedly. But before she could say a word the major was speaking again, his tone cynical and his eyes bleak. "And to think when you walked in here that I actually imagined that you might have had second thoughts, given way to womanly compassion and—" He broke off as the door opened unceremoniously after the briefest of knocks, and a young soldier burst in.

150

"Yes, what is it?" the major rapped out sharply. The soldier looked embarrassed and murmured something to the major that Valeria could not catch and then backed out of the office blushing to the tips of his ears.

Before the door had closed behind him, the major was on his feet, his expression a shuttered mask.

"I'm afraid I shall have to ask you to excuse me, Miss Fitzmount," Valeria heard him say formally, as though they had been engaged in nothing more than a polite exchange of civilities. "I am called away on urgent business," he added by way of explanation, but Valeria could not let him go without at least attempting to fulfill her mission. She knew she would not be able to screw her courage up again; it was either now or never, to plead Perry's case.

"Please," she begged feverishly, her hand almost going out to detain him. "It will only take a minute."

The major seemed to hesitate, his eyes scrutinizing her flushed cheeks. For a second hope welled inside her, only to die as his gaze hardened. "No," he said harshly, "and that is my final word."

What had possessed her to lower her pride before this man? Valeria asked herself, shivering with apprehension and disappointment. Head held high, she walked through the door he had opened for her, not trusting herself to look into his face. If only she could have made him listen. But now the opportunity was gone and with it, her final chance of assisting Perry.

Slowly she retraced her steps. Outside the sun was still shining. Since there was nothing to be gained now from pawning her emeralds—even had the jewelers been willing to advance the money, in Perry's continued absence it was of little use to her—Valeria decided that she might as well collect her jewelry. Everything had gone so dreadfully wrong, she thought mournfully.

This time neither of the two men who had served her before came in answer to the shop's bell. Instead a rather timid-looking individual with a vacant expression, a pair of spectacles perched precariously on the end of his thin nose, came hurrying forward.

"My name is Valeria Fitzmount, and I have come to collect my emeralds," Valeria told him. "I left them here the other day."

"Emeralds you say," the assistant murmured vaguely,

pulling out numerous drawers and peering at their contents. "Were they for repair?"

"Not exactly," Valeria hedged, thinking that it might simplify matters were she to ask for one of the two gentlemen who had attended her on her original visit.

She described them both quickly and then produced her receipt. The assistant shook his head unhappily. "It is obvious that your business was dealt with by my uncle and cousin, Miss Fitzmount, but they are both out of town. At this time of the year they always spend a week in the country with their families. They will not be back for several days, I fear."

"Perhaps not, but my emeralds must be somewhere," Valeria pointed out. "Do you not have a safe of some description where they might be deposited?"

"There is a safe but it will take me some time to go through it. Are you able to wait?" Confirming that she was, Valeria described the emeralds and then sat down to wait.

The shop door opened and two ladies came in. Valeria recognized one of them rather vaguely as being attached to the Viennese Court. She thought she had seen her at the empress's ball. Her companion was also a lady of high rank, although with a pursed mouth and querulous expression. It was she who was speaking as the ladies entered.

"I tell you it is quite true. The Princess Bagration is completely disgraced. She will lose everything. Her jewels, the palace, her reputation—and all because of this affair with the czar. You know she pawned her rubies, the ones her first husband gave her?"

Her companion shuddered. "Pray do not tell me more. The thought of any *lady*, no matter what the reason, lowering herself to actually pawn her jewels is totally repugnant. The princess has completely disgraced herself now of course. The empress has ordered that she is not to be received. You know how strict she is about these matters."

Valeria remained in her chair like one transfixed. Out of nowhere a tiny little shiver of apprehension feathered along her spine. It was ridiculous to suppose that anyone would gossip about her in such a fashion, wasn't it? During the ladies' conversation it had gradually come to her what constructions could be placed on her own behavior by those in a mind to see it in the worst possible light. But of course no one knew she had tried to pawn the emeralds, she reminded

152

herself. Only herself and the jewelers. This thought was less than comforting and when the assistant returned, gravely shaking his head, to whisper that the emeralds were nowhere to be found and suggesting that she call back when his relatives returned, Valeria thanked him and whisked herself out of the shop before he could read the dismay in her eyes.

Of course, it was ridiculous to suppose that the jewelers were retaining her jewels for any ulterior motive. But then, where were they? What on earth was she going to do? There was only one thing she could do, she decided unhappily. She would have to confide the whole in Papa and trust that he might think of some way of repossessing the necklace, at the same time quenching any would-be attempts at blackmail on the part of the jewelers.

She was letting her imagination run away with her, Valeria scolded herself, but she knew this was not entirely true. The attitude of the two ladies in the shop was that which would exist everywhere in society, where the rules governing the behavior of ladies were very strict indeed. And, as Valeria knew quite well, once a lady's reputation was gone, it could never be regained. Every step back to the apartment brought fresh depths of despair, and by the time it was eventually reached, her imagination had painted a picture of such dreadful consequence that Valeria was white to the lips.

Everything had gone so dreadfully wrong. She longed for nothing so much as to cast herself into some comforting male arms and sob out the whole on an accommodating masculine shoulder. However, as Valeria was the first to admit, Sir Edward was not easily cast into the role of understanding father and was far more likely to fly off into one of his tempers. Indeed, there was only one gentleman she could think of who would adequately fill all her requirements, and she swiftly banished *his* image from her mind before it could wreak even more havoc.

After Valeria had gone, Leo Carrington sent for the sergeant on duty and exchanged a few words with him. "He's waiting in the officers' mess, you say?" he inquired sharply of the sergeant. "Did he say anything to you?"

"Not a word. Struck me that he had something on his mind though, sir."

And he knew who was to blame for that, Leo Carrington thought grimly as he strode toward the mess. Valeria Fitzmount had the nerve of the devil. To actually dare to enlist his aid, after all that he had said! The anger he had felt during their interview returned, causing him to frown heavily so that Perry, who had been awaiting his coming rather nervously, flushed guiltily as he walked into the room.

"Adaire, at last. I have had my man scouring the town for you." This was news to Perry, who had not returned to his lodgings yet and made him wonder unhappily if his admission of guilt was going to be too late.

"You know then?" he asked hesitantly. "I should have told you, but I could only think of the disgrace. However, now that I am a married man I—"

"Married? You are married?" he interjected sharply, his brows contracting as he remembered Valeria's plea for him to hear her out, but then he had not suspected that she had come to inform him in person of her marriage!

He crossed the room swiftly, coming to stand opposite Perry, his face the color of parchment.

"You young fool," he said roughly. "Why did you not come to me before? No, don't bother to answer. Having observed your bride's acting abilities firsthand, I can well understand how she took you in."

"You have met Maria then?" Perry inquired in some bewilderment, on the point of taking umbrage at his commanding officer's criticisms of his wife.

"Maria? Is that what you call her? I had thought Valeria an extremely apt name for so strong-minded a female." Underlying the sarcasm was a strong thread of bitterness, but Perry was not aware of it. He was staring at the major in openmouthed astonishment.

"Valeria! Leo, you have it all wrong," he said urgently, protocol forgotten. "I am not married to Valeria."

"Not!" The major was plainly surprised. "Then who the devil have you married?"

"Maria Schubraum," Perry said simply. "I cannot think where you have the idea that Valeria and I are married. Nothing could be further from either of our minds, I assure you."

"From yours, perhaps not," the major agreed sardonically. "But perhaps you would be good enough to explain why Miss Fitzmount should go to the extraordinary length of risking her reputation to raise £20,000 by pawning her emeralds

154

if it was not in the expectation of using the money to coerce you into marriage?"

This time it was Perry's turn for stunned silence. "Valeria did that!" he exclaimed at length turning pale. "Good God, Leo, you jest!"

"You see, you did not know her as well as you thought," the major announced with a certain grim satisfaction. "I assure you that I am not jesting. The jeweler himself approached me to see if I would vouch for her."

Without asking for permission, Perry sank down into the nearest chair. "Of all the foolish, bravest girls," he said softly, more to himself than his companion, guessing for what purpose Valeria had wanted the funds. "Leo, I cannot allow you to malign Valeria any longer. The money was not to entrap me into marriage, but to free me from a trap of a very different kind." Quickly he explained the events leading up to his disappearance from Vienna, his expression grave as he outlined Valeria's part in his story.

The major heard him out in silence, his face very pale and his eyes very dark as the enormity of his own misjudgment was made clear.

"So you see, there was never any question of a marriage between Val and me," Perry finished quietly. "I only wish now I had taken her advice in the first place and thrown myself upon your mercy. Then none of this would ever have arisen. When I think of the risks she has run!"

For a moment both men were silent and then the major roused himself sufficiently to say bleakly, "At least I have the full tale now and am thankful for it."

"I wish only that I could have brought myself to make a full confession before Valeria took it into her head to raise money by pawning her emeralds," Perry admitted frankly. "If that isn't just like her though! No one ever had a more staunch friend. Never a thought in her head for herself when she might help another. She is the most generous of creatures. I only hope she does not suffer through her loyalty to me."

"None shall hear from me of what has passed," the major informed him grimly, unable to forget how close he had come to threatening to reveal Valeria's intention of pawning her emeralds. Thank God that on that account at least he need not berate himself . . . although when it came to his other appalling misconceptions . . .

"I only trust that you have not overestimated Miss Fitz-

155

mount's generosity," he told Perry heavily, "for I stand much in need of it." Slowly he explained how he had misjudged Valeria, making no attempt to paint himself in a good light or try to conceal how prejudiced he had been.

"Not a pretty tale," he concluded grimly when Perry remained silent, "and one I would have given much not to relate."

"I am sure Val will understand," Perry said, quickly moved, despite himself, by the major's determination to tell him just how gravely he viewed his errors. Had it been any other man but Leo who had cast such aspersions on his old friend, he would have felt obliged to take instant umbrage on Valeria's behalf. But in this instance he sensed that for the major to admit his own mistakes would be far graver punishment than anything *he* could offer.

"Would you like me to return the emeralds to Val?" Perry asked helpfully, mindful of how they had come into the major's possession and how embarrassing it would be for him to have to return them to Valeria.

But the major shook his head. "No, I must do that myself, and make my apologies."

He couldn't forget Valeria's white face as she pleaded with him for a moment of his time—and he had refused! Thank God that soldier had interrupted when he did. Otherwise, who knew what his passion might have led him to say?

Sensing that his commanding officer would prefer to be alone, Perry took his leave of him, having begged him to call upon both Maria and himself, whenever he was free to do so, so that he might make his wife known to him.

When Perry had gone, the major sat down and filled his glass from the decanter on the table, downing the contents at a swallow, before refilling it to the brim—an action unprecedented since his green and callow youth.

Later that evening Perry called upon Valeria and her father, in company with Maria, to introduce her to them, and under cover of the general conversation managed to tell Valeria that he had at last found the courage to unburden himself to the major. "He was more generous than I had hoped, Val, and far more understanding." It was on the tip of Perry's tongue to try and smooth the way for his friend's apology, but one look at Valeria's set face at the mention of the major's name was sufficient to make him change his mind.

156

This was something in which no outsider could meddle and instead he contented himself with advising Valeria that he had arranged to sell out of the regiment. "Maria too knows everything, and has forgiven me," he finished, "and I believe I must be the happiest man on earth."

In view of this announcement, how could Valeria tell him of her own fears concerning her missing jewelry? She had still not found the courage to confess the absence of the emeralds to her father, although she knew she dare not delay for too long.

Maria was talking to her, announcing that she intended throwing a ball. "I shall invite the whole of Vienna to show off my wonderful new husband," she exclaimed with a joyful smile. "You will invite the major, Perry," she instructed, "and you must come too, Valeria."

Perry saw her stiffen slightly, but before he could comment Valeria was accepting the invitation graciously. Whilst the newly married couple exchanged doting glances, Sir Edward harrumped noisily and declared to Valeria that he was damned if young Perry hadn't gone and made an excellent choice after all. "I see now that you and Adaire would never have suited. Can't think why I ever thought you might."

"I do hope Lord Adaire will accept Maria," Valeria murmured in reply. "She is so perfectly right for Perry."

"I don't think you need have any worries on that score," Sir Edward reassured her. "Delightful girl."

Valeria echoed his sentiments and said as much to Perry a little later in the evening whilst Sir Edward was talking to Maria. "I am glad you approve, Val," Perry replied simply, "but what about you? Is something troubling you? You looked so preoccupied a moment ago."

"Just daydreaming," Valeria fibbed, unaware that she and Perry had come full circle and her words were but a repetition of his upon her arrival in Vienna.

It was only when Perry and Maria finally rose to leave that she admitted the truth to herself. She had fallen in love with Leo Carrington. It was no use trying to deny it, or telling herself that he would ever return her feelings. She was too sensible to put any trust in fairy-tale happy endings. She could not love him, her brain protested, but her heart told her the truth: she did! From the moment they had met she had been aware of the major's masculine magnetism; had wanted his approval rather than his contempt; and had hoped against hope that he might perceive the truth of his own volition. "Fool!" she chided herself crossly. She was long past the age for romantic daydreams. An ungainly bean pole, he had called her, whilst his eyes swept her with dislike.

If only she had never set foot in Vienna! And, more important, never set eyes on Major Leo Carrington!

Chapter Eleven

The promised military tattoo had generated a good deal of excitement amongst the visitors to Vienna. There had been gossip that Wellington himself might journey from England to lead the British regiments, but this gossip was quashed by Lord Carrington, who did not altogether approve of such a lavish display, and to what purpose? The allies had already beaten Napoleon. Nevertheless, there was fierce competition to obtain tickets for the best seats in the stands erected in the main square.

Hart, as a member of the Foreign Office, had received four complimentary tickets but, as he told Sir Edward, these were for narrow wooden seats, right at the very back of the stands where it would be nigh on impossible to see what was going on and wretchedly uncomfortable.

Instead, he had suggested that Sir Edward, Valeria, Camilla and himself make use of Camilla's barouche, which they could drive to the furthermost point of the proposed route of the tattoo, and from there observe everything in comfort.

Since the direction the parade was to take led through the city to the Prater Park, where the fair had been set up, this suggestion immediately found favor with the others.

At the appointed hour the barouche arrived outside Sir Edward's apartment. Having elected to dispense with the services of his groom, Hart remained outside with the horses whilst Camilla tripped up to the door to see if their guests were ready.

She wore her newest carriage dress of dusky pink jaconet,

a matching bonnet tied over her golden curls, and as Sir Edward came forward to greet her she glanced impatiently at the face of a tiny fob watch attached to her gown.

"Is Hart not with you?" Sir Edward asked.

"Yes indeed, but on this occasion he has decided to drive the barouche himself and so he must remain with the horses. We must not keep him waiting though. The streets are so very crowded already. If we do not hurry we shall be caught up in the traffic and never reach the park. Is Valeria not yet ready?"

"She will be down in a second. I suppose you've heard about young Adaire?"

Camilla nodded her head. The news had reached her via Hart, who had had it from one of Perry's fellow officers.

"Yes it is an excellent match for both of them, although I dare say Lord Adaire will be a little disappointed at first, for he was as anxious for Perry and Valeria to marry as you were yourself."

"Aye, but I think you were in the right of it. They should not have suited. There's no point in denying though that I should like to have seen her settled before we return to England."

"As to that—" Camilla began portentously, breaking off when Valeria appeared at the head of the stairs to hurry to her friend's side. "At last! Hart will wonder what is delaying us. It is not like you to be late, Val."

That was, perhaps, because she had never before experienced such reluctance to fulfill her social obligations, Valeria thought wearily. Had she not known how much the others were looking forward to this outing she would have cried off without hesitation.

The realization that she had fallen in love with the major had had such an effect upon her emotions that she felt completely incapable of rational behavior. Indeed, her composure was so fragile that she could place no reliance at all on being able to treat the major with the cold contempt common sense told her he well deserved. How on earth she had come to fall in love with a man who freely admitted his dislike and distaste for her was a matter passing all comprehension.

At last, some fifteen minutes after she had entered the apartment, Camilla was shepherding her guests toward the waiting barouche. Hart, wise in the ways of females, had sensibly walked his horses up and down the street during his wife's absence, preventing them from growing excitable during the wait.

"A fine team," Sir Edward commented admiringly as he helped first Camilla and then Valeria into the barouche. "Have you had them long?"

"They aren't actually mine," Hart confessed. "One of my own pair went lame yesterday and I had to borrow these from a friend. That is one of the reasons why I decided to drive myself."

Even the weather was conspiring against her unhappy mood, Valeria reflected as they drove down the street, for the morning was golden with autumnal sunshine, a fresh crispness in the air, sunbeams transforming the drab flagways and covering the buildings with a powdering of gold dust.

Despite their early start, the streets were already crowded. As they drew nearer to the main square from which the march of the various regiments was to commence, people were crowded at upper-story windows, leaning dangerously over the sills, the better to perceive what was happening. Every child seemed to have his own small banner. Gaily colored bunting draped every building, the flags of the allied armies displayed at every vantage point.

Vast crowds thronged the busy squares, and when the barouche was forced to a standstill by the press of traffic, Hart insisted on beckoning a flower girl, standing by her cart, and bestowing posies on Camilla and Valeria. Valeria took hers with a small smile. The pastel flowers complemented the soft pale green of her gown, its delicacy emphasizing her own fragile pallor so that Camilla was driven to ask if she was feeling quite well.

Fortunately, before her friend could ask any more awkward questions, the barouche started to move again, a narrow side street giving them a tantalizing glimpse of the orderly rows of soldiers filling the main square, preparatory to the commencement of the tattoo.

The order of the day was that the regiments of the allied armies stationed in Vienna would march past the heads of state before parading through the town and out toward the Prater Park, where several formal displays would be given.

161

For those with little interest in military matters there was, of course, the fair with all its attendant attractions.

When their carriage had come to a standstill for the fourth time, Camilla exclaimed petulantly to her husband, "Hart, we shall miss everything. The emperor is to give the opening speech in five minutes and we are nowhere near the park."

"No, I know. I had not expected the traffic to be as heavy as this. However, I know a short cut which should get us to the park in a few minutes."

"But shall we be able to hear the speeches?" Camilla asked fretfully.

"I don't know, we shall have to see, but we shall certainly have an uninterrupted view of the whole proceedings."

Fortunately, this forcast proved to be quite correct, and just as the first military band struck up a rousing march, Hart was positioning the barouche strategically atop a small knoll, affording its occupants a far superior view of the parade than they would have had from the square.

The czar's personal guard led the parade, a dashing display of elegant white uniforms, trimmed with gold braid glittering in the sunlight; here and there diamonds flashed as the sun caught the gem-studded Orders of St. Michael decorating several of the officers' chests. Each man rode a coal black horse, and the contrast of immaculate white uniforms and black horseflesh formed a picture which caught the breath in admiration.

"Wait until you see our troops," Hart advised the others. "Troops which made this whole congress possible, I might add."

Sir Edward agreed with him and whilst the two gentlemen became involved in a technical discussion of Wellington's tactics during the Peninsular Campaign, Valeria and Camilla exchanged rueful glances.

The Russian troops gave way to the Austrian Imperial Guard, Polish Hussars, and bringing up the rear, the English Cavalry. Valeria's heart missed a beat. How foolish, she chided herself. It was impossible to make out one man's features from such a distance, and yet she could not quite prevent her pulse racing with the knowledge that the major was amongst that gallant throng.

"Castlereagh said that if we were not to lead the parade, then we should come last to show others how it should be done," Hart informed them, referring to the czar's insistence that his troops led the parade. It was these aspects of the congress which Castlereagh most abhorred, considering it beneath a senior politician to involve himself in squabbles of such a nature.

However, there was no denying that the English Cavalry was the highlight of the parade. Down in the square the crowd cheered themselves hoarse, the sound reaching the barouche in ever more audible waves of noise. Looking down on the scene, all one could see was the scarlet uniforms and gray horses, surrounded on all sides by a sea of waving flags as the crowd roared its approval. Not even the enthusiastic jostling of the onlookers broke the cavalry's perfect formation, and Valeria had to swallow a foolish lump in her throat as she gazed upon the scene. That the others had been similarly affected it was impossible to deny. Sir Edward cleared his throat loudly, and Camilla sought wildly for a handkerchief as Hart gave her hand a reassuring squeeze.

"I still say that when it comes to turning out a fighting unit, there's none to beat us," Sir Edward declared to no one in particular, and in her heart Valeria agreed. There was something about those ramrod-straight backs and scarlet uniforms. Perhaps they lacked the dash and verve of the Russian troops, but there was no doubt in her mind as to whom she would rather rely on in a crisis. She visualized the major in the heat of some desperate battle, perhaps fighting for his life, his uniform no longer immaculate but—but no! She must not allow her emotions to gain control of her in such a way. Even so, it was several minutes before she felt able to converse naturally with the others and hoped that no one had noticed her momentary lack of attention.

When the parade was over, the serried ranks of soldiers gave way to compact groups, their uniforms bright patches of color as they mingled with the crowd.

The crowd spread out through the streets like ripples on a pool, the majority heading for the park and the fair. "Someone seems to be heading in our direction," Camilla commented, her sharp eyes noticing the group of horsemen galloping toward them. Valeria looked up only to be consumed with disappointment when she perceived the white jacket of

163

the czar's guard rather than the scarlet one of the British troops.

"It looks like Count Polinsky," Camilla added, throwing her friend a teasing smile. "I do believe he would make you his countess if you would let him, Val."

The horsemen's imminent approach saved Valeria from the necessity of replying, although she noticed her father scowl, as though Camilla's suggestion did not find favor. Poor Papa, he would not like to see her married to the Russian—but then he was hardly likely to, Valeria admitted. Like the count though she did, she could not visualize marriage to him.

The count dismounted, kissing Camilla's hand with old-fashioned courtesy and smiling at Valeria.

"I thought I recognized that gorgeous hair," he commented by way of explanation for his arrival. "Even when it is partially covered as it is today, there is no mistaking it."

Valeria could not believe that the count had picked *her* out of the crowd from as far away as the square, but she let his flattery pass, merely giving him a small smile, and allowing Camilla to take charge of the conversation. It soon became plain that nothing would satisfy her but a full tour of all the fair booths, and Valeria tried to compose her features into an expression of pleasure when Camilla suggested that they leave the barouche to explore the fair on foot. Evidently she had failed, for Hart, always quick to recognize the feelings of others, said that he did not think it would be a good idea to leave the barouche unattended, adding that he felt the fair would be somewhat overcrowded with the press of townspeople. Camilla pouted, unwilling to be denied her treat.

"I promised the children I would take them some little present to mark the occasion," she protested. "Surely you want to see the fair, Val?"

"Well . . ."

"I think it an excellent idea," the count interrupted before Valeria could reply. "Pray allow me to escort you, Miss Fitzmount."

"I suspect Valeria does not relish the prospect of being trodden underfoot by the crowds," Hart said, briskly coming to her rescue, "but I can see that you will not be satisfied, my love, until you have toured every booth for yourself. So, with our guests' leave, I suggest that we form ourselves into two parties: those who wish to visit the fair and those who do not."

Feeling something of a killjoy, Valeria realized that she was the only member of the party who wished to remain with the barouche. Even Sir Edward was keen to examine the fair at closer quarters, murmuring reminiscently that it reminded him of his youth when his parents had had occasion to take him to the York fair one summer.

Perceiving her embarrassment, Hart said lightly that there was no need for her to feel guilty. Someone had to remain with the horses and if Valeria did not mind being used as a substitute groom, he would be extremely grateful to her. "As they are not my own team, I feel obligated to ensure that no harm befalls them," Hart explained. "For they are thoroughbreds and cost their owner a pretty packet I dare swear."

Count Polinsky was plainly disappointed by Valeria's refusal to accompany them, but having sung the praises of the fair quite loudly, he could hardly bow out of the party now.

Having assured Camilla that she had not the slightest objection to being left alone (indeed she would most welcome it), Valeria bid the others good-bye and settled down in the barouche to watch their progress.

Within minutes they had been swallowed up by the crowd around the huddle of booths comprising the fair and Valeria leaned back in the barouche, tempted to close her eyes and relax her tensed limbs. If she was going to react like this every time there was a chance she might come face to face with Leo Carrington, it was just as well that they would soon be returning to England. She thought about Maria's ball. She would have given much to decline attending it, but she knew that to do so would give rise to all manner of unkind comments, not only about herself but Maria as well. It was well known in the British contingent of visitors to Vienna that Perry's land neighbored her father's and if she did not put in an appearance at the ball, some persons might suppose it was because she found his marriage unacceptable. It was bad enough to have people thinking she had pursued Perry before his marriage, without having the added burden of their believing that she was envious of Maria's position as his wife. The knoll on which Hart had stationed the barouche marked the boundary between the cultivated part of the park and the more natural heath, bordering the woods proper; and whilst the sounds of laughter and merry-making wafted to her on the breeze, there were few people about to disturb the peace of the early afternoon. In the distance Valeria could hear the children's shrieks gradually growing louder. She opened her eyes and saw that she was no longer alone. Some children were making use of the relative solitude of her knoll to play ball, tossing the bright red sphere into the air and catching it again with breathless enjoyment.

She watched them for several minutes, marveling at their exuberance. Even as she watched, one of the smaller children tripped, dropping the ball which bounced across the ground in front of the horses, causing them to rear up in a panic, snorting nervously. Alert to the danger, Valeria leaned forward to grasp their trailing reins, but the rocking movement of the well-sprung barouche disturbed the highly strung animals even more, and just as her fingers grasped the leather reins, the horses started to bolt, heading straight for the panic-stricken children.

Too alarmed to be concerned about her own danger, Valeria pulled hard on the reins, forcing the team to swerve sharply to the right. The children were a blur of white faces, merging with the green of the earth and the blue of the sky. The narrow strips of leather tore into the soft skin of her hands, the combined strength of the two thoroughbred horses wrenching the reins out of her grasp as she fought to control the runaway pair.

There was only time for Valeria to thank God that they were heading for the open countryside and not the crowded fairground before a sudden jolt, as the barouche left the road, juddering over uneven ground, threw her to the floor of the carriage. Grasping the door handle, Valeria prayed as she had never prayed before, in her mind a vision of herself lying amongst the splintered ruins of the barouche.

The thunder of the galloping hooves filled her ears, blotting out even the sound of her own heartbeat. Terror formed a cold lump in the pit of her stomach. She had lost the reins, and had no means of stopping the horses. To jump out of the barouche, even if she was able to stand up long enough, was surely to court death; yet, if she remained crouching here on the floor in fear, what hope was there for her? Already the barouche was swaying wildly from side to side as the team picked up speed. Unlike a curricle, the carriage was not built for racing and with every grassy hillock Valeria expected it to disintegrate completely. Sky and earth were a muzzy blur. Frightened tears could not be suppressed. Where was her courage? She closed her eyes, willing herself not to give way to foolish and useless hysterics. If only she could get to her feet she might be able to reach the reins. The horses must surely begin to tire soon. At least she had not mown down those poor children. How frightened they must have been! To lose one's life merely because of a bright red ball.

Gritting her teeth, Valeria tried to lever herself up, grasping the padded velvet seat as she leaned forward. The reins trailed tantalizingly between the shafts. It was a mercy one of the horses had not caught a hoof in them and fallen. If she were to lean right over and stretch out her hand, she might just—

"Lie down!"

So engrossed was she in her task that she had not heard the horseman approach, not seen the shadow he cast along the ground as he raced across the heath. She obeyed the command he gave her instinctively, not daring to trust herself to watch as the powerful animal he was riding drew level with the barouche. The sun touched the gold epaulets of his uniform, his jacket a crimson blur as he shook his feet free of his stirrups, balancing himself in the saddle.

Her mouth dry with fear, Valeria watched. He could surely not be going to attempt to jump from the racing horse into the swaying barouche. But he was.

"Major Carrington," she protested, but her words were swept away on the wind as the major knotted his own reins, swinging himself free of his saddle, poised for a moment as Valeria waited, her heart in her mouth. He would never make it, no one could accomplish such a superhuman feat. He would be crushed beneath the relentless wheels of the carriage, his body mangled and torn. A sob rose to her lips, sternly repressed as she inched across the barouche, giving him what room she could. There was a dull thud, the carriage rocked wildly, and when Valeria opened her eyes the major was dusting down his jacket, his long arms already accomplishing the task hers could not, as he reached down between the traces to catch up the reins.

A densely wooded copse loomed up before them, and the bolting horses changing direction so suddenly that Valeria stumbled, catching her head against the side of the barouche as she fell. From a great distance she heard the major swear forcefully and then all consciousness fled.

When she came round the horses' headlong flight might all have been part of a bad dream. Only the faint lathering of their coats told of their mad stampede; the two culprits grazed peacefully on the cropped turf.

All about her Valeria could hear the familiar sounds of the countryside, a cow lowing placidly in the distance, a bird-song, the lazy drone of a bee near at hand.

A hazy lassitude enveloped her. There was something she should remember but it eluded her. It was comfortable here in the barouche, her shoulder pillowed against something warm and secure, all danger past. On the seat opposite her she could see her own bonnet and wondered drowsily how it came to be there. Surely she had been wearing it? It was too much of an effort to think. All she wanted to do was to sleep. To forget the dreadful, merciless pounding of horses' hooves, to forget those moments when Major Carrington— Major Carrington. She struggled to sit upright, her hair, which had been confined in a loose coil, cloaking her shoulders, the neck of her gown unfastened at the throat.

"Lie still, you are suffering from shock and could easily faint again," a male voice instructed.

This time she did not obey the command, but the arm fastened securely about her waist prevented her from fulfilling her intention of getting to her feet. Instead, she was forced to twist round in her rescuer's supporting arm to beg him to release her.

"Not until I am convinced that you are fully recovered," she was told curtly. "My God, what were your friends about to leave you alone with such a mettlesome pair and not so much as a groom to look out for your safety? When I saw the team bolting and realized it was you—"

"It is fortunate for me that you *did* chance to see it,"

Valeria said shakily, trying to suppress a shiver of fear. "I must confess that I thought my last hour had come."

As indeed it must have, had the major not rescued her. A suffocating awarness of his presence brought a flush of color to her too-pale cheeks, her mouth trembling with remembered shock as she relived those moments when she had been forced to face death.

"Those damned brats," the major cursed angrily, but Valeria shook her head impulsively, denying his accusation.

"They were not to blame, no one was. Hart had no idea that the horses were so unreliable, otherwise he would never have borrowed them. And as for the children—if they cannot play ball in the middle of a park, then it is a poor thing indeed."

"You saved their lives. If you had not grasped the reins so quickly they would have been killed."

"You saw that? I did not realize you . . ."

"My companions were intent on patronizing the fairground, but I had no wish to join them so I rode up here."

Under his tan, his face looked oddly pale and Valeria was swept with a wave of love. How brave he was. To risk his life to save hers, when she knew quite well he must consider it a worthless sacrifice. The thought that he could be so noble washed her with fresh emotion and not wanting him to see her tears she averted her head, gripping her hands tightly together, until she realized that the action was causing the most intense pain. All across her palms were raised weals where the reins had dragged, some of them puffy and raw, bleeding where the soft flesh had been torn. A small gasp escaped her lips, the sight of her own blood bringing a surge of nausea that made the world turn into a spinning black void into which she was inexorably drawn.

Her companion heard the soft betraying sound and cursed again as Valeria's body went limp within his grasp. It was no more than he expected. Indeed he marveled at her courage and quick thinking but then, as he freely admitted, Valeria was full of surprises.

He had ridden out toward the barouche with the express intention of restoring to her her emeralds, having already bumped into her father and Hart by one of the fairground booths. On learning that Valeria had elected to remain behind

169

alone, he had seized upon the opportunity as being ideal for the return of her jewelry and the delivery of his own apology.

He had never dreamed he would be called upon to save her from the direst danger, and as he looked down into her waxen face his mouth compressed into a bitter smile. A tendril of red gold hair lay across the scarlet of his jacket and as he bent to unentangle it, Valeria's eyelids fluttered, her lips forming a name. He bent closer.

"Perry?" Valeria said weakly, "Perry is it you?"

She herself was unaware of having spoken, her ordeal had taken its toll. It was not until Camilla, who together with Hart and Sir Edward had seen the whole dreadful incident, and had hurried to the barouche, uncorked her bottle of smelling salts to wave under Valeria's nose, that the latter began to recover consciousness.

"Oh, my poor dear," Camilla all but wept, her face nearly as pale as Valeria's. "Your poor head. There is a lump the size of an egg! Oh, Hart!" she exclaimed in deep distress, "how did it happen. Those horses!"

"I saw the whole thing," the major's deep voice chimed in, and Valeria was glad to leave the explanations to him. She felt far too exhausted and drained to join in the conversation. Indeed, she felt dangerously close to succumbing to the fits of shivering which seemed to consume her, making it impossible for her to rouse herself to do anything more than assure Camilla that she was still all in one piece. There was a further commotion when Perry and Maria arrived in the baron's old-fashioned coach. They too had witnessed the entire incident, although not realizing at the time that Valeria was the occupant of the carriage.

"How is Val?" Valeria heard Perry ask urgently. The major's broad frame shielded her from his view and as she struggled for the words to assure him that she was quite safe, the major replied calmly that he did not consider that she was suffering from anything worse than shock although that in itself could be a very unpleasant malady.

"No, major, you are wrong," Camilla interrupted worriedly. "There are bloodstains on Val's gown, I saw them myself."

She must have touched her dress with her injured hands, Valeria thought weakly, as the major turned to look at her.

She tried in vain to hide them behind her back, but he was too quick for her. Grasping her wrists and turning her hands palms upward, his face turned gray as he looked down at the raw flesh. The earlier agonizing pain had given way to a nagging throb, but the weals had swollen, leaving her hands, to Valeria's critical eyes, looking dreadfully misshapen and ugly.

There was a moment's silence, when she felt she must have imagined the blazing intensity of the major's scrutiny, and then he was saying in a husky voice, "I suppose that happened when you swerved to avoid those wretched children. You really are the most aggravating female. Why did you not tell me that you were hurt? When you fell in the carriage I thought you might have broken a bone but it never occurred to me to check your hands when I examined you."

Valeria flushed, remembering the open neck of her gown. So she had not imagined the touch of gentle hands, just as she was on the verge of recovering consciousness.

"I shall never forgive myself for this," Hart burst out, his normal calm deserting him. "Warburton never warned me that his horses were not to be trusted. You may be sure that I shall have something to say to him about this. He is damned lucky to be getting his team back all in one piece. A testament of your skill, Leo, unless I am mistaken."

"I suggest we save the apportionment of praise and blame until later," the major replied coolly. "The most important thing now is to get Miss Fitzmount safely home. If I were you, Sir Edward," he added, addressing Valeria's father, "I should lose no time in summoning a doctor. Those hands must be attended to and I am sure a sleeping draught would do much to give your daughter a painless night's sleep. Where shock is concerned, sleep is nature's best remedy. I have seen the effect of it on campaigns and it would be unwise to treat Miss Fitzmount's condition too lightly."

The others all agreed. In vain did Valeria protest that she was quite recovered and did not want anyone to make a fuss. The gentlemen drew apart to discuss how best to transport her safely back to the apartment, whilst Camilla and Maria clustered protectively around her, praising her bravery and exclaiming over her wounded hands and bruised head.

Valeria was still protesting that she was quite able to

walk back to the apartment—a palpable untruth—when the gentlemen returned to the carriage.

"So Perry will escort Miss Fitzmount home in his carriag," the major was saying in clipped accents as they reached the barouche. "And then I shall go straight round to the barracks to ask Doctor Milbourne to call on Val," Perry added.

Hart explained that Camilla and Marie could wait until Perry returned with the carriage, or walk back into the city, whichever they preferred, which caused Valeria to make a shocked protest that she could not deprive Maria of both her coach and her husband.

Maria waved her objections aside.

"Nonsense," she said firmly. "Of course you must use our coach. You could not return on foot or in the barouche."

"No, I swear I positively hate the thing now," Camilla said with a shudder. "I shall never ride in it again. You must dispose of it. Hart, I should never have a peaceful moment if I thought I might have to use it again."

"We are distressing Miss Fitzmount," the major broke in curtly. "The barouche is quite safe, it was the team that was at fault, if anything. Now, Miss Fitzmount." He turned to Valeria, his arms encircling her waist before she could divine his purpose, as he swung her feet down out of the barouche. She might have weighed little more than a feather so easily did he carry her. Her foolish heart pounded like a drum as his dark head inclined toward her.

"Give her to me, Leo," Perry offered, breaking the spell the major's touch had woven about her. But to her mixed joy and fear the major ignored Perry, striding instead to where the old-fashioned coach stood and thrusting open the door with his shoulder to deposit her carefully on the sturdy leather seat.

"Thank you." Her shyly whispered thanks were brushed aside with a brusque shrug, somehow more painful than all his earlier condemnation. There was no time to say any more because Perry was instructing his coachman to drive on, seating himself at Valeria's side, his large hand enfolding her much smaller one in a comforting clasp that was careful of her wounds. The gesture did not go unnoticed by the major. As the coach rumbled slowly out of sight, he stared after it, his mouth bitter.

172

"I'm glad Perry has gone with Val," Camilla said softly at his side. "After her ordeal she must be sorely in need of a shoulder to cry on and I am sure Maria will not grudge her Perry's upon this occasion."

"I am sure she will not," the major agreed, his eyes still on the coach, his fingers clenching over the emeralds he had meant to return to Valeria. He tried not to remember the sight of the barouche rocking crazily from side to side as it raced out of control across the heath—or his own reactions!

Chapter
Twelve

As the major had predicted, the doctor pronounced that Valeria was suffering from a severe shock, coupled with bruising to her head and lacerations to her hands. He bound her hands carefully in strips of clean linen, having first applied a healing salve, and instructed Hester to change the dressings every day.

The morning would doubtless find Valeria with an agonizing headache he told his patient not unsympathetically, but if she would go acting the heroine what else could she expect. Oh yes, he had heard all about it, he told a surprised Valeria. The town was full of the English girl's bravery. Hadn't she saved the lives of four children at the risk of her own.

"I acted automatically," Valeria confessed. "The one person who really acted bravely was Major Carrington. He risked his life to save mine."

"A very cool customer," the doctor agreed, opening his bag to mix an evil-looking sleeping draught, "and what you say is only in accord with everything I have heard about him. Two young lieutenants have every reason to be grateful for his cool head. Were it not for him their bodies would now be rotting on the Spanish peninsula, and I dare say they are not the only ones. Now, you will drink half this concoction tonight upon retiring and the other half the night after. I do not as a rule approve of prescribing sleeping draughts for healthy young women, but it strikes me that these hollows beneath your shoulders and this wan face do not arise purely from the shock you have suffered." He held up a hand as Valeria started to speak.

"No, don't tell me. A couple of good nights sleep should

do much to set you up again." He stood up, snapping his bag closed, bending to peer thoughtfully at Valeria once again.

"Umm. No reading until your headache is quite gone, and no excitement."

Not unnaturally, Sir Edward could not rest until he had spoken to the doctor himself and been assured that Valeria was as strong as a horse and would be fully recovered within the week. Valeria sighed a little as he pronounced this judgment. She had been hoping that her accident might provide her with an excuse not to attend Maria's ball, but it seemed she was to be denied even that.

It was only as Hester helped her to disrobe and handed her the sleeping draught that Valeria remembered the emeralds. The thought gave her a sickening jolt. She would have to tell her father. The moment could not be put off any longer. She must tell him tomorrow, she decided drowsily as the drug started to work. Tomorrow . . .

There were certain pleasant aspects to being an invalid, Valeria decided in amusement as yet another basket of hothouse fruit was delivered to the apartment. It was not yet twenty-four hours since the accident, and yet already all Vienna seemed to know about it. As the doctor had predicted, a sound night's sleep had done much to restore her normal equilibrium, although the memory of those few moments in the major's arms was still enough to set her nerve ends quivering betrayingly.

"Are you sure you don't mind being left on your own?" Sir Edward asked fussily from the door for the umpteenth time. He had an engagement with Lord Charles Stuart, but, as he had assured his daughter, he was quite ready to cancel it if she felt in need of his company.

Since constant inquiries punctuated by fierce denunciations of the owner of the runaway team were his notion of soothing conversation, Valeria was not entirely sorry to see him leave.

Poor Papa, she thought fondly, his was not a nature best suited to the sick room.

A knock on the drawing room door disturbed her reverie. At her command a footman entered.

"Major Carrington is asking to see you, miss," he informed her. Valeria's heart leapt, beating against the confining wall of her chest like a trapped bird. "Please show the major in," she instructed, trying to sound calm. Why had he come? Surely not to revile her yet again.

The answer was soon forthcoming as the major strode into the room, soberly dressed in riding clothes, his face showing traces of stern control.

"You are feeling much more the thing this morning, I hope," he said formally. "The doctor assures me that you have sustained no lasting injury, although your hands will be painful for some time to come."

So he had asked the doctor about her! But then of course his sense of honor would oblige him to do that.

Engrossed in her own thoughts, it was several minutes before Valeria realized that the major seemed ill at ease, prowling round the room examining the paintings, before finally coming to rest by the fire.

"Miss Fitzmount—Valeria—there is something I must say to you," he announced abruptly. "I am sensible of the fact that this is perhaps not the best of times for a confession of my faults and the wrong I have done you, but my guilt weighs heavily on my mind."

"Please sit down," Valeria said unsteadily. "Believe me, Major, whatever wrongs you have done me have been more than wiped out by the way you saved my life."

He gave her a bleak look in response to her tremulous smile, delving in his pocket to produce a familiar leather case.

"First let me give you these and then I shall make my explanations."

"The Fitzmount emeralds!" Valeria declared in bemusement. "But how came you by these? Oh, Major! You have indeed earned my gratitude. You cannot conceive how worried I have been about these jewels. You see . . . well . . ." Rather shyly Valeria looked up at him, too relieved at having the emeralds returned to question either the major's possession of them or the look in his eyes. For some reason she felt compelled to confess to him how foolishly she had acted over the jewels, but even as the words trembled on her lips the major forestalled her.

"Your *gratitude*," he exclaimed bitterly. "Dear God, if you did but realize I know all about your plans for these jewels. Indeed, not so very long ago I was congratulating myself on having cleverly overset those same plans. So sure was I that I was in the right and you in the wrong, that I felt no compunction at all in instructing your jeweler friends to refuse you your loan.

"Oh yes," he continued grimly, ignoring Valeria's dismayed gasp. "That is what manner of man I am, Miss Fitzmount. A man so despicable that he accepts upon the word of a known troublemaker—I refer to my aunt, of course, who is cordially disliked throughout the family—condemning out-of-hand a young girl whose only aim is to help those fortunate enough to call themselves her friends. No . . . please let me finish, Valeria," he said grimly, when she would have spoken. "You cannot have more contempt for me than I have for myself. The only reason I know the truth now is because Perry told me. Indeed, when he called upon me the other night to advise me of his marriage, so deeply entrenched was I in my own misconceptions that I immediately assumed the new Lady Adaire to be you."

There was a painful pause whilst Valeria tried to assimilate what he was saying.

"But I had come to beg you to show Perry a little mercy," she got out through stiff lips.

"I realize that now. When I think how I misjudged you!" He swung around angrily, his face a tight mask of self-loathing and Valeria bit her lip. For a man of pride it must be a hard thing indeed to admit one's self in the wrong; and whilst she could not deny that his attitude had hurt her, it was hardly his fault that she had fallen in love with him.

"I collect a good deal of the blame must lie with Euphemia Gervaise," Valeria said gently. "And indirectly with me, for if I had not annoyed her, I doubt she would have written to you in such a damning vein."

At the major's insistence she explained what had happened between his aunt and herself, and he heard her out in a brooding silence.

"Perry once told me that you were the most generous of females," he said finally. "Dare I hope that that generosity might extend to myself?"

"If you are asking my pardon, then you already have it," Valeria said unsteadily, conscious of the burning intensity of his scrutiny. "After all I am guilty of the same offense in connection with the jewelers. I was convinced that they had kept the emeralds on purpose and intended to threaten me with disclosure of the purpose of my visit. Before you came I was just steeling myself to make a confession to Papa, in the hope that he might be able to recover them. Thank goodness that is no longer necessary."

"Your mistake can in no way compare with mine," the major objected, taking a deep breath and turning to face her. "You have given your pardon but if I—"

What he was going to say was lost as the door suddenly opened to admit Camilla, who stopped short when she observed that Valeria was not alone.

"Oh pray forgive me," she exclaimed in flustered accents. "I did not realize you were here, Major."

"I was just on the point of leaving," the major announced in a clipped voice. "I trust it will not be too long before you are out and about again, Miss Fitzmount," he added formally to Valeria. "Pray do not disturb yourself, I can find my own way out."

Valeria had half risen to escort him from the room but at his words subsided again, stuffing the case containing the emeralds beneath a cushion, before Camilla's curiosity was aroused by their presence.

"Oh, Val, I'm so sorry," Camilla apologized when the major had gone. "If only I had known."

"The major had merely come to see how I was, Camilla," Valeria said as lightly as she could. "Please do not be putting any particular construction upon his visit. It was the merest civility, that is all."

"If you say so." Camilla was plainly disappointed by her friend's calm manner. "Perhaps if I had not entered when I did—"

"You are letting your imagination run away with you," Valeria said firmly, her pulse fluttering at the vain hopes Camilla's suggestion raised. "I know you mean well, Camilla," she added, "but I can assure you that the major does not cherish the slightest *tendre* toward me. As you yourself pointed out, he has a mistress who—"

"Who no longer exists," Camilla declared triumphantly. "I heard it from Lady C. It seems the lady was a trifle presumptuous and was clearly given her *congé*. She has not lost much time in finding another protector I hear—one of the Russians this time. And although Hart declares that it is not a fitting matter to discuss with me, I gather that they

179

parted with no regrets—on the major's side at least. So you see—"

"I see only that you are determined to throw the pair of us together," Valeria said, firmly directing the conversation into less dangerous waters. What had passed between the major and herself must forever remain undisclosed. She was glad that he now knew the whole truth and no longer saw her in a bad light, but mere approval could in no way appease the hunger in her heart, which demanded a far stronger emotion.

Camilla remained for another hour, chatting about this and that, and exclaiming that they must both have new gowns for Maria's ball.

"You may be sure that Hart has spoken most strongly to his friend regarding the instability of his horses," she told Valeria as she prepared to depart. "You are so brave, Val. I confess that had I been the one in the barouche I must surely have died from shock. It puts me in a positive quake merely to think about it."

"The incident does not hold particularly pleasant memories for *me* I can assure you," Valeria said with a slight grimace, but when Camilla had gone she admitted that her assertion had not held the complete truth. Terrifying though her ordeal had been, there were several moments that would live in her memory forever—moments when for a few seconds she had been in the arms of the man she loved, felt the strong beat of his heart next to her own.

A sigh quivered past her lips and she felt under the cushion for the emeralds, opening the box to stare down at the stones which had been the cause of so much misunderstanding. They glinted with green fire. Deep in thought Valeria continued to stare unseeingly into their depths. The door opened.

"Val."

"Perry! I did not hear you come in. Today must be my day for visitors. I shall have to incur accidents more frequently."

"I see that one of your visitors was Leo," Perry commented, glancing meaningfully at the emeralds. "He was in quite a state when he discovered how badly he had misjudged you. I told him at the time that he must have been blind to imagine that you, of all people, would be guilty of such underhanded behavior."

"Yes, he has told me the whole. I cannot deny that at first his attitude upset me, but it is over now."

"Yes, I doubt you will see him again," Perry said cheerfully, unaware of the blow he was dealing. "He too is to sell out, and he has urgent business in England. The estates he has inherited have been neglected for too long and are in need of attention."

"So he will not be attending your ball?" Valeria asked in a low voice. Until that moment she had not realized how much she had been hoping against hope that somehow a miracle might occur.

"I shouldn't think so," Perry agreed, "although Maria did invite him. I dare say it won't be long before Sir Edward returns home either. Has he made any plans?"

They talked for several minutes, although afterwards, Valeria could not remember a word of what had been said. When Perry had gone she huddled back against the cushions, her face paper-white.

She would not cry, she told herself. It was not really the end of the world. But her heart refused to be persuaded.

By the date of Maria's ball, Valeria was completely recovered in body if not in spirits. Camilla had called every day whilst she had been recuperating but on no occasion had she mentioned the major, and Valeria could not bring herself to ask if he had definitely quitted the city.

He must have done, she admitted wretchedly as she prepared for the ball, for otherwise Camilla must have surely made some mention of his attending the function. With this admission, her fragile hope that he might have called to take his leave of her finally faded. The fault was her own, she chided herself, for reading too much into his apology which, after all, had been no more than what it purported to be—an admission that he had been guilty of misjudging her on the flimsiest of evidence, and a request for her forbearance.

Without the promise of the major's presence to raise her spirits, she had no enthusiasm for the ball. Her new gown was a creation of beauty, layer upon layer of tawny silk which floated ethereally around her when she put it on, the material the color of autumn leaves. A silver thread had been woven into the fabric, glittering as she moved; the candles turned her hair the same color as her gown. "The spirit of autumn," the modiste had fancifully called her creation. Valeria thought it most apt, for autumn was the time of death and decay, and her heart already felt as bare and wintry as the trees outside.

Sir Edward had hired a chaise to convey them to the town house owned by Maria's parents, and as it rattled over the cobbled streets Valeria prayed that the evening would be concluded without anyone suspecting what ailed her.

The house was an elegant building constructed in the classical fashion with an impressive portico supported by Greek columns, leading into a marble hall where a wrought-iron staircase curved upward to an overhanging gallery.

To accommodate all the guests the two main salons had been thrown together, and the ballroom itself gave out onto the gardens, prettily decorated with colored lanterns and an illuminated fountain.

"Such a pity the weather has turned so cold," Maria complained as she welcomed Valeria. "I dare swear no one will be tempted into the gardens now. It seems such a waste."

"Oh surely not," Valeria comforted her. "With the ballroom curtains open it makes such a lovely picture, I'm sure the gardens will be much admired, even though it may be from within rather than without."

"If you think so," Maria began doubtfully, breaking off as she espied Camilla. "I shall leave you two together," she told them. "That is the worst of being a hostess, as I am just discovering. One must continually be making sure that everyone *else* is enjoying the party."

Valeria laughed dutifully. In point of fact Maria was the epitome of the blissfully happy bride, her brown eyes sparkling with happiness every time they rested on the face of her new husband.

"Maria tells me that she has had a most cordial letter from Perry's grandfather," Camilla commented when the other girl had moved away. "I am glad that he has accepted the match, for her sake."

"So am I," Valeria agreed, "and Perry could not have made a more charming choice."

"It is a pity that you could not return to England betrothed," Camilla remarked wistfully. "Count Polinsky would have made you his countess had you encouraged him a little."

"I know, but life in Russia did not appeal," Valeria responded, unwilling to admit the real reason why she was so disinterested in her admirers. Once one had experienced love, every other emotion was but a pale shadow, she thought sadly, and she could never countenance a marriage without love now that she had tasted its heady sweetness.

"I suspect I am destined to remain an old maid," she confided to Camilla, but no one seeing the gentlemen clustering round her ten minutes later, begging for the chance to write their names on her dance card, could have placed much credence upon this assertion.

The musicians Maria had hired played waltz after waltz, but neither the dance nor the music had the power to thrill her as it had once done. Not even Count Polinsky's teasing chatter could rouse her from her misery.

Halfway through the evening, whilst Valeria was dancing with Perry, it was announced that the next dance would be the supper waltz. Valeria had saved this dance for her father, thinking that Sir Edward would want to take her in to supper. Perry made some comment about how pleased Maria had been by his grandfather's kind letter, and Valeria turned toward him, intending to make some affirmatory response. Instead, the words froze on her lips, her face draining of all color as she stared at the man crossing the floor toward them.

"Good Lord, it's Leo!" Perry exclaimed in surprise, drawing Valeria away from the other dancers so that he could talk to his friend. "I thought you had left for London."

"Not yet," the major said curtly. "I had some unfinished business." He turned to Valeria. "I wonder, Miss Fitzmount. Am I too late to secure the pleasure of a dance?"

As Valeria already knew, the only dance she had free was the supper waltz. Common sense urged her to refuse his request, but her heart pleaded for this last painful pleasure . . . the precious memory of those moments, stolen from time, when she would once again feel his arms enfold her . . . and her heart would not be denied.

"There is only the supper dance, and I was saving that for my father," she began hesitantly, but the major interrupted her.

"Then Sir Edward's loss is my gain," he announced firmly, quickly penciling his name against the empty space before Valeria could give in to the urgings of sanity.

"I shall leave Val in your capable hands then, Leo,"

Perry exclaimed as the supper waltz was announced. "I have promised to share this dance with my wife."

If only the music would never stop, Valeria thought feverishly as the major took her in his arms. Never had she seen him looking so handsome. Like the other gentlemen he was wearing formal attire, and Valeria was distressed to discover how affected she was by his maleness. Appalled by her own reaction she forced herself to concentrate on her steps, willing her body not to tremble betrayingly at the proximity of his.

"You are not in uniform," she commented inanely. hoping to break the spell cast by the music and the touch of his hand.

"Because I have sold out. I have enjoyed my years in the army, but now all that must come to an end. I confess, though, that I am looking forward to returning to England."

"I had not expected to see you here this evening. Indeed, I thought you had already quitted Vienna."

He frowned, his expression almost causing Valeria to miss her steps, whilst her traitorous heart pounded unsteadily. "You thought I would go without taking my leave of you? I suppose I am well served for my own stubborn prejudice and have no one but myself to blame if you think me unmannerly."

In her distress that he should think any such thing, Valeria trembled a little. Her companion's arm tightened about her waist instantly to steady her. Its charged pressure did not change even when she had herself fully under control, and Valeria had to confess that the sensation of being held so close to the major's broad chest was an extremely pleasurable one.

Outside the lanterns twinkled in the trees, swaying in the breeze. The sky was studded with stars as bright as any diamonds, the scents of autumn crisp on the cool air wafting through the open windows, haunting and elusive, overlaid with the melancholy that autumn always brought.

"You look very pensive. Is something troubling you?" the major asked. His question brought a vivid flush to Valeria's hitherto pale face.

"No, no, it is nothing. Do you expect to remain in Vienna much longer?" she asked, hoping that he would not guess what prompted the question. It was one which she ought not to ask, she knew, but somehow she could not refrain. These previous moments were not enough; already her heart was clamoring greedily for more.

"I don't know," the major replied. "As I said to Perry, there is some unfinished business which detains me. It is foolish of me to linger perhaps, but I cannot go until it is settled."

The music drew to a close and couples drifted off the floor in the direction of the dining room where supper tables had been laid out.

The major put his hand under Valeria's elbow, guiding her through the other guests, but it was not to the dining room that he led her. Instead, he ushered her into a small salon off the ballroom, where he closed the door firmly behind them, saying, "Do not be alarmed. I mean you no harm and have not taken leave of my senses, but drastic situations call for drastic measures. As a soldier one soon learns that."

Drastic situations . . . drastic measures . . . what could he mean?

A fire burned brightly in the grate of the small room, an elegant chaise positioned invitingly before its warmth, family portraits lining the walls of what was essentially a delightfully cozy drawing room.

"Please, I do not understand," Valeria stammered a little nervously.

"A situation drastic to me at least," the major continued as though she had not spoken. "For I confess that hitherto I have been a complete stranger to the emotion which now dominates my every waking thought and most of my sleeping ones as well. Indeed, the very affliction I have often derided in others—an affliction I have scorned and reviled—now has me in its toils and will allow me no peace. Do you know to what I refer, Valeria?"

It was impossible for her to look at him. Impossible for her to meet his eyes lest he read the truth in hers. At his words, all her own hopeless yearnings had surfaced, causing her the most agonizing of pains.

"Valeria, look at me!"

She did not want to obey, but somehow she could not resist doing so; a look of such tenderness blazed in her companion's eyes that her breath stifled in her throat. And then he was closing the gap between them, taking her in his arms and declaring in muffled accents that he had done with words and would *make* her love him, as his mouth descended upon hers, banishing all coherent thought and flooding her with the sweetness of wild honey.

She must be dreaming, Valeria thought hazily. This could not be Leo kissing her with such tender sincerity, whispering soft endearments in her ear, as his lips moved from cheek to brow, his arms those of a lover as he strained her against him in mute plea.

Her emotions thrown into utter confusion, Valeria could only tremble within the circle of his arms, scarcely daring to believe what her senses were conveying to her.

"Tell me it is not too late and that there is still hope for me," Leo urged huskily. "I swore I would not torture myself by coming here tonight, to watch you dance by in the arms of someone more fortunate than myself—someone who had the wit to see you as you really are and not as his embittered imagination had painted you. But in the end I could not deny myself the painful pleasure of being in your company, even if it was only at a distance. Am I the greatest fool alive, Valeria? Did I only dream your response to my kiss or can it be that fortune has decided to favor me after all that you return my regard, unworthy of your love though I undoubtedly am."

"You are not," Valeria declared stoutly, if somewhat shakily. "You saved my life, but I don't understand."

"Then let this be my explanation," the major said softly, bending his head for a second time.

This time it was no tentative embrace, but a kiss of searing need, passion held in fine check beneath the pressure of his mouth, and Valeria's own lips responded to the demand of his, silently acknowledging the love she had previously sought to hide.

There was no need for words. Their lips and eyes said them all.

"You cannot pretend now that you do not know that I love you," Leo told Valeria unsteadily, when he reluctantly released her lips.

"Or you that I return that love," Valeria whispered shyly. "But all these weeks when you have made it plain that you held me in the greatest contempt . . ."

"I may have made it plain to *you*," the major said ruefully, "but my heart was far from convinced, I promise you. That first time we were introduced I looked at you and knew, and then I heard your name and remembered where

I had seen it before. I was glad to have some reason for despising you so. You see, long, long ago I said I would never fall in love, never subject myself to the wilfull caprice of any woman—so great was my dislike of your sex, that I was convinced the entire race lived only to deceive men. Foolish, bigoted, call it what you will."

"Your feelings were based on sound reasoning," Valeria said gently, not wanting him to torture him any further. "Camilla told me about your brother. His death must have grieved you terribly, and in such a wasted cause. I can well understand how it was that you decided I was tarred with the same brush. On the face of it, the circumstances were damning. People who have known me virtually all my life believed I was determined to marry Perry, so why should you not suppose the same?"

"You are too generous," the major said huskily, dropping a kiss on the palm of her hand.

"Even though I do foolish and improper things like trying to pawn my jewelry?" Valeria asked tremulously.

"I do not consider what you did in any way improper," her companion replied firmly. "To me it was the act of a true friend. But if you ever pawn any of the jewelry *I* give you, I shall beat you."

"I thought you despised me," Valeria confessed. "Every time we met, events seemed to serve only to lessen your opinion of me."

"When, in reality, they served only to increase my longing for you," Leo told her. "A longing I fought against long and hard until I could fight no longer. I wanted to tell you the truth when I returned your emeralds, but you looked so pale and drawn, and then Camilla arrived." He turned her hand palm upward, tracing the faint scars of her injuries, before pressing his lips to her soft skin. A quiver of delight shivered through her.

"Tell me quickly, Val. Will you marry me?" he asked roughly. Her face told him her answer.

She was gathered up against him and kissed until she could not get her breath. One small cloud still lingered, refusing to be banished. Forcing herself to appear unconcerned, she asked hesitantly, "You do not think me too tall?" Only the faintest tremor betrayed the importance of the question as she stared resolutely at the major's cravat.

He regarded her bowed head gravely for a few seconds

and then captured her chin, forcing it upward, so that he could study her unguarded expression.

"Neither an inch too many nor one too few," he proclaimed softly. "Only conjecture the inconvenience it would cause me were it necessary to risk a crick in my neck every time I wished to kiss my wife—an inclination I suspect I shall succumb to with increasing frequency, and you know how I dislike to be inconvenienced."

As he spoke, he bent his head experimentally, a teasing smile lighting his eyes. The touch of his lips melted away all her lingering doubts. "There," he declared wickedly, releasing her to contemplate her flushed face with every evidence of amusement. "Exactly right! Forgive me those unkind, uncalled for words, my love," he added on a more sober note. "My only defense is that at the time I was half-mad with jealousy. Am I forgiven?"

In answer, Valeria reached up shyly to touch her lips to his cheek, her heart in her eyes. There would be time enough later for them to talk of events leading up to bitterness which had marred Leo's lifetime for making plans for the future. For now she was content to be held in his arms, wrapped in the security of his love. There was only the firelight to witness their love, and strike sparks from the oval sapphire Leo was withdrawing from his pocket. Flanked by diamonds, the stone caught and held the light, mirroring the warm flames.

"This was my mama's," Leo explained. "I should like you to wear it for me, but if you would prefer something else . . ."

"I love it," Valeria told him gently, "for it is exactly the color of your eyes."

ABOUT THE AUTHOR
Caroline Courtney

Caroline Courtney was born in India, the youngest daughter of a British Army Colonel stationed there in the troubled years after the First World War. Her first husband, a Royal Air Force pilot, was tragically killed in the closing stages of the Second World War. She later remarried and now lives with her second husband, a retired barrister, in a beautiful 17th century house in Cornwall. They have three children, two sons and a daughter, all of whom are now married, and four grandchildren.

On the rare occasions that Caroline Courtney takes time off from her writing, she enjoys gardening and listening to music, particularly opera. She is also an avid reader of romantic poetry and has an ever-growing collection of poems she has composed herself.

Caroline Courtney is destined to be one of this country's leading romantic novelists. She has written an enormous number of novels over the years—purely for pleasure—and has never before been interested in seeing them reach publication. However, at her family's insistence she has now relented, and Warner Books is proud to be issuing a selection in this uniform edition.

YOUR WARNER LIBRARY OF
REGENCY ROMANCE

#1 THE FIVE-MINUTE MARRIAGE
by Joan Aiken (D84-682, $1.75)

#2 LADY BLUE
by Zabrina Faire (D94-056, $1.75)

#3 PHILIPPA
by Katherine Talbot (D84-664, $1.75)

#4 AGENT OF LOVE
by Jillian Kearny (D94-003, $1.75)

#5 ACCESSORY TO LOVE
by Maureen Wakefield (D84-790, $1.75)

#6 THE MIDNIGHT MATCH
by Zabrina Faire (D94-057, $1.75)

#7 THE ROMANY REBEL
by Zabrina Faire (D94-206, $1.75)

#8 ENCHANTING JENNY
by Zabrina Faire (D94-103, $1.75)

#9 THE SEVENTH SUITOR
by Laura Matthews (D94-340, $1.75)

#10 THE SMILE OF THE STRANGER
by Joan Aiken (D94-144, $1.75)

#11 GWENDELINE
by Jane Ashford (D94-247, $1.75)

#12 THE WICKED COUSIN
by Zabrina Faire (D94-104, $1.75)

#13 THE PINK PHAETON
by Juliana Davison (D94-270, $1.75)

#14 THEODOSIA
by Katherine Talbot (D94-142, $1.75)

#15 THE AIM OF A LADY
by Laura Matthews (D94-341, $1.75)

YOUR WARNER LIBRARY OF REGENCY ROMANCE

#16 VELVET RIBBONS
by Juliana Davison   (D94-271, $1.75)

#17 ATHENA'S AIRS
by Zabrina Faire   (D94-463, $1.75)

#18 PETALS OF THE ROSE
by Juliana Davison   (D94-272, $1.75)

#19 BLUESTOCKING
by Jane Ashford   (D90-509, $1.95)

#20 LORD CLAYBORNE'S FANCY
by Laura Matthews   (D94-570, $1.75)

#21 BOLD PURSUIT
by Zabrina Faire   (D94-464, $1.75)

#22 A BARONET'S WIFE
by Laura Matthews   (D94-571, $1.75)

#23 PRETTY KITTY
by Zabrina Faire   (D94-465, $1.75)

#24 HOLIDAY IN BATH
by Laura Matthews   (D94-741, $1.75)

#25 MAN OF HONOUR
by Jane Ashford   (D94-797, $1.75)

#26 LOVE'S CLAIMANT
by Jillian Kearny   (D94-671, $1.75)

#28 TIFFANY'S TRUE LOVE
by Zabrina Faire   (D94-466, $1.75)

#29 COUNTESS BY CONTRACT
by Juliana Davison   (D94-789, $1.75)

#30 TOBLETHORPE MANOR
by Carola Dunn   (D90-943, $1.95)

#31 PRETENDER TO LOVE
by Zabrina Faire   (D94-467, $1.75)